SILVER ANNIVERSARY CONGRATULATIONS

"It's a treat to wish Faith Fairchild a happy anniversary. May she be around for many more! The world—the real one, as well as the world of books—needs more people who are smart and compassionate and can cook."

—Lois Lowry

"Book by book for more than twenty years, Katherine Hall Page has earned a place among the best American mystery writers."
—Joe Meyers, Hearst Connecticut Media Group

"Congratulations to Katherine Hall Page on the publication of the twenty-fifth installment in the delicious Faith Fairchild series! Fans of the traditional mystery will be doubly rewarded by this terrific new book."
—Diane Mott Davidson

"The Faith Fairchild series is as good as it gets in the traditional mystery genre. They—both the author and her wonderful creation—have been reader favorites in my bookshop for a quarter of a century."
—Otto Penzler, proprietor of
The Mysterious Bookshop

"I cherish Faith Fairchild and her creator, Katherine Hall Page. . . . Thank you, dear Katherine, for fine whodunits, delicious recipes, and, most of all, thank you for you. Happy Silver Anniversary."

—Carolyn Hart

"Cheers and good wishes for a landmark twenty-fifth anniversary for Katherine and Faith. Here's to another great twenty-five, for a very special lady and her creator!"

—Charles Todd

"The twenty-five mysteries that Katherine Hall Page has cooked up for her sleuth, Faith Fairchild, make for delectable reading. What a body of work! Dig in."

—Gregory Maguire

THE
BODY *in the* WAKE

By Katherine Hall Page

THE BODY IN THE WAKE
THE BODY IN THE CASKET
THE BODY IN THE WARDROBE
THE BODY IN THE BIRCHES
SMALL PLATES
THE BODY IN THE PIAZZA
THE BODY IN THE BOUDOIR
THE BODY IN THE GAZEBO
THE BODY IN THE SLEIGH
THE BODY IN THE GALLERY
THE BODY IN THE IVY
THE BODY IN THE SNOWDRIFT
THE BODY IN THE ATTIC
THE BODY IN THE LIGHTHOUSE
THE BODY IN THE BONFIRE
THE BODY IN THE MOONLIGHT
THE BODY IN THE BIG APPLE
THE BODY IN THE BOOKCASE
THE BODY IN THE FJORD
THE BODY IN THE BOG
THE BODY IN THE BASEMENT
THE BODY IN THE CAST
THE BODY IN THE VESTIBULE
THE BODY IN THE BOUILLON
THE BODY IN THE KELP
THE BODY IN THE BELFRY

ATTENTION: ORGANIZATIONS AND CORPORATIONS

HarperCollins books may be purchased for educational, business, or sales promotional use. For information, please e-mail the Special Markets Department at SPsales@harpercollins.com.

KATHERINE HALL PAGE

THE
BODY *in* WAKE
the
A FAITH FAIRCHILD MYSTERY

wm

WILLIAM MORROW
An Imprint of HarperCollinsPublishers

This is a work of fiction. Names, characters, places, and incidents are products of the author's imagination or are used fictitiously and are not to be construed as real. Any resemblance to actual events, locales, organizations, or persons, living or dead, is entirely coincidental.

THE BODY IN THE WAKE. Copyright © 2019 by Katherine Hall Page. All rights reserved. Printed in the United States of America. No part of this book may be used or reproduced in any manner whatsoever without written permission except in the case of brief quotations embodied in critical articles and reviews. For information, address HarperCollins Publishers, 195 Broadway, New York, NY 10007.

First William Morrow mass market printing: March 2020
First William Morrow hardcover printing: May 2019

Print Edition ISBN: 978-0-06-286326-3
Digital Edition ISBN: 978-0-06-286327-0

Cover art by Nadine Badalaty
Cover illustrations © Getty Images: FScottMattern; blacklight_trace; mysondanube; IvanNikulin; Palomita22; befehr; joto; kolotuschenko; ulimi; and © Kovalov Anatolii/Shutterstock
Author photograph by Jean Fogelberg

William Morrow and HarperCollins are registered trademarks of HarperCollins Publishers in the United States of America and other countries.

20 21 22 23 24   QGM   10 9 8 7 6 5 4 3 2 1

If you purchased this book without a cover, you should be aware that this book is stolen property. It was reported as "unsold and destroyed" to the publisher, and neither the author nor the publisher has received any payment for this "stripped book."

For my husband, Alan, and my son, Nicholas
From the luckiest woman in the world

Wake n.
the visible track of turbulence left by
something moving through the water

Wake n.
a vigil for the dead

Till human voices wake us, and we drown

T. S. ELIOT, "THE LOVE SONG OF
J. ALFRED PRUFROCK" (1915)

Acknowledgments

My thanks to the following for help ranging from a pot buoy plot device and medical expertise to navigating the currents of getting this book published: Dr. Robert DeMartino; at Greenburger, my agent Faith Hamlin, Stefanie Diaz, and Edward Maxwell; my editor, Katherine Nintzel, and other Harper treasures: Danielle Bartlett, Vedika Khanna, Gena Lanzi, Shelly Perron, and Virginia Stanley; in Maine: Jean Fogelberg, Steve and Roberta Johnson (Bert and I Charters), Stephen Pickering, Elizabeth Richardson, and Tom Ricks.

Special thanks to Holly and Trisha Eaton for their high bid to name a character at the Maine Center for Coastal Fisheries auction fund-raiser, which gave me a chance to include their adorable son Sam!

Throughout the series so far, I have been fortunate to have had the following editors: Ruth Cavin, Carrie Feron, Zachary Schisgal, Jennifer Sawyer-Fisher, Sarah Durand, Wendy Lee, and Katherine Nintzel. Their expertise and friendship have been treasures.

One

"If one more person tells me to relax and stop thinking about it, I swear I will commit murder. I'll get myself off. Justifiable homicide. Why else did I go to law school? It will be a win for women everywhere who are *trying*—and I hate that word with its suggestion that you just aren't *trying* hard enough—to get pregnant!"

Sophie Maxwell set the glass of iced tea she had been drinking down on the small table next to her with such force, the lemon slice shot out onto the floor of the porch where she was sitting with her friend Faith Fairchild. Sophie scooped it up and set it next to the pitcher, which had been full an hour ago when the two women had come outside hoping for a breeze off Penobscot Bay's Eggemoggin Reach. It was the third day in a row of record-breaking heat. The sailboats, colored dots of varying sizes, were either not moving at all, or motoring with sails down.

The wraparound veranda of The Birches, Sophie's family's turn-of-the-twentieth-century summerhouse, sported the usual Down East assortment of Bar Harbor rockers made famous by John F. Kennedy and wicker of all sorts and vintages. Sophie and her great-uncle Paul had been almost living on the porch, taking meals there and sitting in the dark until the mosquitos, made even more vicious by the heat, drove them inside. Sophie hadn't had a decent night's sleep in ages, tossing restlessly on top of the sheets and searching in vain for a cool spot on her pillow. Uncle Paul was relying on an ancient dangerous-looking fan with blades as sharp as a guillotine. He'd offered to search one out for her in the attic, but she had declined. On Sanpere Island a few people From Away had air-conditioning, but natives and longtime summer people considered it unnecessary, as it usually was, or showy.

"And when you are pregnant," Faith said, "you'll face even more personal comments from family and strangers alike. That carrying high means a boy, except when it means a girl. Or even worse, pats on the belly once you show, getting beyond the plum stage to melon. Where did the fruit comparisons come from I wonder? One woman actually put both her hands on my honeydew bulge while I was in line at the post office and told me she was transmitting her aura to my unborn infant." Faith was trying to distract Sophie, keep things light. "That aura thing was a bit creepy, though. For weeks after Ben was born I found myself looking for telltale signs of possession—not mentioning the whole thing to Tom, of course. When the Linda Blair phase arrived, it turned out to be colic."

"I would never bring up something as intimate as, well, I guess family planning is the best way to put it," Sophie continued to fume. The heat and lack of sleep were making her cranky. "I mean, when they say 'trying,' you know what they really mean!"

"'Roll in the hay,' 'shagging'—I'm told that's Old English, by the way—'nookie,' of course, and then there's 'mattress dancing.' I prefer 'making love' or just good old 'sex.'"

"Faith, for a minister's wife you seem extremely conversant with all these terms." Sophie laughed.

The two women had known each other for a long time—Sophie had been an occasional babysitter for the Fairchilds when she was in her teens—but they became more than close during their unwitting involvement in solving two murders. The first was several summers ago on Sanpere. In the course of those dark days, the bright spot was Sophie's meeting her future husband, Will. After the wedding the following fall, performed by Faith's husband, the Reverend Thomas Fairchild, the couple moved to Will's hometown—Savannah, Georgia. The new bride had barely mastered which square was which when she was caught up in the kind of ghost story that fit right in with Savannah's reputation as the most haunted city in the South. When Will had suddenly disappeared, Faith came to Sophie's aid as they learned the spirits were all too real. It wasn't the type of bonding common between most female friends, particularly since Faith was older and in a different place in life, but as they now sat in companionable silence drinking sweet tea—the Savannah influence—Sophie thought that aside from Will, there was no one she was closer to than Faith, who knew what was dominating Sophie's thoughts now. The big three oh was looming closer and closer, weeks away, and her biological clock was ticking at warp speed.

"It must be hotter than Hades in Savannah," Faith said. "When is Will going to be able to get back here?"

"He says he should tie things up in another two weeks, three at the most. I feel a little guilty leaving him, but the house and his office are air-conditioned. He says he's used to the heat. And what little work I need to do can be done from here." Sophie had become a partner in Will's family firm while he opted to stay independent with his PI agency, which specialized in investigating white-collar crime.

"In that case, you really *can* put all this out of your mind. If you get pregnant it's going to be a second immaculate conception or an indecent scandal."

Sophie stretched and stood up, smiling. "Thank you, Faith, I knew you'd cheer me up. Not that I'm at the stage where a Pampers commercial makes me sob, but I *have* been blue. The heat hasn't helped. Let's go to the Lily Pond for a swim. I know you won't go off the dock here no matter how hot it is." Sophie had learned in the past that Faith considered a plunge into Sanpere's cold salt waters unthinkable unless she found herself at the end of a plank with the tip of Captain Hook's cutlass between her shoulder blades. The Lily Pond was fresh water.

The Fairchilds had bought a small piece of land on Sanpere some years ago and put up a cottage of their own, but it wasn't a cottage like The Birches, which had more in common sizewise with the "cottages" in Bar Harbor and Newport. Sophie's great-grandparents, Josiah and Eleanor Proctor, had built at the same time as other rusticators from Boston, New York, and Philadelphia, selecting the large scenic site overlooking the Reach on a sailing trip as newlyweds, captivated by the nearby lighthouse, the rough granite ledges, and a deep-water mooring. Once the house was completed, they never missed a summer. They came up from Boston by train, changing in Portland for the coastal steamboats that carried them to Sanpere, where they indulged in early-morning bracing swims, yachting, long walks in the woods, and other Teddy Roosevelt–type roughing-it activities while making do with plenty of servants to help them lead such simple lives.

Except for the outdoor activities, this way of life had vanished. The rusticators' descendants now arrived by car, usually four-wheel-drive Subarus— the Maine state car—with kayaks on the top. The army of servants had been replaced by part-time help like Marge Foster, a local island woman, who was pushing the screen door to the porch open now.

"Thought you'd need more tea and I've got some molasses cookies I made this morning," Marge said. Sophie jumped up to get the tray and was glad to see that Marge had brought a glass for herself.

"You have to stop baking in this heat—not that we don't appreciate it. But, sit and relax please! It's a little cooler out here."

Marge was an ample woman and filled the

rocker Faith pulled up for her. "With just you and Mr. Paul there is scarcely anything for me to do. Might as well bake, as you only want cold suppers," Marge said, taking the glass of tea Sophie had poured for her.

Sophie had insisted that she take care of meals, but Marge in turn had told her that cooking was part of the job, and they settled on having Marge leave what she called the "fixings." She also considered cleaning the house and doing the wash part of what was supposed to be a half-time job. Sophie occasionally found herself in a race to get to the housework before Marge. However, she was a godsend when the house was full, as it had been over the Fourth of July. Sophie's Uncle Simon, her mother's only sibling, and his family were a throwback to an earlier era and considered anything more than mixing a drink "not my job."

Marge drank thirstily. "That was some good, and yes, thank you, I'll have more. Missed seeing your mother, Sophie. It's not like her to skip the Fourth, or be this late coming."

Babs, Sophie's mother, was a favorite of Marge's—and of the whole island. She started life as Barbara Proctor, Josiah and Eleanor's granddaughter, never missing a summer either, and Marge was right. To Sophie's almost certain knowledge her mother had rarely been absent for the Fourth.

Sophie was the happy result of Babs's brief marriage to Sandy Maxwell, one cut short by the discovery of a receipt from Firestone and Parson for a diamond bracelet Babs never received that Christmas, opening the promising small box to find a silver one from Shreve's instead. Babs didn't have any more children but did have plenty more husbands. Her current full name was Barbara Proctor Maxwell Rothenstein Williams Harrington. She'd told her daughter that in her day you married your beau rather than "jump between the sheets." Yet, with this current marriage, which had lasted the longest, Sophie was pretty sure that her mother had finally found "The One" in Ed Harrington, an easygoing venture capitalist with a good sense of humor and his own hair (one of Babs's requirements). They traveled a great deal, as Ed liked to golf in exotic places and Babs liked to shop in exotic places. They'd been to the Mission Hills Golf Club in Guangdong, China, and others from New Zealand to Abu Dhabi. At the moment they were in Greenland. She imagined her mother would be restless by now, as Greenland was not known as a shopping destination once you'd purchased something fashioned from musk ox wool.

"She's planned to be here for a few weeks before Samantha's wedding, so I'd say soon—early August—although she'll probably spend some time at the Connecticut house when she gets back from Greenland," Sophie said. Babs may have changed husbands the way other women changed nail polish, but through them all she'd held on to her magnificent house overlooking Long Island Sound on the Connecticut shore, where Sophie had grown up.

"The wedding's over Labor Day weekend, right?" Marge asked. "I told Mrs. Miller I could help and she's about asked every other woman on the island to keep the dates clear."

Pix and Sam Miller were the Fairchilds' closest friends and neighbors in Aleford, Massachusetts, and on Sanpere, and their daughter, Samantha, was marrying Zach Cohen. Pix had been in panic mode since the couple announced their engagement the previous fall. No matter what Faith, or Sophie, also a friend, said, Pix was sure they'd run out of food or there would be a Nor'easter or there would be a flu epidemic or a meteor would crash down on the venue, Edgewood Farm . . . the list was endless.

" You two better get that swim in before it rains," Marge said.

"But there isn't a cloud in the sky," Faith pointed out. "And the weather report didn't say anything about showers. I wish it would rain and cool things down."

"Oh, you can't trust weather reports," Marge

said complacently. "My knee was acting up this morning and it's a sure sign."

"Leave everything, please," Sophie said to Marge. "You've stayed long enough. Go home and say hi to that nice husband of yours from me."

Marge's husband, Charlie, fished, like most men on the island, and he *was* a very nice man who turned up, usually unannounced, to help Paul with all sorts of tasks from splitting wood to repairing the roof. He just seemed to know. Like Marge.

Sophie's words brought a grin to Marge's face. "I'll tell him. 'Nice.' He'll get a kick out of that. Now, Sophie, I overheard what you were saying before. Can't say I ever had trouble in that department nor did Mumma. 'All you need to do is lay a pair of men's pants across the bottom of my bed' and nine months later the cradle would be full, she used to say."

"It's a thought," Sophie said. "Why not give it a try? I'll tell Will to bring some particularly sexy trousers up with him."

Marge gave her a look. "Silly girl, that's just an old wives' tale. Like sleeping with a piece of wedding cake under your pillow or planting parsley. What I'm telling you is to go off and have fun. And no, I did not say 'relax.' Don't want you turning into a murderer." She closed the door behind her with one last slightly wicked look over her shoulder.

Faith and Sophie dissolved in giggles. "Parsley! Wedding cake and pants. Those are new ones to me, and I thought I'd heard them all," Sophie gasped. "We are definitely not paying Marge enough."

Faith nodded. "Let's go swim. I have to get my suit back at the house so I'll meet you at the pond."

The Birches was actually located on Little Sanpere Island, a much smaller—only four miles long—piece of land connected to Sanpere by a causeway. As Faith crossed it now she noted the new guardrails that the state had finally installed on the narrow twist of road, a favorite for drag racers with often horrific consequences. Sanpere itself, with roughly two thousand year-round residents, was many times larger than Little Sanpere. The population in both doubled in the summer, a phenomenon giving rise to a local saying that you knew it was June because of the dual invasions of blackflies and summer folk. There were two towns on Sanpere, Sanpere Village and Granville, much bigger and home to the largest lobster fishing port in Maine. Last summer Sonny Prescott, a local dealer, told Faith the total year's haul was over seventeen million pounds. In the summer months, tourism coexisted with the working port. Newcomers expecting only quaint picture postcard fishing scenes were disabused by the first gigantic tractor-trailer truck passing them on a curve.

She turned off Route 15, which circled the island, onto the road that led to the Point, which she now considered home. She'd been in Aleford all her married life, but they lived in a parsonage that belonged to the church, not the current occupant. A few summers ago she and Tom had decided to buy a plot in Mount Adams cemetery, so the island would be her dwelling for a long time. The Millers had a large family plot not far from the Fairchilds' choice, and the Proctor plot already had a number of occupants, starting with Sophie's great-grandparents. Faith took comfort knowing that she could at the very least count on some good conversation in the hereafter.

She thought back to her first summer on the island. Ben, now entering his second year at Brown, was a toddler. The Millers had convinced the Fairchilds to rent a cottage on Sanpere, their beloved Maine island. Faith had given in, faced with such enthusiasm, especially Tom's. He'd grown up on Massachusetts's South Shore and thought exploring rocky beaches with side trips to canoe on the North River or hike in Myles Standish State Forest was heaven on earth. Faith's plan was to be a good sport—especially when she heard there was a bridge to the mainland—then call in her chips and head for the Hamptons or even Provence the following summer. Instead, looking back she was sure Tom and the Millers had slipped something in the well water at the farmhouse rental they'd found for them on a white sandy cove with a view straight out toward Mount Desert Island and sunsets more magnificent than Faith had seen anywhere. She found herself gathering wildflowers and sticking them in mason jars, marveling at the number of varieties of ferns, listening for the cries of gulls and terns. Above all she cooked. The setting could not have been more different from Manhattan's Upper East Side, where she had grown up and chosen a more elaborate culinary path leading to her own catering firm, Have Faith, which became one of the most sought after in the city. It was at a wedding she was catering that she met Tom. He was in town to perform the ceremony, changing for the reception. Daughter and granddaughter of clergy, Faith was adamant about avoiding the fishbowl life of a parish spouse, but the heart knows not reason. Faith found herself in a small town west of Boston, the land of boiled dinners and soft bagels. But her feeling for New England changed definitively that first summer on Sanpere, with a richer bounty than Dean & DeLuca and Citarella combined at her fingertips. Lobster, mussels, clams, scallops, halibut, haddock, peekytoe crab, chanterelles and other wild mushrooms. Local goat cheeses and fresh eggs from Mrs. Cousins were a short walk down the dirt road. Maine meant a late growing season, but as first peas, then strawberries, blueberries, and all the rest of summer's bounty arrived, Faith found herself savoring each with renewed appreciation. She made things like blueberry buckle, green tomato chutney, and all sorts of chowders in the farmhouse's kitchen.

As she pulled into the empty gravel driveway, relishing the pleasant memory, Faith thought how different a summer this summer was from previous ones. First, no Ben, who had opted to stay in Providence and accept his professor's offer of a summer research spot. After entering college intent on linguistics, Ben had become interested in biochem, especially as it related to life in waters like Sanpere's, and had switched majors.

The other difference was having Tom on the island all the time rather than for sporadic visits. He had a contract with Harvard University Press to turn his divinity school thesis on the history and theology of the twelfth-century French Albigensians into a shorter and more accessible book. An editor had come across the thesis and was intrigued by Tom's conclusion that the successful, extremely brutal Crusade by the church to obliterate the Albigensians, or Cathars, was the first example of genocide in the Western world with far-reaching historical implications. He'd arranged to take a leave from First Parish for two months, working with the assistant minister and calling in guest preaching favors from fellow clergy to do so.

Faith had been delighted, picturing the two of them with free time for picnics, boat trips, and other fun they'd never had uninterrupted hours for, but Tom soon realized he couldn't work at the cottage because of both the delightful distraction that was his wife and the slow Internet. Friends with a techie's wired dream house who would not be on Sanpere until the fall had offered it as an office for Tom. This left Faith with daughter Amy, entering her junior year at Aleford High School. But Amy was following the time-honored Fairchild summer job tradition at The Laughing Gull Lodge's kitchen. Laughing Gull was now Sanpere Shores, a conference center. Last summer, its first, had proved very successful. The new owners, who had two other similar facilities in New England, had added tennis courts, a spa, and a pool. They had also changed the Rec Center that had served as a kids' camp and hangout space for families into a lounge with a bar, billiard table, Ping-Pong, and a flat-screen TV the size of Rembrandt's *The Night Watch*. The rustic cabins had been upgraded—no more knotty pine—and there was plenty of high-speed Internet. Companies used Sanpere Shores for training retreats, and professionals booked time to offer courses in every-

thing from digital photography to how to trace
your family tree. To distract herself From Here
to Maternity, Sophie had signed up for a writing
program starting soon.

Sanpere Shores provided three meals a day: a
hearty continental breakfast, box lunches, and a
full-course dinner with menu choices. Amy was
determined to follow in her mother's culinary footsteps, despite Faith's admonitions—hard work,
long hours, difficult customers, and so forth. Amy
had left Nancy Drew and Lemony Snicket behind
years ago for M. F. K. Fisher, Elizabeth David,
A. J. Liebling, and Ruth Reichl. Sanpere Shores was
close to the house Tom was using, so the two of
them left after breakfast each morning like com-
muters. Faith didn't know what she would have
done without Sophie and Pix. She was unaccus-
tomed to the experience of free time.

She dashed into the house, changed into her
bathing suit, and threw one of Tom's old tee shirts
over it—Yankee thrift was part of the Fairchild
DNA, and she saved a couple of threadbare items
from his wardrobe she hadn't managed to spirit
away to wear for times like this. The tote she kept
with towels, sunscreen, and a book was already
in the car.

Faith was surprised to see so few people on the
pond's small beach, or in its waters. Maybe it *was*

going to rain. She set her things down and realized that the woman sitting next to a little girl filling a bucket with sand was the mother of Samantha's best friend, Arlene, and the child was Arlene's three-year-old, Kylie.

"Hi, Marilyn," Faith said. "Wow, Kylie seems to be growing taller—and cuter—every time I see her. She looked adorable in the parade." The theme for this year's Fourth of July parade had been "Our Island Paradise," and Kylie, riding on Larry Snowden's float, had been a lobster with a grass skirt.

Marilyn gave a big smile. "Took me forever to sew that thing. That Larry comes up with some foolishness every year, but this took the cake."

"And the blue ribbon I heard," Faith said. "Is Arlene swimming?" She shaded her eyes to look out at the water. It was a long pond surrounded by birches and other trees. Water lilies encroached upon the clear water, and Faith didn't like to swim too close to the sides. Besides the lily pads there was an abundance of other aquatic plants that seemed to have tendrils waiting to grasp her ankles.

"No. She was feeling a little poorly today," Marilyn said, her smile dimming. "I said I'd take Kylie, but I've got to go now. I have to get supper on." Island meal times were considerably earlier than the ones Faith kept. She wondered if Arlene might be pregnant. If so, it would mean drastic alterations to her matron of honor dress. Kylie was also in the wedding party—the flower girl—and Sam Eaton, the little son of other island friends, was the ring bearer. The kids would steal the show, Samantha said when she showed Faith pictures of their outfits. They *would* look precious, especially if Sam could be persuaded out of his beloved rubber clammer's boots. Faith, however, knew all eyes would be on the bride. Samantha had selected a gown from Anthropologie's bridal collection that looked like something from *A Midsummer Night's Dream,* floral appliqués over layers of tulle with a pale rose-colored satin underskirt. Instead of a veil, she planned to make a simple white floral wreath to crown her shoulder-length dark hair.

"Say good-bye to Mrs. Fairchild, Kylie," Marilyn said, and the little girl came over, planting a sandy kiss on Faith's cheek.

As she waved good-bye Faith remembered the car accident Arlene had been in late last winter and chided herself for not asking how Arlene was doing in more detail. On their way to pick up Kylie at Arlene's parents', Arlene and her husband, Mike, who was driving, hit black ice, and the car flipped over. They had been wearing seat belts, and both the front and side airbags deployed forcibly. Mike was tall and avoided injury, but Arlene's nose and left cheekbone had been broken; she'd sustained a hairline jaw fracture—plus several teeth had been knocked out. Samantha had told Faith that Arlene had worried she wouldn't be healed in time for the wedding. For months she had looked like someone from a horror movie. It had been a long process and many trips to various doctors, but Faith thought Arlene had looked amazingly good on the Fourth at the parade. No wonder she was "poorly" though. The long drawn-out recovery had to have still left her feeling tired, especially with a lively little one.

Sophie was coming down the path onto the beach, and after exchanging quick greetings with Marilyn and Kylie, she called out to Faith, "I'm dying to get in the water! Race you to the end of the pond and back?"

"You're on!" Faith said and sped into the pond. After a shallow dive took her to the deeper water, she quickly moved into a fast crawl, heading straight down the middle. She could hear Sophie closing in behind her and quickened the pace. She reached the end of the pond and flipped to return, then realized she was about to get tangled up in a reedy thicket filled with fallen branches and trash, a bundle of old clothes. She started to swim away.

Until she saw two bare feet sticking out of a pair of jeans.

"Sophie, come help!" she screamed and dove underwater, grabbing the legs to free the whole body from the tangled mess. Faith tugged hard, and it broke loose and slid across the water like a cork from a bottle. Facedown with pale blond hair.

At Faith's side in seconds, Sophie immediately grabbed the head and neck, lifting them above the surface. "I can't feel a pulse!! I'm going to float him over toward that mud flat and start CPR. Can't wait to get him to the beach. Go call 911!"

As Faith started toward the opposite end of the pond at a competition pace she tried to get her mind around what was happening. Sophie had said "he." The body was a man. He couldn't have been in the pond long. No discoloration. His slender feet and ankles were bare—no bloating. Nearing the shore, she started yelling for someone to call 911 and was relieved to see a man instantly take a phone from his pocket. The pond was near the new cell tower and one of the few reliable places on the island for a signal.

Getting out of the water, she cried, "A man has drowned! At the end of the pond!" Someone draped a large towel around her. Someone else gave her a can of sugary Mountain Dew and told her to drink it down. In what seemed like no time at all, she heard the ambulance's siren signal its arrival, and the volunteers instantly went into action, two of them swimming out to help Sophie transport the body ashore. As they closed in on her and the body, she yelled, "I think there's a pulse."

Onshore the EMTs strapped an oxygen mask to his face and then the ambulance sped off, leaving Faith, Sophie, and the other few who had been at the pond sitting close together. It was over.

"Anybody know him?" asked a man Faith recognized by his distinctive beard as Bill Haviford, the president of the historical society. They had all had a good look at the victim as he was taken away.

No one answered at first and then Sophie said, "I'm pretty sure I saw him and some other guys at the market last week. They looked in their twenties, maybe a little older. Around my age." One of the ambulance corps volunteers had tossed blankets out for Sophie and Faith to wrap around themselves, and despite the temperature Sophie was still clutching hers close. "They were buying beer. Four of them. I didn't really pay much attention until they left the parking lot. They were all on motorcycles—Harleys I think—and roared off."

"You gals need to go home and dry off," Bill said.

Faith nodded in agreement. "Yes, come to my

house, Sophie. We'll get your car later." She was thinking dry clothes were in order plus some brandy. The image of the young man in the water like a grotesque Ophelia wasn't going to go away for a long time though.

"Give me your keys, and my wife will follow with our car. We don't live far from you," Bill said. Faith wasn't surprised he knew where she lived, although she had no idea where he did. It was the island after all.

"Thank you, that would be a big help," Faith said. Sophie was still shaking, and Faith was sure the young woman was in mild shock.

Since leaving the pond Sophie hadn't said a word, but now as they drove through Sanpere Village, she shuddered and, barely audible, said, "Did you see his tattoo?"

"Yes," Faith said. "I did." Tattoos were so common now and she'd thought she'd seen them all, but this one was unique: a lifelike green adder snaking up his right forearm, its fangs dripping blood and a few Gothic letters in red spelling something Faith couldn't make out before he was taken away. A *Y* at the end? And she was pretty sure the first letter was an *L*.

She stepped on the gas.

Pix Miller stepped out onto the porch at The Pines. She closed the screen door gently in case her mother, sitting in her favorite canvas sling back chair, was dozing. The Pines, built by Pix's grandparents next to the Proctors' Birches, was a large gray-shingled "cottage" with the same magnificent view of the Reach and lighthouse as its neighbor's.

"Pix? Is that you? Creeping up on me," Ursula said, turning to look at her daughter with a welcoming smile. Pix gave her mother a kiss. This year she had started bringing the mail from their post office boxes every afternoon along with the *Island Crier,* the weekly island newspaper, on Thursdays. Pix had thought Ursula, who had always fetched both for herself, would protest. Driving The Pines's 1949 Ford Woody station wagon, kept in perfect shape by Forrest "Fod" Nevells, had been octogenarian Ursula's particular delight. Pix knew giving this up was hard. She had friends who had had to hide elderly parents' keys and, in one case, declare the car stolen (with a buyer all lined up). But Ursula had never said anything except to say in the beginning that Pix must have better things to do than drive all the way from her cottage every day, that a couple of times a week would suffice. Pix had pointed out that Sam wasn't coming until August, nor were any of her children around, so she really *didn't* have anything to do. In fact, she treasured this quiet time with her mother.

"Get yourself something cold to drink," Ursula said. "I sent Gert home. Too hot to work. She insisted on baking cinnamon raisin bread this morning. Told her I couldn't have her passing out from the heat, and that convinced her." Gert Prescott was surely close to Ursula's own age, Pix reflected. She'd been working at The Pines since she was a teen, coming to give Ursula, with two small children, a hand. Pix disliked the kind of summer person who referred to the women and men who worked for them as "just like family" while underpaying and overworking them, taking advantage of the fact that these jobs only existed seasonally and were a much-needed source of income. But Gert truly *was* family, and a few years ago Ursula had hired a young woman to do the housework and tend the garden over Gert's protests. Gert was possibly more excited about Samantha's wedding than anyone. Arlene, the matron of honor, was a niece, and Gert was seeing to the refreshments at the shower that Arlene was giving close to the big event.

"I'll get you something, too," Pix said, noticing her mother's glass was empty. "Lemonade?"

"Yes, and hurry up. Want to see what's been going on this week."

Pix laughed to herself. While the paper was a news source, Gert knew what was happening on

Sanpere before the island actually did and wasn't so much a part of the grapevine as the root itself.

When they were settled with their drinks, Pix opened the paper and as usual started with the column "From the Crow's Nest." Ursula had unearthed a Japanese fan and was wafting it to and fro in front of her face, sending puffs of air toward Pix, who was feeling extremely content until the thought of the wedding intruded. She sighed. Her mother waved the fan hard. "I heard that! I have half a mind to give them a large check and tell them to elope if you can't stop worrying. It's all going to be fine. Faith is taking care of everything, and what she isn't, Samantha is."

"I know, but I wish Samantha was here."

"She will be in a few weeks. In plenty of time for the ceremony, which is what counts. You know they can't get away from their jobs."

Taking the scolding in stride, Pix brightened up. "Maybe they'll be here sooner. Samantha loves Fishermen's Day even more than the Fourth, and Zach has never been. I wouldn't be surprised if they drove up after work tomorrow and back on Sunday after it's over. It never goes much past three."

"There now. Keep a good thought and open the paper!" Much as Ursula loved her one and only daughter, she was fast losing patience with

Pix's wedding woes. This was a woman with such fine-tuned organizational skills that she was on the phone booking rooms at the inn and other lodging scarce on the island less than an hour after hearing the happy news from Samantha and Zach. "Now, what's going on?"

Pix started reading aloud. "'The Maguire family is having their reunion this weekend and expect seventy, one member coming all the way from Australia. Six generations represented.'" Ursula nodded. Family reunions were what kept those who left for whatever reasons closely tied to the island. No matter where you lived, you showed up. Pix continued, "'The Granville Community Center is having an auction to raise money for the Island Food Pantry and is looking for items.'"

"I'm sure we can find some things in the attic once the heat breaks," Ursula said. Clearing out the attic had been on The Pines to-do list roughly since the 1930s.

Pix read more—what was coming up in gardens and the Fisheries Log, which was pessimistic about the lobster catch equaling last season's. Lobsters liked cold water, and the increasingly warm Sanpere waters due to climate change meant many crustaceans were staying far from the traps in water more to their taste.

"Let's see. Your Sewing Circle Fair is featured in 'Coming Events.' No Planning Board announcements; they're not meeting next week." Everyone on Sanpere scrutinized these announcements. Fair warning if your neighbor was planning to put up a dock across your view or add an addition blocking your time-honored shore access.

She turned to the obituaries. "Oh dear." Her voice caught.

"Who is it? Tell me quickly," Ursula said.

"No one we know. But young. Only twenty-four. Fished, graduate of Sanpere High School, beloved son, father of a four-year-old. There's a picture of the two of them. Heartbreaking." Pix looked up at her mother and then out to the Reach. "It's another 'died suddenly' one," she said.

"We're losing a whole generation," Ursula said in despair.

Two

Gin and tonic seemed to fit the weather better than brandy. Once she had found dry clothes for Sophie, Faith mixed two drinks with plenty of lime, adding to the tray a plate of cheese and crackers plus some smoked mackerel spread she'd made. Drink, yes, but food at times like these was equally important.

They sat on the deck watching the tide come in. It was swiftly covering the mounds of mud and deep troughs the clammers had left after hours of backbreaking digging. The cove in front of the Fairchilds' was a good spot. Tom and the kids enjoyed clamming, but after getting her foot stuck and unable to free herself because of the suction Faith opted to prepare the bivalves instead. Her rubber boot was still buried somewhere out there.

Faith took a swallow of the cool drink and looked over at Sophie. Her friend seemed fine now, popping a cracker with the mackerel spread into her mouth with relish. But obviously what had just happened was foremost in her mind, Faith's, too.

"It's quite shallow at that end of the pond, especially off to the side where he was. Maybe he couldn't swim?" Sophie said. "Although you keep hearing that swimmer or not, you can drown in your bath or in a teacup of water. Although why you'd be swimming in a teacup is puzzling."

Sophie was making jokes; the shock was wearing off. Faith smiled as her friend continued talking. "He wasn't dressed for a dip in the pond—not even shorts—although he wasn't wearing shoes or socks. He must have taken them off to wade and then slipped in too far? Then again, even though the bank is muddy, it's not all that slippery, especially with the recent temperatures."

"True, but there have been several other drownings in the Lily Pond over the years, fortunately not many," Faith commented.

"Will made me promise not to swim alone, although I'm not sure what Uncle Paul could do. He does like sitting on the dock when I go in. He unearthed an ancient life buoy that may possibly have come over on the *Mayflower*. He brings a thermos of martinis, and given that it's almost empty when I get out I don't think it's meant to be an emergency restorative." Faith laughed as Sophie made herself another cracker with the spread. "You have to tell me how you make this. A secret family recipe?"

"Nope, and so easy, it's embarrassing," Faith answered. "I get the Ducktrap smoked mackerel at the market in Blue Hill, take the skin off, flake the meat, and blend it with cream cheese plus a touch of mayo with a fork or the back of a spoon. It turns too mushy in the food processor."

"I'll never tell, but I will copy it." Sophie set her drink down, sat up straighter in the chaise, and said, "Okay. I've been doing a rewind of the guy from the market. He wasn't from Maine, or at least his bike wasn't registered in this state. He, and the others, had Massachusetts plates and a lot of gear strapped on the back. Maybe they'd just come here to ride because there's no helmet law and they wanted to feel the wind whistling in their hair. Or detouring onto the island on the way to Acadia is common. But if the others took off to Mount Desert, he obviously stayed behind."

"Or none of them went and are still on the island. When was it you saw them?" Faith said.

"Late in the week. Friday? Yes, Friday because

people were coming for dinner and I had to pick up a few more things."

"Anything else?" Faith asked. "Did you notice the tattoo then?"

Sophie shook her head and closed her eyes briefly to try to recall more details. "He was wearing a long-sleeved black tee shirt and a blue jean jacket with the arms cut out," she said slowly. "And one of them may have been a girl. That person was wearing a bright pink bandanna covering his or her hair and a leather jacket with a red rose stenciled on the back. Not exactly macho." She realized that she was remembering more and more. Maybe it was the gin.

"About how old were they?"

"One of them seemed older than the rest. Thirties, maybe even forty. But the others were mid to late twenties. Not kids."

"We know they were all over twenty-one. The market checks every ID unless you are very obviously old enough to buy." When places in both Maine and Massachusetts had stopped asking Faith for her ID it had been somewhat traumatic. Like the gray eyelash she'd discovered more recently. "Anything else?"

"They weren't talking much to each other and not to anyone in line or at the checkout. Nobody said hi, so probably not from the island."

"Or not favorites," Faith said. While she had

always found Sanpere a congenial place, especially after coming for so many years, she knew that there were grudges that had lasted generations.

The two sat silently for a few minutes. The moon would be close to full tonight, and that meant a higher than usual tide. It was coming in at a steady pace, and Faith, as usual, found it calming.

"I didn't see motorcycle tire tracks at the end of the pond," Sophie said, "but then I wasn't looking anywhere but at him. Did you notice any?"

Faith shook her head. "Besides, you can't get a vehicle through the woods and brush there. Maybe a bicycle, but definitely nothing larger. The closest road stops well before that end—there are no houses nearby—and the surrounding area is pretty much acres of swamp. Seth Marshall and other builders have been trying to figure out a way to drain it for houses for as long as we've been coming."

"Maybe he left his hog on the main road?" Sophie suggested. "I was running late and wanted to jump in the water, so I didn't notice any vehicles except yours." To get to the Lily Pond, you had to park on the side of a road and then walk in on a wide lane created in an earlier era when the pond was a source of ice for icehouses. "Did you see one?"

"No, although it could have been parked under

some trees. I did notice how few cars there were for such a hot day, but a lot of families like Sand Beach better—so much larger and real sand. And it would be cooler today, since it's on the ocean." Faith stood up. Their glasses were empty. "We need fresh drinks. I know you're driving, so lots of tonic, ice, and more fresh limes." She'd said this noting a slightly worried look that crossed Sophie's face. But it wasn't about driving.

"Faith, do you think there's any possibility he made it? I thought at one point I was getting a faint pulse."

"We can call the hospital in a while." Faith knew how much Sophie needed to hear that a life already in existence had not been lost.

When Faith heard a car on the gravel drive, she expected to see Tom's. He might have sequestered himself, but she was sure that by now someone on Sanpere had relayed the information that his wife had been involved in finding yet another body.

Except it wasn't Tom. It was Sergeant Earl Dickinson who got out of a Hancock County Sheriff's patrol car and strode toward the deck. Earl and his wife, Jill, were close friends of both Sophie's family and the Fairchilds. Earl was in uniform and looked as fresh as a daisy. Not a wrinkle, except the knifepoint crease in his trousers. He and Jill were still renovating one of the nineteenth-century houses in Sanpere Village that had been built by a schooner captain, and Faith hoped Mrs. Dickinson was ironing with all the windows open in this heat.

"Fortunately it was one of my days on the island," he said. The sheriff's office was the only police presence on Sanpere. There was no chief, force, or hoosegow. Earl pulled up a chair and sat down. "I am so sorry. It must have been a terrible shock. Sophie, I understand you did everything you could to revive him."

"I'm okay. Well, not really. I think you're saying he definitely didn't survive," Sophie said.

"Yes." Earl put his hand on Sophie's arm. "He was already gone when they put him in the ambulance. Bill Haviford told me you thought you'd detected a pulse and had started CPR in the water. I got in touch with him after I learned he was the one who had made the emergency call. He also told me where the two of you were."

Earl continued talking in his slow, steady voice. "We won't know until after the autopsy, but the guess is he'd been in the water for a while. Maybe most of today and even last night."

He took out his trademark little spiral notebook and clicked a ballpoint. "If you feel up to it, could you tell me everything you two noticed at the pond? And, Sophie, Bill said you saw the victim at the market last week with some other people?"

"We've been sitting here going over it all," Faith said, "but let me get you something cold to drink and freshen Sophie's." She planned to make it a stiff one. Earl could drive Sophie home. And Faith herself wasn't going anywhere.

When she returned, Sophie was telling Earl what she'd already related to Faith about last Friday and the pond. She sounded calm—resigned.

"You've been a big help," he said, "but there's a lot more we're trying to figure out. Number one: What was he doing in that part of the pond? Number two: How did he get there? I knew about the motorcycle from what you told Bill, but there's no sign of one anywhere there or on any nearby roads. We're looking all over the island now. What you said about the gear, possibly camping gear, helps. And the Mass. plates. We'll send his finger-prints down there immediately."

"You know he was barefoot, right?" Faith said. "Walking through that part of the woods would have killed his feet. Unless you found his shoes near where we found him." It felt odd to keep re-ferring to the dead man as "he." A man without a name.

Earl shook his head and reached for some crack-ers and cheese. "We haven't done a major search of the area, but there was nothing on the ground near the end of the pond except what you'd expect in the way of rocks, weeds, the odd broken bottle or two—didn't look recent. And there was nothing on him neither. No wallet, no keys, no phone. Tight jeans, so they couldn't have fallen out in the water. It's shallow and clear there. We raked it some and will go back, but so far no clues to his identity at all."

"Except the tattoo," Sophie said.

At first Pix thought an extremely loud mosquito had taken up residence in her ear. She brushed at it, but the noise continued. She opened her eyes and sat up. An early riser, this was early even for her. Not yet six. She shook her head. The noise continued.

Realizing that the sound was a chain saw—one close by—Pix jumped out of bed fully awake and headed out the door to the deck. The sound of chain saws was common on the island, and the ratio of males to that particular kind of machinery was probably one to three—that is three chain saws for every guy. Sam had one, although Pix lived in fear every time he decided to attack the alders or dead branches he claimed might hit the house. After a storm, the whole island buzzed as the opportunity to clear up the "damage," that is, expand your view, was seized.

After their first child was born, the Millers had bought their own summer place on Sanpere, an old farmhouse that was in good shape with shore frontage and surrounded by what Realtors always refer to as mature plantings—spruce, balsam, birch, bayberry bushes, *Rosa rugosa*s, and juniper. A small meadow in front of the house was filled with blueberries and tiny mountain cranberries in season. When the Millers arrived each year, the space was a mass of lupine in a variety of colors. They'd added onto the house as their family increased, linking the small barn to the main house as well as extending a deck off the expanded living room.

There were only a few houses on their road, the nearest one a small cabin—what local people called a "camp." The Spoffords had built it in the 1950s when their children were small, and they moved there from their year-round one in "town" each summer. Ed commuted all of five miles to his job at the shipyard. When he retired they winterized the cabin and sold the house in Granville. Pix loved having them as neighbors, as did the Miller children, who called Edith the "Cookie Lady," returning from a visit next door with huge old-fashioned hermits and snickerdoodles clutched in their hands. Finally the day came when Edith told Pix sadly that they had to move closer to their daughter in South Portland—she made it sound like the other side of the moon, and it certainly would be different from the island. They'd get used to traffic and there was a big mall, she'd added. It had become too much for Ed to keep the cabin, small as it was, up to his standards and Edith had drawn the line at his plan to put on a new roof by himself. When none of the children wanted it, they regretfully put it on the market. It sat unsold for several seasons. The living space was tiny by most standards, and the house sat well back from the shore atop a narrow strip of land. There was a fine view at the shoreline, however, and their two Adirondack chairs overlooking the cove were a permanent part of the landscape. Most early evenings found them there enjoying the sunsets and the beer Ed brewed with a group of his friends. They called themselves The Old Hopsters.

Standing on the deck in the weak morning light, it didn't take long for Pix to pinpoint the direction of the noise that had awoken her so abruptly. The sound, louder outdoors, was coming from the Spoffords'. Only she knew it wasn't the Spoffords anymore. Edith had called in June to say they had finally found a buyer, a couple from New Hampshire who planned to use it as a vacation home. Cameron and Drew Crane. And no, Edith didn't know which was Mr. and which was Mrs. The Realtor had handled everything. She did know that Mr. was recently retired from owning some kind of business. Edith was a whiz when it came to island history, complicated family trees, selling things on eBay, and of course baking; but she could sometimes be vague as to other particulars.

Pix started down the short steps at the end of the deck heading in the direction of the noise. There was a path near the shoreline, well-worn over the years, through the small stand of trees that separated the two properties. She stopped. Perhaps showing up dressed in well-worn PJs that originally belonged to one of her sons was not the way to make the best first impression on new neighbors. She dashed inside, threw on jeans and a tee shirt, shoved her feet into docksiders, and went back out. She wished she had a pie or some other offering to take, but the continuous noise meant serious cutting and Welcome Neighbor would have to wait.

A few feet from the property line she stopped again.

In horror.

Mr. Crane had clear-cut a swath starting at the shoreline. He wasn't a large man, but he was wielding the biggest chain saw Pix had ever seen as though it was a bread knife. His wife was dragging the cuttings to a brush pile that looked like a prop for *The Towering Inferno*. They were both wearing the kind of headphones professionals wore, and Pix was forced to jump dangerously close to the man, frantically waving her arms in his face. Mrs. Crane put down the branches she had scooped up, but after briefly flicking his eyes in her direction, Mr. Crane kept on working. His wife walked over and tugged his sleeve. Pix could see both reluctance and irritation on his face as he turned the saw off.

"Yes?" he said.

"Hi, I'm Pix Miller. We live next door." She pointed behind her. When no one replied, she took a breath and soldiered on. "I'm a bit concerned about the clearing you are doing. The Shoreland Ordinance provides specific guidelines for what can and cannot be done in this zone. For instance, taking down a tree that size"—she pointed to a large pine already neatly cut into logs—"is not allowed."

"And your point is?" He had a crew cut—surely not done with the saw, but an equivalent—and the kind of face that was so bland you would never be able to describe it, say, after a robbery. Well, officer, he had two eyes, a nose, mouth . . . His wife was a bit more memorable. Short red curls were escaping from a craft brewery cap she was wearing. Good sign, Pix thought, then remembered that Ed Spofford had bought them in bulk and must have left a few in the cabin.

Mrs. Crane's face was shiny with sweat. Pix decided the best thing to do was invite them to her house for coffee. Mrs. Crane looked like she might want a break. Pix knew she had enough muffins left from the dozen Faith had brought over yesterday morning for the three of them.

"Why don't you come back with me now for some coffee and we can talk about all this?" she said brightly.

"Nothing to talk about," Mr. Crane said. "It's my land and I can do whatever I want with it. I'm exactly ten feet from the property line." Mrs. Crane had not uttered a word so far, but Pix did not think the smug smile that appeared on her face boded well.

"That may be so, but you are breaking other laws—and there are fines. Plus you are destroying both of our privacies!"

Mr. Crane's response took the form of switching the saw on and moving it menacingly close to Pix before limbing up a tree as far as he was able to reach, which was quite far. His wife got back to work, too. Pix started to stomp away and then remembered her phone was in her jeans. With a defiant glance at both of them she snapped photos of what they had done so far. She was so angry she felt sick to her stomach.

Back at the house she called Sam on the landline. The quixotic cell service on the island meant she could text him but not call. She sent all the photos as she waited for him to answer. He would still be asleep. When he picked up and heard her voice, it was a few seconds before she was able to assure him that she was fine—in body, but not in soul. It only took another few seconds for Sam to be as furious as she was. And this was before he saw the pictures arriving on his cell. Miles away in Aleford, his voice was so loud he sounded as if he were next to her. "Print out the regulations and go back there. No, don't go back there. We have no idea what this man is capable of." Pix knew they were both thinking scenes from a Stephen King novel. "Stay away. But call the Code Enforcement officer. Too bad Hubert's retired. Call him anyway if you can't get a hold of the new person this early."

Hubert Billings had been the island's Code Enforcement officer for more years than most current residents had been alive and knew every inch of it. He was fair, but strict. As he was wont to say, "Gone is gone." Whether it was a tree, acreage, or frontage. He had spoken highly of the woman who had taken his place after he told the town he flatly refused to keep going, having given in to their entreaties to stay just one more term too many times.

"I will," said Pix. "I'm going to the farmers' market in Granville and if I can't reach her by phone, I'll go to the town offices."

"Okay. I'll hit the road as soon as I can. The calls I have to make I can do pulling over. No one will be at work yet."

"But can you take the time off? I thought the case wasn't finished."

"All tied up yesterday. Thought I might come up for Fishermen's Day anyway."

Pix hung up, and despite the whine of the chain saw, which mimicked a never-ending dental drill, she felt better. Sam was coming. Sam and she would handle the Cranes, Cameron and Drew—he and she or she and he. Until then Pix wouldn't let herself think about what damage they would do before Sam's five-hour nonstop drive.

Chainsaw Massacre. Those were the only words for it.

Sanpere had a real farmers' market with vendors selling vegetables, fruits, eggs, cheese, smoked sausage, and other products of their own toil. No cardboard boxes shoved in the backs of pickups with places of origin far from Maine. The only craft items were wool from a woman who owned sheep and a man who made cutting boards and spoons from his woodlot. Therefore, it was smaller than some in the state, but as word had spread, Granville had had to open the ballfield behind the old elementary school now consolidated with Sanpere Village's to accommodate all the cars.

Over the years on Fridays, Faith and Pix left their families when they could to meet up at the Harbor Café before the market opened at ten. The late opening was to allow sellers who lived on the other side of the bridge a chance to get to Granville at the same time as island purveyors. Fair was fair.

Pix hadn't been able to reach the Code Enforcement officer, but she'd left a message. She'd also left a message for Hubert. Granville's Town Hall was next to the Café, and she popped in there to leave word, too, enjoying a few minutes venting with the sympathetic town clerk before meeting Faith.

Faith had scored a booth at the Café. "Sorry to keep you waiting," Pix said. "I'll explain in a minute. But first of all, how are you and how is Sophie?" Faith had called her after Earl and Sophie drove off, knowing Pix would hear the news about their grisly discovery—if she hadn't already—and worry. Pix had immediately walked over. She knew bringing any sort of food would be coals to Newcastle, so she arrived bearing a large bottle of Tanqueray gin. Tom pulled into the drive alone not long after. Amy was working late. Apparently, no one had wanted to disturb him with the news, so Pix had left it to Faith to fill him in. As she let herself out, she heard her friend say firmly, "I'm not going to be involved in any sleuthing."

Adding a splash of real cream to the Café's excellent coffee, Faith said, "I'm fine. Tom calmed down right away, and your gin helped. I owe you. I talked to Sophie this morning, and she's fine, too." Faith was sure that like her, Sophie must have been trying to push it all far to the back of her mind, answering "fine" to inquiries. And the one she uttered now, even to Pix, "A tragic thing, but we didn't know him. But you're not fine. What's going on? The wedding? Don't tell me Edgewood Farm has double-booked?" This, Pix had told Faith, was the kind of problem that kept her up at night no matter how many times she was assured it couldn't happen and had a contract to prove it.

"The wedding?" For a moment Pix had trouble remembering. What wedding? "Oh, no. Worse." And it was. If Mr. Crane didn't stop chopping, the Millers would be looking straight into his property and vice versa.

"Would you like me to go over and chain myself to his chain saw? Hug a tree?" Faith offered after hearing what had happened.

"I thought of doing both, but the noise stopped shortly after I left them. I mentioned fines, and maybe that was a deterrent. Although he also may have simply needed more gas."

"Let's go up to the market," Faith said.

Pix finished her grilled strawberry rhubarb muffin and her coffee—the fourth cup of the day, which might not have soothed her nerves, but holding the warm mug had been comforting.

It was much cooler than it had been all week, and the farmers' market was packed. The two women parted ways to stand in different lines. Pix figured that if Sam left Aleford when he said, he'd get to the island a little after noon or close to one o'clock with a stop. He'd want lunch. She knew he didn't consider salad of any kind a meal, so instead she got bread from Tinder Hearth and smoked gouda for grilled cheese. She stood in another long line for several kinds of Anne Bossi's delectable goat cheese and husband Bob Bowen's slab bacon and eggs. Dinner would be easy; she had steaks in the freezer and stood in another line for new potatoes, zucchini, peppers, and chard. She grew only patio tomatoes and herbs herself now, having declared the deer and slugs the winners years ago.

Seeing Faith in conversation with Sophie, she headed over to them. Faith's trug was overflowing with purchases, including veggies Pix had no idea how to turn into something edible.

"I've been telling Sophie about your new neighbors from hell," Faith said.

"If you like, I can see whether there's some kind of injunction you can get quickly," Sophie offered. "I'm not familiar with Maine's environmental laws, but there must be a county or state tree warden's office. Unfortunately, I do know that people clear-cut and pay the relatively low fine. Still, there may be something about having to replant if it is too extensive."

"I'm relying on Sam," Pix said. "The only place he's ever lost his cool to my knowledge is on the tennis court. He should be here in a few hours and can reason with them."

Faith nodded. "I've seen him in action dealing with crazy-making questions at Town Meeting, so this should be a walk in the park—or woods." Sam was one of Aleford's selectmen.

Feeling better after both comments, Pix changed the subject. "I thought you two would be surrounded by groups of discreet individuals wanting to know all about yesterday."

"We have been a bit," Faith said, "but you know how people are here. It's like when Julia Child used to visit her friend, and now Meryl Streep has rented on the Pressey Road. Live and let live."

"That's not to say there isn't a buzz," Sophie said. "Bob Bowen, never one to shy away from any topic, first commiserated and then related all the rumors of sightings of the victim on the island and the Hancock peninsula for a week or more— that he was here looking to buy property, make a movie, find a job, or compete in the codfish toss on Sunday. Take your pick."

Faith and Pix laughed. "And I'm sure that's only

a few of the rumors," Faith said as she started to head for the ballfield where she had parked her car. Pix followed.

"Pix," Sophie said, putting her hand out to stop her. "Faith and Tom are coming for dinner tomorrow night. Why don't you and Sam join us?"

"I know he'd agree, so yes. And I can bring hors d'oeuvres. I bought a whole Fleur de Bossi, the cheese with herbs Anne makes that won best chèvre in the state a while ago, and I'll pick up some smoked mussels at Clearwater Seafood."

She was glad to be free. Like the Fairchilds', Pix and Sam's social life in the summer was hectic as everyone took advantage of the proximity of friends who were spread out during the rest of the year.

"Great," Sophie said. "Uncle Paul wants to set some sailing dates with Sam, so he'll be very happy."

"See you tomorrow then," Pix said and went home to wait impatiently for her husband, a Daniel who would tame the lion in the den next door.

Sam didn't want to take the time to eat anything. Pix had returned to the sound of the chain saw and it was still going on when Sam arrived.

"I printed out the state handbook," Pix said, handing it to Sam. "Do you think it's better to go alone or should I come?" It was hard to think what the proper approach should be—nice couple living next door only concerned about a few, more than a few, trees or furious couple concerned about same. "I don't think I offended them, but you never know . . ." Pix really, really didn't want to confront the Cranes again, but if Sam thought it was best, of course she would.

"No, you've had a try, and we don't want them to feel threatened by two against, well, two but one problem. Give me the printout, and if I'm not back in an hour or you hear screams, call Earl."

Rather than take the shortcut, Sam walked up the road. He was back in ten minutes. It took five minutes to reach the cabin. The conversation must have been brief.

Pix quickly started lunch as Sam expressed his feelings using language never employed in front of the children, even though said children were now adults.

"He wants an open view," Sam seethed. "Oh, and he's Cameron, she's Drew. He said, 'Drew and I,' hence . . ."

"What can we do?" Pix realized she was letting the sandwiches burn and quickly took them out of the iron skillet.

"I don't know, honey. All I know is it will be expensive. We'll have to get Mainescape down here to put in a staggered row of evergreens twelve feet from the property line to be sure legally and maybe some sort of fencing up here by the house if that area is cleared, too." He sat down and eyed the oozing sandwich with obvious anticipation. "Now let's try to forget about it for now. Tell me about this body Faith and Sophie found."

"How did you find out?" Pix asked. "Oh, Tom, right?"

"Yes. He called last night. Wanted to know what I knew, which was nothing. However, I reassured him his wife wasn't getting mixed up in anything again or else you would have called me."

Pix gave him a brief description. She was distracted by the noise from next door. Sam's attempt at reasoning with them seemed to have only increased the volume.

"I just saw Sophie and Faith at the farmers' market," she said. "They seem to have put it all out of their minds. Sophie's invited us to The Birches for dinner tomorrow with Faith and Tom. Oh, she mentioned Paul wants to set a sailing date." As she'd predicted, Sam was pleased. "I'll call him right now," he said, "and see if he wants to go sailing during the day."

"He'd love that," Pix said. Delighted to have her husband sooner than expected, Pix cleaned up the kitchen while Sam called The Birches. Worries about the wedding and even the trees were pushed aside, and she looked forward to a lazy afternoon on the deck with a swim once the tide was high enough. Next door had grown blessedly quiet.

And then the noise started up again.

Sam stormed into the room. "Come on, let's go to Blue Hill and price out some trees! We can't stay here!"

Considerably out of pocket, but with assurances that the work would be done quickly, the Millers decided to stop at El El Frijoles in Sargentville on the way back to the island. Michele Levesque, the chef, and husband Michael Rossney had created a unique place—Mexican food goes Down East. Sam was addicted to their spicy lobster tacos, and Pix equally to their crab quesadillas. El El, as it was known, had a BYO policy and Sam had gone to the Eggemoggin Country Store to pick up cold beers while Pix ordered. She remembered she'd forgotten to take the steaks out of the freezer and had a sudden yen for meat. She ordered the taco for Sam and a carne asada burrito for herself, deciding on an order of nachos to start. When Sam returned, they took the nachos—layers of beans, guacamole, crema, and salsa topped with melted cheese, a meal in itself—to the screened-in area with picnic tables behind the small restaurant. There were a few small tables inside, but it was beautiful out, and the screens took care of the mosquitos.

Sam took a long drink. "It will take a while for the trees to provide the privacy we had, but if we plant some low-lying junipers in between, it will look like a screen sooner." Pix nodded agreement—her mouth was full. She was feeling happier than she had for hours. Just getting away from the noisy reminder of the problem helped.

"Faith told me it took her a few summers before she got the El El Frijoles joke—L.L. Bean." Pix laughed. Sunday, the day after the wedding, Ursula was hosting a brunch at The Pines, and it had been her idea to hire El El's Michele to cater it. They would serve plenty of what was on the regular menu, but it would also be a showcase for Michele's considerable skills as a professional chef across many borders. El El's garden supplied much of their produce and the rest came from the local, high-quality sources they had discovered—even the black beans and, of course, the seafood.

By now the wedding really was as organized as Pix, mistress of the art, could make it. Faith was doing the rehearsal dinner Friday night, an old-fashioned clambake with a few of Faith's own touches. The guest list had expanded to include anyone who had already arrived from out of town in addition to the wedding party. The next afternoon following the outdoor—Pix said a silent prayer to the weather gods—ceremony at Edgewood, with its spectacular view across Penobscot Bay, there would be a sit-down dinner, catered by Blue Hill's Arborvine, followed by dancing. Samantha had told her mother that she and Zach were taking swing dance lessons at a dance studio in Cambridge. Reluctant at first, Zach had gotten into it and Samantha said now he was better than she was.

"I can't eat another thing," Pix said. "Home?"

"Absolutely—and I have a few ideas about what we can do for fun," Sam said with an attempt at a roguish smile.

The night was blissfully quiet. Since Cameron and Drew Crane were up with the lark, perhaps they went to bed with the birds as well.

The only thing that disturbed the Millers was the surprise arrival of their daughter and her fiancé shortly after one o'clock. The couple had crept in silently, but Pix—after years of fine-tuned awakenings if a child so much as sneezed—heard them, made sure they weren't hungry, and went back to sleep, elated to have so much of her family under one roof.

It wasn't a lark that awakened the Millers shortly after dawn the next morning, but loud banging on the front door and an angry voice shouting for them to get up. When Sam opened it, followed closely by Pix, he found their new neighbor on the other side.

"You bastard," Cameron Crane yelled at Sam.

"What are you talking about?" Sam was stunned. "I think you need to calm down!"

"Oh, you don't know what I'm talking about, do you?" Cameron grabbed Sam's arm and pulled him toward the drive, where Drew was sitting in a large Mercedes 4x4. "Get in."

"Now just a minute, pal," Sam said, wrenching his arm free.

Pix had never seen her husband so mad. Hastily she said, "Sam, put some shoes on and we'll go see whatever it is that's upsetting Mr. Crane." Somehow saying Cameron sounded too friendly, and he was frightening her. She pushed that feeling away and let anger take its place. Standing very straight, she said in a chilling tone, "We can walk over to your house. There are plenty of openings now."

As she'd intended, it was a red flag. The man looked as if he was going to deck her.

"Let's get this over with," he snarled, turned around and got into the car, backing out of their drive fast, scattering gravel.

"What's going on?" Zach came down the stairs. "Sounded like a fight."

"Go back to bed, dear," Pix said. "We'll explain later."

"Okay, but if you need me . . ." Zach rubbed an eye.

"If we do, we'll come back. We just have to go next door for a bit."

Pix followed Sam on foot down the path, and they arrived before the Cranes. "What on earth could have happened?" Pix wondered as the car pulled in.

"I have no idea, but this is not a person I ever want to have any dealings with and certainly not as a neighbor. We just have to wait and see what's triggered this, then keep a distance."

What triggered it was soon clear as Cameron virtually dragged them to the shed Ed Spofford had put up years ago for his tools and a small workbench. With his wife by his side, Cameron flung open the door and pointed to the cement floor. His chain saw was lying in a slick pool of something and covered with the substance as well. He didn't need to point at the cause, but he did, almost foaming with rage.

The floor was strewn with empty containers of Gorilla Glue.

Three

Both Millers were aghast. "You can't seriously believe we had anything to do with this!" Sam exclaimed.

Cameron Crane folded his arms in front of his chest. "And you can't seriously believe that last night some random passerby happened upon our shed armed with the stuff and thought destroying a chain saw would be a fun thing to do. Whereas you and your wife"—he made it sound dubious, Pix thought indignantly, as if she were something else—"had every reason in your perverted minds for committing this act of vandalism. I've called the police and my lawyer. That saw was an Echo thirty-six inch and put me back almost nine hundred bucks. I'll be expecting the replacement immediately."

Pix watched in alarm as Sam's face turned bright red. "Now just a minute! I'm not paying a dime and you can tell that to your lawyer. Judging by the way you've acted toward us, I'm sure there are plenty of people out there who would like to do this kind of thing to you!"

The windowless shed was feeling very cramped, Pix thought, even without the monster chain saw taking up room in pride of place. Plus the smell of the glue was nauseating. "Let's go home, Sam," she said. There was no point in continuing the conversation.

"Don't go far," Crane shouted after them. "The police are going to want to talk to you!"

"There goes that trip to Paris," Sam said sarcastically. He started to turn back, but Pix kept a firm grip on his elbow and moved him along.

Out on the road she said, "I think we'd better call Earl right away."

Going back to sleep was impossible, so she made a large pot of coffee and batter for blueberry pancakes. Zach and Samantha would sleep in, given how late they arrived, but Sam needed sustenance now. She was too upset to eat but poured herself a large mug of coffee.

"We know we didn't do it," she said to her husband, who was sitting at the kitchen table staring gloomily out at the cove. "So who did?"

"They haven't been on the island long, but I'm sure with his attitude he's managed to piss off any number of people. You can get that glue at Barton's, although there was such a lot of it maybe it was from the Home Depot in Ellsworth." Barton's was the lumberyard and hardware store located between Granville and Sanpere Village. It stocked anything you could possibly need, but not in large quantities. "You said he started cutting early. Sound carries over water, especially that kind. Could have been someone on the other Point or farther."

Pix set a stack of pancakes and warm syrup in front of him.

"We don't have to find out who did it. The police will, and it won't be a secret long on this island. Eat your breakfast."

Sam shook his head. "No matter what, he'll never believe it wasn't us. Damn. We should have bought the place from the Spoffords ourselves. But I'd always pictured someone like them buying it, and it's nice to have neighbors."

Pix sighed. She'd been thinking the same thing since her confrontation with the Cranes yesterday. "It's annoying—more than annoying—now, but we'll plant and in a few years we won't see them and before that we *really* won't see them."

"So no inviting them for dinner?" Sam reached for his wife and pulled her onto his lap. "No bringing over crabs when we have too many from Ed Ricks?"

Ed Ricks, Dr. Edwin Ricks, was a well-known New York City psychiatrist, quoted in the *Times* and elsewhere, and often appearing on PBS. A few years ago he'd given up his practice and retired year-round to his Sanpere summer home. He had a license to put out a few traps and always dropped off the crabs that he caught with the lobsters, knowing they were favorites with the Millers and too much work to pick for other friends. Pix could not envision the Cranes at this time-consuming task. They seemed to prefer immediate results.

"I wonder what Ed would make of Cameron?" Pix said.

"If he wants to meet the man, it will have to be on other than our turf, what is left of it," Sam said. "And speaking of turf, I'd swear that lawn was new sod. Did you see there were no twigs or weeds marring the surface? Looked like a golf course, or maybe AstroTurf."

"The only flowers I saw were impatiens by the front door in terra-cotta pots—fakes. I can always tell, no mold or chips." Pix tended a wide perennial garden along the front of their house but let nature supply the rest of the floral landscaping. After the lupine, the uncultivated lawn was covered with daisies and then black-eyed Susans. Queen Anne's lace was coming in now. They mowed occasionally to keep ticks away but tried to steer around the clumps of flowers. Pix liked marking summer's progression by looking out the window at what was growing. Goldenrod and wild asters marked its end. "I haven't been able to figure what Mrs. Crane, Drew, might be like. She hasn't said a single word so far, and her only facial expression has been the kind of smarmy smile that girl who used to bully Samantha in middle school had."

"*He's* certainly a bully, so two of a kind," Sam said, mopping up the syrup on his plate with the last bite of his pancakes. "I'm going to go check online what recourse we may have. Not about the chain saw but about reporting the clear-cutting and possible fines. We've made an enemy so might as well follow through."

"So nice to have legal counsel close at hand," Pix said, kissing the top of her lawyer husband's head. "Give a shout when the kids are up. I'm going to take Arty outside. Don't clean up. I'll do it all at once." The Millers were down to one beloved golden retriever, Arthur or Arty. Pix hoped to have him by her side and at the foot of the bed for many more years.

"'When the "kids" wake up'? I don't think we can call them that anymore," Sam said.

"Well, the bride and groom then," Pix retorted. All three of her children and their significant others would always be "kids" in her mind.

Two pills. That was it. She shook them out of the vial into her hand and saw that it was trembling. She made a tight fist.

Two round white pills.

Nowhere near enough, but enough to make do for now. She closed her eyes and felt the tears. Hot tears that streamed down her cheeks.

He'd noticed she was losing weight, but she said it was so she'd look good in her summer clothes. Like a bathing suit. She almost laughed aloud. No way was she going swimming.

Her mother was worried that she was doing too much, because she was so tired all the time. Well yes, she was doing too much. She started to laugh again. Up. Down. Sunshine and tears. She'd never been that kind of girl. Miss Responsible. Steady as a rock.

She was alone in the house. It would be okay. There was plenty of time. She could already feel the rush. Feel herself relax like a ragdoll. Soon all the bad stuff would go away. All the thoughts of the kind of person she really was. Poof. Gone like magic. Gone

*like her own personal Tinkerbell had waved a wand
and sprinkled her with fairy dust.*

*She'd been sitting on the side of the bed and lay
down, slowly stretching out on top of the quilt her
grandmother had made for them. Wedding Ring.
That was the pattern.*

*She opened her fingers. Only two. She had to get
more. That meant going off-island. Too dangerous
to score here.*

*The bad thoughts were starting to come. They
were like snakes. Horrible snakes that wrapped
around her brain.*

She took the pills dry.

Sophie was sitting on the porch, watching the
start of what promised to be a stunning sunset
and waiting for everyone to arrive. Uncle Paul was
taking a shower—getting "gussied up" he'd told
her. Sam Miller had called early that morning inviting them for a sail. Sophie had declined, but
Paul had enjoyed a long trip out to North Haven
with Sam and Zach. Before he went up to change,
Paul had given Sophie a quick version of the sticky
chain saw incident, and she was sure she'd hear a
full account once the Millers arrived.

So many angry people, Sophie thought, pushing
world and national events firmly away. The island
was never one big happy family, but the various
groups—natives, people from away, and summer

people—coexisted in a kind of surface harmony. But this summer she'd noticed some cracks. Not the same kind of mingling at the parade or chatting about the weather in line at the market between someone who had come out of a pickup and someone from a BMW. A local she didn't know yelled at her for parking in the post office lot, pointing to her out-of-state plates. Sophie had held out her post office box keys and started to say the family had had a box just about forever, but the woman got in her own car and slammed the door. Sophie had talked about it with Will on one of their late-night chats. He'd said it was the same everywhere and compared life now to a kind of large-scale road rage. Sometimes, he had said, you really were cut off, but mostly the rude gestures were because of what else was going on—nothing that had anything to do with the rules of the road. Worry, fear, not enough time or money. She'd agreed.

And now here was another island mystery—the title not *Who Drowned in the Lily Pond?* but *Who Glued the Chain Saw to the Shed Floor?* It would be funny if it were happening to people she didn't know.

As for the man in the Lily Pond, she had lied to Faith, Will, and others. She wasn't fine. Not now and not during the two long nights after her failed attempt to bring him to life. When she did drift off to sleep, she woke at once. The adder that slithered down his arm had slithered into her dreams. She could no longer picture what his face had looked like, but she could feel the texture of his hair as she gripped it, trying to breathe for him. Long strands. Down to his collarbones. Although wet, fine as silk. His eyes were closed. She remembered that and was glad. No stare to haunt her waking and sleeping thoughts. Will had sensed her true feelings and pressed to come. She had amped up her objections. The weekend would be tantalizingly short. She was surrounded by friends. She was fine.

I am fine, Sophie told herself again and put on a smile as her uncle came through the door.

"You cannot make this stuff up," Sam said. Pix was driving, so the martini Paul had offered—and he mixed the old-fashioned James Bond kind—plus the Peak Summer Ales Sam was having with dinner had created his jovial mood.

"What did Earl say when you called him?" Sophie asked. She'd been putting the finishing touches to the seafood risotto and arugula salad with grilled pears that was the main course and had missed the law enforcement part of the story.

Pix picked up the thread. "Earl got the voice mail we left this morning and I spoke to him this afternoon when he called back. The Cranes had immediately phoned the sheriff's office, but Earl was in Ellsworth at the courthouse, so he didn't speak with them. Whoever it was took down the details, and said someone would come when they had an officer free and advised them to get a lock for their shed. Then they called twice more and their lawyer once in the next hour, so somebody drew the short straw and came down. Given what has been happening all over the peninsula, a vandalized chain saw was not a top priority on the department's list. If one that expensive had been stolen, that would have been another thing—and who on earth would pay that much for one? Anyway, Earl had relayed our message to the patrolman who went to the house. He took photos and even dusted for prints at Crane's insistence—there were none, which had them accusing us all the more, apparently."

"Pix is such a lady. She always wears gloves," Tom teased.

"Go on," Sophie said. "Then what?"

"Then nothing," Sam said. "Except the Cranes have now been reported by us and the sheriff's office for clear-cutting. The sheriff's office also reported them to the Bangor office of the Department of Environmental Protection for possible infractions. Guess there might have been some Cameron Crane attitude going on." He sounded gleeful.

Zach turned to Samantha, who was sitting next to him. "And you told me this was a peaceful place. I believe your words when you first told me about Sanpere were 'island of calm.'"

"It is," she protested. "Mostly. I mean, it's like anywhere else. Things happen. But calmly. They happen calmly. Look at the way my parents are taking this. Other people in other places would be suing the Cranes for slander or worse by now."

"Calm it is. A paradise. No problem." Zach put his arm around her. "And if you're not going to finish that risotto, I will."

"In your dreams!" she said and then put a big spoonful on his plate. "But no sharing my fried clams tomorrow on the pier. Or the fries and onion rings."

"Children, children," Paul said. "I happen to know for certain that there will be more than enough food. Marge told me this morning that the Rebekahs have been shucking mountains of clams and slicing a truckload of onions and potatoes for vats of chowder and the wickedly good food that is so bad for you."

"Are there that many women named Rebekah on the island?" Zach asked.

His future wife punched him lightly on the arm. "You went to the Blue Hill Fair with me last year and had strawberry shortcake. I know for sure I told you the women who cooked all those biscuits, hulled berries, and whipped cream were the Rebekahs, women's branch of the Odd Fellows!"

"It's all coming back." Zach did not sound convincing.

"What is?" Faith asked as she came through the door with a pan of Blueberry Buckle (see recipe, page 324) and a bowl of ice cream.

"Don't ask," Tom said. "If what you're bringing is what I think it is, it needs to be eaten immediately."

Faith laughed. "It's Blueberry Buckle, and I almost make it for the name alone! But what I think you're really talking about is the bowlful of the Ice Cream Lady's Madagascar Vanilla. And yes, both have to be eaten immediately while one is warm and one cold. Sophie, cut the cake and I'll serve the ice cream."

For years the Ice Cream Lady was another island mystery. A good one. Her flavors changed with what was in season—strawberries, blueberries, blackberries, peaches—but she always maintained a few classics like the vanilla, a dense dark chocolate, peppermint stick, and ginger. She was finally identified but still preferred a low profile and stuck to small batches at only a few stores. Happily the IGA was one.

After dessert, everyone helped clear and no one wanted coffee. The women shooed all the men from the kitchen back out onto the porch so they could talk about things of little interest to their male counterparts and vice versa. There wouldn't be port and cigars outdoors, but Paul did have some single malt on offer. In the kitchen while they were cleaning up, the women sipped mint tea courtesy of Pix's herb garden.

"Faith showed me a picture of your dress," Sophie said to Samantha. "It's a dream. I loved my dress, too, and they have a custom in Savannah and other parts of the South where you get to wear it on other occasions during that first year—and even longer if you push it. And Pix," she added, "yours is gorgeous, too. Just the right soft green for your lovely dark locks." Mother and daughter were brunettes, as Ursula—now snowy white—had been, too.

"I think my mother will steal the show—aside from the bride and those adorable children," Pix said. "She went to her lady at Saks and found a pale gold beaded cocktail dress, ballerina length, that looks like something Princess Grace would have worn during her movie career."

"What do you think Millicent will wear?" Samantha said. "I haven't dared ask her. I hope it doesn't smell of mothballs."

Sophie had heard about Millicent Revere McKinley, who was as much a part of Aleford as the town green. A distant descendant of the famous rider, she lived in a small clapboard house strategically placed with a sightline down Main Street. Claiming septuagenarian status for the last ten plus years, she was spry—and the arbiter of all things proper—in her opinion. "It's Miss McKinley, not Ms. Thank you very much." She was Ursula's closest friend and equally attached to the Millers and Fairchilds. Sophie loved hearing the tale about what happened after Faith dared to ring the Revere-cast bell in the Old Belfry her first year in Aleford. The fact that Faith, with baby Benjamin in a Snugli, had just discovered the still-warm corpse of a parishioner there cut no mustard with Millicent. In her very vocal opinion, Faith could have sped down the hill and screamed. The bell was tolled only on Patriots' Day and for the death of a president or of a descendant of those lucky enough to bear arms against the Redcoats that April day. Thinking about it now, she thought how New England it was and also that she couldn't wait to meet Millicent in person!

"She wore a kind of long velvet dress that may have been purple once to Ursula's eightieth," Pix said tentatively. "I think it may have been her mother's, judging from the style. Crushed velvet is in now, but I think Millicent's did not start out that way."

"I'll talk to Granny," Samantha offered. "She'll know what to do. Where is she tonight? I would have gone over to The Pines earlier but assumed I'd see her here."

"Her calendar is more filled than ours," Pix said. "Tonight she's at a friend's over in Sedgwick. It's the woman's camp reunion weekend—Camp Four Winds. Mother never went there nor did I, but she's always been considered an official Old Girl."

"How did Arlene like the matron of honor dress?" Faith asked Samantha. "I can't imagine she didn't love it—and look great in it. We saw her mother and Kylie the other day. Kylie is growing up so fast. It feels like we were just at that baby shower."

Samantha finished drying the plate in her hand. "Mike had to work and Kylie was running a low fever. Arlene's mother was working, too, so Arlene needed to stay home. I offered to bring the dress over but she didn't want me to catch anything if Kylie turned out to have that flu bug that's going around."

"There's always a flu bug going around in New England," Faith said. "No matter what time of year. Nobody ever had the flu in Manhattan when I was growing up."

Tom walked in on his wife's remark. "All the flu bugs were probably killed by exhaust fumes."

"Time to go?" she asked, exasperated as always

for his lack of appreciation for any apples, Big or small, except New England ones.

"Yes, you know me and Scotch. My eyelids are getting heavy."

"Cheap date," she told the others and went to say good night to the men on the porch.

The Millers, Zach, and Samantha left soon after. Sophie joined Paul outside. It was still so warm she was tempted to swim. On a clear night like this the stars appeared as if an unseen hand had upended an overflowing astral basin. There was scarcely room among the points of light for the velvety dark.

Paul handed her a glass with a finger of Scotch. "Drink this. And I want you to sleep tonight. If you can't, come get me. We'll sit out here."

She reached across and took her uncle's hand, obediently sipped the drink, and felt its warmth travel down through her body. Maybe she *would* sleep. A star shot across the night sky. She closed her eyes and made a wish.

Pix was surprised to see Arty coming down the stairs the moment the kitchen door closed behind them. Normally the dog would be snoring softly at the foot of their bed. She went over, bent down, and stroked his soft head, noting how many more white hairs there were on his snout. "Doggy nightmare? What's the matter, sweetheart?" When she stood up, Arty promptly took her dangling sweater sleeve in his mouth and pulled her toward the stairs. Everyone laughed.

"Oh no, I think Timmy's in the well," Zach said.

"I guess I'd better go get him settled," Pix said. "I'll be down in a minute."

She was down in less than a minute with Arty at her heels. "There's a strange woman asleep in the guest room! Strange, I mean, as in I have no idea who she is."

"I'm assuming it's not Goldilocks," Sam said. "And I don't think we need to count the teaspoons if the perp stayed on the premises."

They all headed up the stairs quietly with Pix leading the way. She opened the door and they saw that there was indeed a woman fast asleep under a sheet and light summer blanket in the spindle bed. "Never saw her before," Sam whispered. "And even if I had I wouldn't recognize her with all that goop on her face and the mask."

Samantha poked her father. "It's an eye mask and moisturizer. Lots of women use a night cream."

"Not mine," he said. "Do most women wear that kind of eye thing, too? Never got that kind on a plane."

The eye mask was pink satin decorated with exaggerated long sequin lashes. Besides that, the woman had a kind of turban wrapped around her head, presumably to keep from getting bed hair.

"Why are we whispering?" Pix asked. "I don't want to seem inhospitable, but I think we should wake her up, ask her who she is and what she's doing here."

"Let her sleep," Zach said in a weary tone. "It's my mother."

After Zach's statement, Pix closed the door gently behind her and they all filed downstairs.

Zach sat down on the sofa and Samantha snuggled close to her fiancé, putting her head on his shoulder. He stroked his fiancée's hair, then sat up straight. "You know my family situation. You could call me an orphan except my parents are both very much alive," he said. "Marrying into a family like yours is kind of like a dream. Samantha would be enough. But gaining sibs and parents-in-law like you is amazing—I'm getting sappy, but seriously, I didn't know what I had been missing. You don't miss what you never had. I last saw my father at my high school graduation because he happened to be in the area. Before that there never seemed to be the right time to go out to the coast and meet his new wife and their kids. Particularly since he wasn't exactly sending me a plane ticket. I'm a reminder of a very acrimonious marriage and worse divorce. As for my mother, she always made sure I was in the right boarding school and at the right summer camp, so problem solved year-round. She'd swoop in unexpectedly—like now—and then take off. I have an email address for her and at various times addresses for apartments she's owned in New York, London, and Paris, but I don't have an address for her at the moment. She could be living anywhere. She was in Mongolia at Christmas in some sort of luxurious yurt. I know because she sent a postcard. Once I turned twenty-one a trust—don't think millions—kicked in and has kept me in ramen."

Pix immediately got up and sat on his other side. "I knew you didn't have much contact with your parents, but I had no idea! Samantha never said." All her maternal juices were flowing. "You poor boy!"

He gave her a somewhat crooked smile. "I guess I turned out all right though. Thanks to friends, especially the Fairchilds. Growing up on my own has made me stronger I think. Anyway, there wasn't much choice. At least my parents made sure I got a great education. The big question now is what is Alexandra Kohn doing here and how did she track me down? We have different last names, by the way—she changed *Cohen* to *K-O-H-N* for some reason. Pretty sure she didn't start life as 'Alexandra' either, but her birth certificate would be the last thing she'd let me see. She's in her thirties, which would make her about five when I was born. Now how about a beer and Scrabble? I play better when I'm slightly buzzed."

"Great idea," Sam said, standing up. "I'll get the beers and—" Whatever he was about to say was cut off by the sound of footsteps coming down the stairs. And they weren't doggy ones.

Everybody froze as the woman they had just seen asleep stood in front of them, hands on her hips. She was wearing an elaborately embroidered fuchsia silk dressing gown, and the sleep mask had been pushed up on top of her forehead, but rather than incongruous, the unsmiling figure was imposing.

"Do you have any idea the hell of a time I've had finding you, Zachary?" She didn't even pause for breath. "I get a computer invitation to your wedding—no earlier word that you were planning to get married. And not a proper invitation in the mail. What will my friends think?"

There *were* proper engraved invitations that the Millers had sent out. The evites went to Zach's and Samantha's friends, who were far more used to this form of communication. Zach hadn't had a snail mail address for his mother, he'd told Pix, so he'd sent the evite with a note about Samantha and her family, also reminding his mother that he had mentioned Samantha a while ago as a serious girlfriend. His mother either had not read it, had forgotten it, or was choosing to ignore its existence, possibly all three. He sent the formal invitation with a note to his father, whose address he knew, and received regrets with an Amazon gift card almost by return mail.

"I didn't have—" Zach started to protest, but his mother cut him off, actually putting her hand up, as if stopping traffic.

"We'll discuss this later." Her eyes swept the room, as if wondering who the interlopers into this one-on-one conversation were. "Fortunately I had your apartment's address, so I went straight there from the plane—don't even ask about that nightmare trip—they only had business class available not first. Your roommate told me you were on this island, so back to the airport I went and I ended up in Banger or some such place. No address for what I presume is the bride's family's house." There was another sweep of the eyes, but this time slower, taking in all three Millers and the rustic cottage with what could only be called mild distaste. "I had the cab take me to the venue on the invitation—a farm! What could you have been thinking?—and the people there directed me here. No one was in obviously and I'm terribly jet-lagged, so I'll be going back to sleep. Just coffee, dark roast, and wheat toast in the morning. Good night."

Zach jumped up. "Wait a minute. The wedding isn't for several weeks. What are you doing here?"

His mother sighed deeply, walked over, and patted her son on the shoulder. "To plan a proper one, of course."

She left bewilderment, anxiety, and the fragrance of Patou's Joy in the air.

It never rained on Fishermen's Day. At least not in the island's collective memory, which was extremely reliable when it came to weather. On this sunny Sunday morning, Samantha was sitting at the kitchen table with her future mother-in-law, wishing desperately that Zach or her parents were there, too. Her mother was already at the pier helping out with the festivities, which would start at ten o'clock. Zach and her father were grabbing some time on the boat polishing the brightwork, a never-ending chore. No one had expected Alexandra to be up this early.

"Alexandra." She'd immediately told Samantha to call her that, striding into the room dressed for the Hamptons or maybe the Riviera in snowy white capris, a turquoise silk shirt, wedged espadrilles that added inches to her height, and Jackie O sunglasses perched on her perfectly coiffed chin-length streaked blond hair—not the work of Supercuts and Clairol. A heavy gold-link necklace and several similar bracelets completed the look. She was carrying what Samantha knew was a Birkin bag. Whatever Alexandra was doing at night, and other times, to enhance her appearance was working. She was a striking woman who seemed much younger than Samantha knew she must be.

"'Mother Kohn' sounds like a patent medicine," Alexandra had added. "And I haven't been Mrs. Kohn for a very long time."

Samantha had been cleaning the cast-iron skillets they'd used for eggs and bacon. Alexandra had immediately observed that Samantha and Zachary might want to update their *batterie de cuisine* on their registry. "I'm assuming you have cookware listed? Calphalon and Creuset or my friends in Paris can send from Dehillerin," she'd said as Samantha hastily made toast and a fresh pot of coffee. Alexandra had looked on approvingly as Samantha ground beans, only asking whether they were fair trade or not. "Zachary can tell you that I am very concerned about the planet."

Now they were across from each other and Alexandra was grilling—there was no other word for it—her future daughter-in-law. Where had she gone to high school? What college? Job history? Why did she leave Manhattan for Boston? Why was she still living at home in—what was the place? Aleford? How many siblings did she have? What did they do? On and on and on until Samantha felt as if her skin were being peeled away layer by layer to reveal every fault, every defect minor or major. Shouldn't Zach's mother be happy that he was happy? About to marry the woman he loved? And simply accept her future daughter-in-law with open arms? Extremely well-toned and tanned ones Samantha noted.

Just when she thought she was going to crack and confess to shoplifting a bottle of glitter nail polish in sixth grade, Zach and her dad returned.

"Hi, honey," Samantha said gratefully. "Your mother and I have been having a, um, nice talk."

"Good," Zach said, and away from his mother's gaze, he raised his eyebrows and Samantha nodded, her mouth a tight line. "Well, Mom . . ." She didn't care for that name—"too Brady Bunch"—and had suggested Mater or Mother, even "Alexandra," but Zach had stuck with "Mom," claiming a tiny piece of his own territory. "We're all heading out to Fishermen's Day down on the pier in Granville if you'd like to join us. Granville is one of the largest lobster ports in the Northeast and every year they celebrate the industry and honor the fishermen."

"Sounds charming, but we don't have time," Alexandra said, pulling a Smythson leather notebook from her bag. "First of all, the place. Such a miracle, but I was able to pull some strings and get the Taj in Boston for the reception. The ceremony could be at any number of churches if you must, but also right there—so convenient. I assume you've already got some sort of dress"—she made it sound like a little number run up on the Millers' Singer—"but again, helps to have friends. Jenny, Jenny Packham, can send a toile as soon as I get your measurements and she'll do a custom rush job or Vera will. I think I'll have Vera do my gown and I can take your mother with me for hers. Men in morning coats I assume, unless you want an evening wedding and black tie? Really it would be best to move it to Manhattan. Florists to die for. Caterers, too. Glorious Food does such yummy things, but I suppose it has to be in Boston . . ." She was scribbling away as Zach sat down at the kitchen table next to her.

"Mom. Our wedding is all planned. For here. On the island. Everyone will be clothed just fine. The food will be delicious, and Mary, a professional gardener here, is taking care of the flowers. All you have to do is show up. I'm glad you'll be there." He put his arm around her, but she stiffened.

"You are my only child and I assume this is going to be your only wedding. I'm sure once I tell Samantha's mother the kind of wedding her daughter could have, one every little girl dreams of—you're very pretty, dear, and will make a lovely bride—all will agree that we need to change the plans."

Sam Miller had been listening quietly, standing away from everyone, and now he walked over to Alexandra. "We are happy to finally meet you and happy to have you as a guest, starting with the festival today. I'm sorry you had trouble getting here and that we couldn't welcome you properly last night. As for the wedding, I know my wife will enjoy telling you the details about what has been arranged."

Alexandra was savvy enough to recognize a stalemate when she saw one, equally savvy at knowing what biding one's time could accomplish. She looked at her son's intended. No girl in her right mind would turn down a wedding gown from Jenny Packham or Vera Wang, same for a reception at the Taj, formerly Boston's historic Ritz-Carlton.

She switched on a high-voltage smile. "Lead me to this fish thing, then. Just so long as I don't have to actually catch one."

Traditionally Fishermen's Day started with a moment of silence for those in peril and those lost at sea, following which individual fishermen were inducted into the Hall of Fame. The honorees had spent many, often colorful, years on the waters of Penobscot Bay. Occasionally the award was posthumous. As Faith, Tom, and Sophie walked past the photos posted on the fencing that lined one side of the pier they recognized, and missed, old friends.

The serious part over but not forgotten, the day started with a pet show ranging from tiny kittens to Great Danes with guinea pigs, hamsters, and the occasional iguana as well.

"It feels so odd not to have a kid with us," Faith said. "No one to cheer for in the watermelon eating or fish face contests."

"I'll enter," Tom offered, making an exaggerated one.

"I think not, Reverend. Too realistic!" Faith joked. "Besides, I would not be able to resist the temptation to text a photo to the church secretary for the next parish newsletter."

"The Wacky Row Boat Races are at noon," Sophie said. "Samantha and I are entered. I haven't seen her though. I hope she and Zach didn't decide to leave early."

"Who's rowing and who's signaling?" Tom asked. The race was aptly named, with the rower blindfolded and guided around a short course in the harbor only by his or her partner. It seemed simple enough, especially for an experienced rower. Just follow the commands, right, left, straight; but the roar of the crowd complicated the task. People shouted encouragement for their favorite team and made distracting comments like "My grandma could beat you without oars, just paddling with her hands!" The Fairchilds' neighbor on the Point, Freeman Hamilton, had told them years ago the trick he'd devised with his sister—a tap on one knee for right, double tap for left, and piercing whistle for straight.

The pier was packed, and Faith felt herself relax into the day as she greeted friends, stopped at booths set up by various island organizations, stocked up on Karen Cousins's beautiful photo cards, and bought, always in vain, still more quilt raffle tickets. One of these years . . . The air was filled with tantalizing smells—the chowder and fried seafood, fried dough, and kettle corn. At the very end of the pier people of all ages were dancing to the tunes of the Merry Mariners, who were set up on a flatbed trailer. The Mariners were known for their versatility, and so far Faith had heard and watched the twist, the macarena, and now an enthusiastic group of line dancers in synch to "Achy Breaky Heart." She was tempted to join, but her tendency to turn the opposite way from everyone else kept her where she was, humming along instead.

"Samantha!" Sophie cried. "I was afraid you had left. It's okay, though. The races haven't started yet."

"No way, this is our year," Samantha said, but Faith thought she didn't look too excited at the prospect. This was not the cheerful bride telling jokes at dinner the night before.

Sophie picked up on it, too. "What's wrong? We don't have to do this. No problem."

Samantha's eyes filled with tears. "Zach's mother was at the house when we got back last night. Asleep in the guest room, but she got up and then . . ." Samantha gulped. "We had a big talk this morning, just the two of us—or rather she talked and I listened. She's over there with Zach, Mom, and Dad. She's drinking a Diet Coke." Samantha pointed out a stylish woman Faith had noticed earlier, wondering how she had strayed so far from Seal Harbor on MDI, Martha Stewart country.

"She wants to move the wedding to Boston! To the Taj. She's 'pulled strings.'" Samantha made the motion with her fingers. "Everything has to be changed. Even my dress. She's ordering a toile and rush job from Jenny Packham, you know that British celeb designer, and 'Vera,'"—she made the quotation marks again—"as backup."

"But, sweetie," Faith said, putting an arm around Samantha. "It's *your* wedding. All the plans are set for here and it's going to be perfect. Nice of her to take an interest at last, but don't worry." Faith was inwardly furious. So Zach's mother, who couldn't be bothered to see him or even be in touch much for all these years, had decided to come steal his show.

Samantha was shaking her head. "I hope you're right, but you haven't met her. She's one of those unstoppable type of people, a tsunami in the making. My dad tried to tell her the wedding plans were fixed and not going to be changed, but she wasn't buying it. Said she'd talk to Mom."

Faith hugged her. "Oh, I think Pix will be more than a match for her—and I'll be standing right next to her."

While they had been talking Sophie had been looking back and forth from Faith and Samantha to the other group, with Alexandra very much in the forefront. "I think this may be a time for reinforcements," she said.

"Reinforcements?" Faith asked.

"Babs. I think this is a job for *my* mother."

Four

Correctly divining that his mother would not be a fan of the two-person codfish toss—an occasional fish missed its intended recipient and veered into the crowd—Zach hooked his arm through hers and suggested they walk to the far end of the pier to look at the view of the Fox Island Thoroughfare and islands beyond. It earned him a big smile.

"I haven't had a chance to talk with you at all. Is there someplace I could get a latte?" Alexandra said. "I need some more caffeine."

"I think you're going to have to get your boost from the view. It's pretty spectacular."

They walked past the booths, some of which

were already packing up. The only event left was the Granville versus Sanpere Village tug-of-war. Rivalry between the two towns had existed since each was incorporated. Granville had always been home to most of the island's industry—the quarries, sardine cannery, fishing fleet—while Sanpere Village's was a brief heyday around the time of the Civil War with lumber mills and easily accessible schooner landings along Eggemoggin Reach. For the most part the rivalry was a friendly one, but it flared up from time to time, most recently a few years back when the state had ordered the consolidation of the schools at a site in Sanpere Village instead of Granville.

"You know," Zach said, "that Samantha and I are driving to Boston in about an hour. I thought you could come, too. It would give you a chance to get to know Samantha better, and you have friends in the area you must want to see. Or we could take you to the airport if you wanted to go to New York."

Zach felt his arm tighten in hers. Tighten a lot. "Oh Zachary, that won't work at all. I had a long chat with Samantha this morning and she is very *nice* I'm sure, like her parents—although I must say her father seems like one of those men used to getting his way. Of course he's a lawyer."

Zach could feel his temper start to rise. The tone his mother had given the word *nice* was not nice. It was dismissive. It was a put-down. It was maddening. He wanted to tell his mother what an extraordinary person Samantha was, and her whole incredible family. How he was the luckiest guy in the world. In the universe.

"Samantha's—" But before he could get more than a word out, Alexandra cut him off.

"Oh, Zachary, you don't have to say a thing. She's your choice and you're old enough to make one. Certainly the phrase *making one's bed and having to lie in it* is apt here. No." She pulled her arm away from his. "I'm staying here. It's my job to see to it that the wedding is done properly. It's not always about you. A wedding is for the parents as well. To introduce the new couple to their friends and family and establish ties."

Zach felt like one of those cartoon characters with visible steam erupting from his ears. "First of all, when it comes to family, for all intents and purposes I only have one parent. Dad, whom I last saw before I was shaving I think, declined immediately. Both of your parents are gone, you don't have any siblings I've ever heard about or even cousins. Next, I have never met any of your friends. And last, Mom"—he stretched the disliked moniker out—"our wedding plans are not going to be altered in the slightest."

In front of them the late afternoon sun was streaming down, creating a mosaic of large and small islands surrounded by liquid gold water. His mother was silent, and for a moment Zach thought he'd won.

She took his arm again. "We'll see. Now we should be joining the others. I don't want to seem rude."

The moment Pix saw Zach's face she knew his very obvious plot to squelch his mother's grandiose plans had failed. Not that Pix had thought he would succeed. The tug-of-war was over—Tom and Sam had signed up to pull for Sanpere Village and were now crowing about the team's victory, the first in years. It had seemed to her that both teams were lacking the younger muscle usually displayed. Twentysomethings and even teens had dominated the teams in the past. Where were they all?

Pix heard Samantha call out, "Hey, Mike." The crowds were on their way up the steep hill to the ballfield where the cars were parked. She saw Arlene's husband, Mike, with their daughter, Kylie, on his shoulders. She was closer, so she quickened her pace and reached him first.

"Hi, Mike. Samantha is trying to get your attention."

"Hi, Pix," he said and stopped, swinging Kylie down. "Great day. I think this one may go to sleep before I can get her home."

"Not tired!" Kylie said, rubbing her eyes, smearing face paint that had turned her into a very colorful clown.

"I'm glad she was over whatever she had yesterday," Pix said.

Mike looked puzzled. "I didn't know she was sick."

"I think she was just running a little temp. Samantha had wanted to bring the dresses over and Arlene didn't want her to catch anything."

"Well, with kids it seems they're either getting something or getting over something," Mike said. "She's fine today."

Samantha caught up to them and Kylie immediately ran into her arms. "Wedding today? My pink dress? Mommy said pink."

"Very pink and you will look like a princess, but not today. Soon," Samantha said, hugging her. "Hi, Mike. Where's Arlene?"

"Nice to see you, too," he said. Mike and Samantha had been friends since Arlene first started dating him in high school. He was a foreigner, they'd teased him, since he was born in Brooksville on the other side of the bridge. "She had to help her mother. Too good a job to turn down. They're getting double time because someone took it today for family coming in tonight." Marilyn worked cleaning houses for one of the island vacation rental agencies, and Arlene helped her out on occasion. She was hoping to go back to her job at the bank once Kylie was in kindergarten. Mike Brown was a Marine Patrol officer. He'd been torn between being on the water fishing and law enforcement. This job, he said, made for the best of both worlds. Arlene had gone to Husson for an associate's degree in accounting. They'd both wanted to come back to live on the island and trained for jobs that would allow it.

"Zach, I know it gives us a late start, but could we drop the dresses off where Arlene is working, although she may be home by now, right?" Samantha asked. Her phone didn't work in Granville even to text. No cell tower.

"I think they were not going to be done until supper," Mike said. "And I'm sorry, but I have no idea where they're working."

Pix had been listening to the conversation. "Leave them with me, honey, and I'll bring them over this week. Don't worry. If either of the dresses needs altering we can do it. There's plenty of time."

Sensing that his mother was about to tell them to forget about these particular outfits, Zach said, "Good to see you again, Mike, and tell Arlene we missed her."

Samantha shook a finger at Mike. "Tell that matron of honor BFF of mine that I'm expecting the bridal shower to end all bridal showers! She'll know what I mean!"

Faith and Pix started to laugh before Samantha had finished talking. They'd seen the X-rated bridal shower lingerie catalog that Arlene had sent last spring. Pix had remarked at the time that her shower had been at Ursula's beloved Chilton Club in Boston, formed by a group of women in 1910 and named for Mary Chilton, the first woman to step off the *Mayflower*. As Pix had described the dainty finger sandwiches, white iced petits fours, and a bridesmaid appointed to thread all the ribbons from gifts through a hole in a paper plate to create a bridal bouquet—gifts that included four fondue pots and a bun warmer to "keep your Parker House rolls hot"—Samantha had commented it all sounded like the nineteenth not the twentieth century.

At the ballfield, Zach and Samantha said goodbye to everyone. They were stopping at The Birches for a short visit with Ursula before the long drive back. As he hugged her Zach whispered, "I'm sorry," in his future mother-in-law's ear. Pix whispered back, but in a very different tone. "Don't be silly. You have nothing to feel sorry about. Everything is going to be fine. Sam goes back Tuesday and I'll be all by myself. It will be fun to show your mother the island, and we can go up to Bar Harbor or even Canada if she wants to take a trip. Marriage means not just the union of two individuals, but their families."

A few minutes later, waving from Zach's Mini Cooper as they turned onto Route 15, Samantha said, "Want to elope?"

"Got a ladder?" Zach replied.

When Faith walked into her house, she saw the message machine was blinking. Two messages. The first was from Ursula, inviting them to a welcome dinner the following night for Alexandra Kohn. She offered the next night if the Fairchilds couldn't make it, but she was hoping for Monday, since Sam was leaving Tuesday. Faith started to call her back and say yes, thinking how typical this was of Ursula. Not exactly making a silk purse out of a sow's ear, but some other image. From the amount of luggage she'd brought—Pix said it completely filled the guest room, and where it would all go when unpacked was a problem—Alexandra had been planning to stay for the month from the start. Filing away the question of why the globetrotting socialite would want to spend so much time on a small unfashionable island, Faith checked the other message. It was from Earl and markedly discreet. "Give me a call when you have a chance. I'm home for the rest of today."

Faith realized she hadn't seen either Earl or his wife, Jill, at Fishermen's Day. She called back immediately. Jill answered.

"Hi, Faith, I'll get Earl."

"Is everything all right? I didn't see you at Fishermen's Day."

"We went early for the Hall of Fame ceremony and then came straight back here. We started stripping wallpaper from the upstairs bath and discovered there are about seven more layers underneath. It's the kind of thing that once you start you just want to keep going."

Not a DIYer herself, Faith found it easy to envision stopping, particularly to call someone else to do it. "I'm sure it will look wonderful when you're finished."

"Here's Earl now, bye," Jill said, the eagerness to get back to her task unmistakable.

"Hi," Earl said. "Two things. We have the autopsy results and a positive ID. I think it's unlikely that it's someone you or Sophie know, but I'm assisting the state police, since the body was found—and seen alive—on the island. We'd like you to look at a photo."

"All right," she answered. "How do you want to do it? Should we go to Ellsworth? To the office there?"

"We want to make it as painless as possible for you, so I brought all the relevant material here. If you and Sophie are free tomorrow morning, how about coming to the house? I can guarantee a good cup of coffee, and Jill has picked so many blueberries she's been using the ones she hasn't frozen for baked goods. Muffins, pie, coffee cake—the works. I left word with Paul for her, but haven't heard back. He thought she could make it though. Nothing on the calendar in the kitchen, he said."

There was a Currier and Ives illustrated calendar with large squares next to the phone on a kitchen wall at The Birches. It even looked worn, but the dates were current. Faith had no idea where Sophie or someone else got it every year.

"Okay. Nine o'clock?"

"Fine. And, Faith, he didn't drown. There was no water in his lungs. He was dead before he went in."

She was good at this. Lying that is. But then she had always been good at everything. High honor roll, sports star, made most of her clothes, even her prom dresses, and the person friends came to when they needed a shoulder to cry on. She gave a little laugh. Not that she needed a shoulder now. She was handling everything fine. The trick she'd figured out right away was to make sure each lie had a large component of truth. Like today. She was where she'd told people she would be—just not for as long.

He'd been waiting at the McDonald's in Belfast and as promised he'd had a prescription he swore was real. She didn't care, just so long as it could be refilled and had her name on it. She had an old license that was still valid with that name, since she'd have to show it. The price had gone up, he told her, but it was cheaper to get the pills this way, even with what he charged for the script, than buying them directly from him. She'd started to protest but then was afraid he'd leave. Leave with that piece of paper she'd do anything to get. He offered to buy her a hamburger, but she told him she didn't have time. She wasn't hungry anyway. She was never hungry. Just thirsty. She'd been drinking so much water she was surprised she didn't make a sloshing noise when she walked. She bought a bottle now and headed for the big Hannaford. It had a pharmacy. She'd be all set and on her way home—back before anyone began to compare notes. Before they knew she was gone. Very gone.

The owners of Sanpere Shores, Sidney and Pamela Childs—he a retired dentist, she a Realtor—had developed a winning formula some years earlier. They'd started by purchasing a crumbling former resort in foreclosure near Gloucester, Massachusetts, and turning it into a luxury conference center that also served as a venue for special occasions. It had a view and enough outdoor space for tennis courts, a pool, even a croquet lawn. An eighteen-hole golf course was within walking distance. Their aim was to combine the best of the old—historic inn, lots of wicker, window seats, large public rooms, and high ceilings—with cutting-edge new technology, a spa and fitness center, plus gourmet food and plenty of it. The Gilmore Gloucester, named for the original owners, became the destination of choice for firms seeking a location for working retreats and for marketers as a place to pitch groups on everything from financial services to weight loss plans.

Once it was clear that the spinning-straw-into-gold strategy worked, the Childses turned to New Hampshire and found a similar derelict *grande dame* near Portsmouth, reproducing Gilmore Gloucester as Hampshire Haven. Sanpere Shores, smaller, was their third venture. This was its second summer of operation.

Amy Fairchild at sixteen, "and almost a half" she insisted—the age when she could get her junior driver's license—was going into her junior year at Aleford High, and the only conflict she had with her parents was her fervent desire to skip a liberal arts college and go straight to a culinary institute upon graduating. They wanted her to keep her options open and experience a wide range of subjects. The argument was on hold this summer, and Faith hoped that once all her daughter's friends began picking colleges she would change her mind.

At the moment Amy's long corn silk hair was in a braid and tucked up into a chef's pillbox cap. She was coating rounds of goat cheese with a mixture of fine bread crumbs and fresh herbs. Just before plating on a bed of local mixed microgreens, they'd go into the oven to bake briefly—crisp on the outside, runny in the middle. Being in the kitchen at the Shores—everybody shortened the name—was her dream job. And last week it got even better when the sous chef declared he couldn't stand the island's isolation any longer—"I mean, what kind of place doesn't even have a movie theater"—and left. Having watched Amy, the chef hadn't hesitated to promote her, especially since he didn't have to pay more than a token increase. Early on he'd realized Amy would work for nothing, or even pay, to be in a restaurant kitchen, and he took as much advantage of her devotion as possible—long hours, more work. She was in heaven and snapped at her mother's protest that the Shores was using her unfairly. "Welcome to real professional cooking, Mom! This is what chefs do." Slightly stung by the obvious implication that a caterer wasn't a real chef, Faith kept her mouth shut and made sure Amy took her day off and slept.

"The cheese is done, Chef," she said. "What next?"

"Add mustard to the leftover breading to make a paste and we'll use it for a crust on the rack of lamb."

Chef Dom, short for Dominic, had ruled each of the Childses' kitchens, another strategy that paid off for the couple. He trained staff and developed essentially the same menu for each location, so buying nonperishable ingredients was done in bulk. The manager at the Shores, Cindy, had also been at the other two places. Dr. and Mrs. Childs rotated among the three, never announcing their visits. It kept their employees on their toes. The big problem at Sanpere Shores, and the other two resorts to a lesser extent, was finding local staff for the dining room, housekeeping, grounds, and kitchen. There had been four dishwashers alone so far this summer, each fired or in one case just didn't show up the next day.

"How are you feeling tonight, Chef?" Amy asked. He had terrible allergies and kept a giant box of Kleenex in the small half bath off the kitchen.

"Fine and happy to have such a charming and talented chef in the making at my side," he said. Amy breathed an inward sigh of relief. There were nights when she swore he was related to Jekyll and Hyde. Hard to believe one person could have two such different personalities.

They continued to work rapidly. Breakfast was a plentiful buffet that Darlene, a local woman, took care of, baking the day before then cooking eggs and other menu items, like French toast, to order.

Amy liked to come in early to pick up tips like using soda water for the lightest scones. She also liked hanging out with Darlene—the chef slept in. Depending on the group currently in residence at the Shores, lunch was either box lunches for excursions or served in the dining room. Dinner was formal for the island, with gourmet choices of appetizers; meat, fish, or vegetarian entrées; and desserts—one always chocolate in nature.

The air-conditioning in the kitchen kept it cool. During the day some of the staff nipped in for coffee, but the chef only encouraged a few favorites to linger—all of whom had worked at the other resorts. Chief among them was Cal Burke, head of maintenance. He was a favorite with others as well. Long, lanky, with rusty brown hair and deeply tanned from working outdoors, he looked like a handsome cowboy who should be riding the range instead of fixing them. He was island born and bred, although he'd left after high school and only returned when Sanpere Shores opened last summer. He projected an air of mystery—hinting at adventures all over the world, regaling Amy and others with tales of fighting pirates off the coast of Africa and leading perilous expeditions down the Amazon. He'd been working for the Childses for the last few years as a "vacation," he'd said. Keeping the grounds in shape and unclogging drains was nothing compared to fighting for his life armed only with a penknife—this yarn set in Snake Island off the coast of Brazil. Cal was popular with the guests, especially the ladies, and besides the thousand and one anecdotes had a well-rehearsed gig accompanying himself on the guitar after dinner while interjecting Bert and I–type Down East humor between Beatles songs and other oldies.

Cal walked into the kitchen now and grabbed a Coke from the fridge while snatching a brownie from a cooling rack.

"Hey," Amy said. "We need those for the brownie sundae special tonight."

"Aw, come on, you've got plenty, and I need to keep my strength up. Just saw the bosses. They want a firepit on the beach with a sing-along after dinner."

Amy liked the Childses the few times she'd had contact with them. They came into the kitchen several times during their stays and had always been appreciative of her work. She was sure they, and the chef, would write letters of recommendation for her. She gave the coating for the lamb a final stir.

"What next, Chef?"

As soon as she hung up the phone, Faith called Sophie. She was home and had just gotten Earl's message from her uncle about meeting in the morning. Faith told her that she had talked to Earl directly.

"Earl has a photo of the dead man that the police in Massachusetts sent," she said. "You saw him in the market, so I'm sure they want you to make a positive identification—that it was the same person. Other than that, I can't think what else Earl might want."

"Nor can I," Sophie said pensively. "We've told all we know."

Pix woke up early as usual, but to silence, except for the sound of her own rapidly beating heart. She'd walked past the Cranes' twice yesterday, early and late. It appeared that the couple was away. Their car, which looked more like a tank on wheels, was gone. For the rest of the summer, Pix hoped, but it was unlikely they would depart the scene of the crime, having taken such a firm stand on the chain saw incident's perp, that is, Pix's beloved Sam.

But no, it wasn't the new neighbors that caused her to wake with her blood pounding, but the new occupant of her house, who seemed to have settled in for the remaining summer days.

Alexandra had gone to bed early, claiming jet lag. Before that she'd taken a small bite of the halibut and vegetables Sam had grilled and outright rejected Pix's rice pilaf—"no carbs, nothing white." She did not turn down nourishment in the form of most of the bottle of pinot grigio Pix had put in the fridge to go with the halibut, however.

When she was sure the woman was upstairs and out of earshot, Pix had said, in a lowered voice just in case, "What on earth are we going to do with her? Me, mostly. And why doesn't she go to the inn?"

Once Alexandra had made it clear she was staying on the island, Zach had described the inn to his mother, extolling its high-end private en suite rooms furnished with antiques and mentioning some of the famous people who had stayed there. To no avail. "Thank you, darling, but this is family time," she'd replied with more than a hint of reproach.

Sam poured his wife a glass of what was left of the wine, looked at the dribble, and got another bottle. "I'm so sorry, darling. But we can be thankful that this particular apple fell very far from the tree. We're getting a wonderful son-in-law and everybody comes with some baggage."

"She's come with enough Vuitton to pack twice my entire wardrobe, throwing in yours as well," Pix snorted, reaching for the glass Sam was handing her.

"I'll try to get back as soon as I can, and remember Samantha will be here for more than a week before the wedding. And earlier for the shower."

Pix had tried to feel reassured. "I know. But, Sam! What am I going to *do* with her?"

She slipped out of bed gently, although it would take considerable noise to wake her snoring husband, grabbed clothes, and went into the master bathroom to get ready to face the day. Over the years they had added onto the original farmhouse, but it was still small by what she assumed were Alexandra's standards. At least there was a separate guest bathroom, although it didn't have a tub, and her future in-law struck her as the long-soak-with-bath-oils-and-maybe-scented-candles type.

Dressed, she crept downstairs. She needed coffee. A lot of coffee. Taking a steaming mug out onto the deck, she let the view settle her nerves and was just beginning to feel like herself again when she was startled by Alexandra's arrival. She was dressed in what Pix recognized from her yoga class as head-to-toe Lululemon, which she'd wanted for warrior pose and cat/cow herself until she discovered the price. Sleek as a greyhound, Alexandra's face was becomingly covered by a film of sweat that indicated her morning run had been much more than a stroll.

"Hi," she said. "I don't suppose there's anyplace more level around here? A track? Though dodging the potholes was great for my calves."

"There's a kind of track at the high school," Pix said, but she had no idea what it was like. "Could I get you some coffee? And I have some anadama bread for toast. Samantha said you didn't eat much breakfast."

"Such a thoughtful girl to remember. Anadama bread. How quaint. I'll just go shower and change first."

By the time she came back down, dressed in what Pix knew was called "cruisewear" from various catalogs, Sam was up and eating what he called a Full Maine in imitation of a Full English or Irish—bacon, sausage, eggs, home fries, and toast.

"A beautiful morning," she said. "Now, I have my notebook here and we can get started on plans. It's terribly late, but crunch time is my specialty!"

Sam put his fork down. "Kind of you to take an interest, but we're all set, thank you." He was using what Samantha called his scary lawyer voice and what Pix called channeling Perry Mason. "It's a fine day for a sail," he continued in a kinder tone, "and the tides are right for a good long one. We can pack a lunch. Do you like to sail?"

"I adore sailing! Richard—Branson that is—said I was a natural-born sailor, and of course when in the Greek Isles, a yacht is the only way—"

"Great," Sam interrupted. "So that's a plan. Leave in half an hour? Our *boat* is on the other side of the Point where there's deep water. Oh, and bring a jacket. It can get cold on the water." Pix noted the emphasis Sam put on the word *boat* with amusement. The *Owl,* their Hinckley Sou'wester Jr., a scaled-down version of the larger wooden Sou'wester sloop, purchased shortly after they were married, wasn't exactly a rowboat at thirty feet, but then again it wasn't in league with the yachts Alexandra must know.

Wondering what kind of picnic she could whip up that did not include carbs, Pix added, "We have caps and sunscreen on board, but you may have a brand you like." She was sure Alexandra had one and equally sure it wasn't from CVS.

"Jill went to the store early and was sorry to miss you," Earl said, opening the door to Sophie and Faith. Years ago, Jill Merriwether Dickinson had started a small gift and bookshop, The Blueberry Patch, in what had originally been her grandfather's cobbler shop. It abutted the parking lot for the Sanpere Village post office, and this strategic location—the mail was sorted, give or take, by ten o'clock—was one of the keys to the store's success. The Patch, as it was known, provided a gathering place, especially in bad weather, if the mail was late. In addition, the shop was the only place in town for newspapers, postcards, souvenirs, and most important, jars of penny candy for kids. Although nostalgic adults were known to dip into them for Bit-O-Honeys and Jujubes.

Sophie was feeling nervous as she followed Faith and Earl into the kitchen. She'd been edgy since she woke up and there was no reason for it, she told herself sternly. She'd been feeling this way most days, and it seemed a permanent condition.

Jill and Earl had accomplished wonders with the house. Sophie remembered it from her childhood as a tumbled-down eyesore built in the mid-1800s by a ship captain for his large family. The Dickinsons didn't have any kids, but their house was like a child—cared for. Lavished upon even, and much beloved.

Earl poured out three mugs of coffee and set a plate of blueberry scones with butter and blueberry jam on the table.

"This won't take long. Sophie, Faith probably told you that we know the victim's name now or the one he's been using for a few years: Dwayne LeBlanc—and that he did not drown. There was no water in his lungs. Judging from some of the other results, we know he was an addict, and the assumption now is that he died of an overdose of heroin, possibly laced with fentanyl. Somebody, or several people, dumped him in that part of the pond, probably figuring he wouldn't be found for a while and when he was would be thought a drowning victim. The fact that he had no identification makes it likely that they didn't want him traced back to any individual, or again more than one."

Sophie nodded. "Good to know this, Earl. I appreciate it. But so sad. He must have been young, from what I remember of his face the time I saw him in the market."

"He was. Only twenty-five. Since you'd noticed the out-of-state plates on the motorcycle, we started by sending his prints to Massachusetts and got an immediate hit. I have his driver's license photo—and mug shots. He'd been arrested over the years for DUI, possession of controlled substance, daytime B and E—did a brief amount of time for that. At the time of death, he was on probation and not supposed to leave the state. He lived in Lowell and grew up there as far as we know." Earl saw the look that crossed Faith's face and said, "Yes, lots of fine people live there, but I'm guessing you know it is part of the pipeline that starts in Colombia and comes here through Mexico, the Southwest, and up to us primarily from Lowell and Lawrence through Portsmouth and Portland."

"Show me the pictures, Earl," Sophie said. She really wanted to get this over with.

He pulled them from a manila envelope, and it only took a few seconds for her to recognize Dwayne. "Yes, his hair was longer, but that's the man I saw in the market."

"These are some of his known associates. Any familiar faces?"

Sophie looked longer. "Maybe that one." She pointed to a heavyset man with dark hair and a tattoo of something that covered his neck up to his chin. "I remember the tattoo, but a lot of people have tattoos like that and I can't be sure about the face."

Tattoo. The word triggered a question from Faith. "Did the Massachusetts police recognize the tattoo on his arm, the snake? Was it gang related?"

Earl shook his head. "It was a new one to them, and us, too." He put everything away. "Okay. Done. Now I suggest you two go have some fun."

"We intend to," Sophie replied, smiling weakly, "but no swimming today."

Arriving for the dinner party, Faith pulled Pix aside, letting Sam escort Alexandra to the front door of The Pines. She knew Ursula would not like the guest of honor to be ushered in through the kitchen door, the one everyone normally used. "How did today go?" Faith asked.

"Surprisingly well. She really is a good sailor, and that's a sure way to Sam's heart. Mine, too. Once she stopped talking about all the America's Cup ones she'd been on, even crewed when she was younger, and because whenever wedding talk came up Sam changed the subject, it was just another great day on the water."

"What did you do for a picnic?"

"Packed crudités enough for a fleet, hummus, and fruit salad. I also made two roast beef sandwiches for Sam and slipped in cookies Gert sent over once she heard Samantha was coming for the weekend. I kept Alexandra company, and I'm starving now."

"So, it's going to be all right?"

"Not really. As soon as she gets me alone she starts to twist my arm about changing from the island to Boston and other things."

"Like what?" Faith hoped she could mask the annoyance, no make that anger, she was feeling, over dinner. Pix had been worried about small things like hurricanes. Nobody could have envisioned the one named "Alexandra."

"She wants Samantha to register at all sorts of places that are so not the kids: Tiffany, for example. When I explained that they had registered only at Heath Ceramics for dinnerware and that midcentury modern was more their style than Waterford and Wedgwood, she looked as if I had said they were going with the Dollar Store. She insisted they would need more than dinnerware to start married life and I said that registering even with Heath had only been because people were asking what to give. You know that on the invitation they requested gifts be made in honor of the occasion to organizations of guests' choice, like Doctors Without Borders, but some people have wanted to give them something personal in addition."

"Alexandra must have seen that on the evite Zach sent and sensed what they are like!"

"Faith, sweetheart, this is a woman who only sees what she wants to see. And gets what she wants," Pix added ruefully.

"Don't be too sure of that," Faith said.

Besides the Fairchilds—including Amy, who was off tonight—Ursula had invited Ed Ricks, Paul, and Sophie. As Faith looked around the dining room, she imagined that it had not changed much since Ursula's grandparents built the house. Beadboard wainscoting and William Morris Willow Boughs wallpaper, which had been renewed from time to time, a classic still being produced. The dining table was more than ample for the ten of them, and Ursula was using the best china—a simple white Haviland Limoges. It was obvious that Ursula wanted the welcome party to be elegant but not ostentatious. A hard look to achieve at The Pines—unless you examined the rooms and valuable decor closely. The Tiffany table and hanging lamps were authentic, the flatware sterling, and the paintings that vied with family photos and framed pressed flowers on the walls represented well-known artists of several periods, including contemporary painters like Fairfield Porter, John Heliker, and Jill Hoy. Hoy's exuberant view of the Reach, a gift for Ursula's eightieth, dominated the dining room, at home with the Arts and Crafts sideboard below.

Faith noticed that Ursula was wearing one of her good summer outfits, a cornflower-blue sheath that made her silver hair appear platinum. Candlelight cast a flattering glow on everyone. The room wasn't dark, however, thanks to Pix's brother's installation of subtle recessed lighting some years ago after he mistakenly tried to eat a papier mâché shrimp his small son had made as a decoration for the plates.

The evening started with champagne, local oysters, smoked mussels in a dill mustard sauce, and for those indulging in carbs, Gert Prescott's cheese straws. If Alexandra was surprised by the offerings—the champagne was Möet & Chandon— she did not show it.

Amy had offered to serve even though Gert wanted to stay—as much for a glimpse of the guest as to help out. There had been peas at the farmers' market, and Faith brought the first course, a cold fresh soup of pureed peas with a hint of mint. (See recipe, page 320.) Amy had asked if anyone wanted a dollop of crème fraîche, and Alexandra—the reason for the inquiry—had predictably declined. The rest found a delicate white spiderweb traced on the bright green surface, a trick Faith had taught her daughter—pulling a sharp knife from the middle to the sides and across.

After clearing the empty soup dishes, Amy served her grandmother and Alexandra, who was at Ursula's right in the place of honor, the main course. Ursula said, "I'm afraid we eat a great deal of fish here. I hope you like scallops."

"I adore fish. So good for us, too. The chef at the Taj does a marvelous poached salmon that could be one of the entrée offerings."

Ed Ricks immediately began talking about the scarcity of lobster in his traps. "And to think that at one time they were so plentiful on the coast, you could pick them off the rocks at low tide and prisoners in the state penitentiary refused to eat any more of them, demanding anything but, even oatmeal instead."

"I'm pretty sure that's an urban—or what's

the equivalent? Rural?—myth," Faith said. "Not about how common they were back in the day, but the prisoners protesting. The food historian Sandra Oliver wrote a great piece about it as an example of how this sort of tall tale becomes fact."

With the subject changed abruptly, Alexandra gave in—for the moment—and said, "This looks delicious, but I'm afraid I don't eat pasta."

Amy grinned, setting another plate down in front of her mother. "It's not pasta, it's zucchini. With a little fresh basil and EVOO. The scallops are poached in white wine, not butter."

Sensing Sam's annoyance at the way they were catering to their future in-law's food foibles—he loved pasta—Pix explained, "Gert has a spiralizer. A pretty nifty kitchen tool that turns zucchini and all sorts of other vegetables into pasta-like strands. She saw one on the Home Shopping Network, and we've all become converts."

"We have one at the Shores, too," Amy said. "There are always going to be some guests—" A look from her mother stopped her short. "Some guests who want new things." She hastened to the kitchen for the rest of the plates.

"I'd like to have a look at that gadget," Alexandra said. "Although I don't cook myself."

As everyone ate, the conversation was genial, revolving around the great turnout for Fishermen's Day, the new coffee shop that was roasting its own beans in Sanpere Village, and of course the weather. Having finished her food, Amy put down her fork and joined in.

"So," she said, "did they ever find out who that dead body in the Lily Pond was?"

Five

As a conversation stopper, it was a lulu. Sophie looked across the table at Faith. Tom was looking at his wife as well. Faith did not always feel it was necessary to bother her husband with the details of her everyday life—as in meeting with Earl this morning, or even Earl's message on the machine, which got erased when she deleted Ursula's. She'd heard them both, she reasoned. Historically Tom took a dim view of Faith's involvement, however tangential, in crime. But clearly her daughter's question—note to self, talk to Amy about topics for dinner party conversation—had to be addressed. To wipe the look of absolute horror off Alexandra's face for a start.

Faith directed a reply to Alexandra. "We had a tragic, fortunately very rare, accident last week at the pond. I believe he has been identified. From out of state. Massachusetts it seems."

"Oh, Massachusetts," Alexandra said, as if that settled the question. "I know a few people in Boston and Cambridge, and dear friends near Lenox in the Berkshires, but as for the rest I'm afraid I would be quite at a loss." Faith avoided her friend Ed's eyes. She knew he was feeling what she was. If Alexandra didn't know the man or the place he lived, it was no never mind to her. "Drowned I presume. People are so careless," Alexandra continued.

"Dessert," Ursula announced. "We're having it in the living room or on the porch if the bugs aren't too bad."

The bugs were bad, so Faith, Amy, and Pix set the array of desserts that had been prepared for all tastes on the large round table in front of the bay window. With the porch lights off, the summer sky just past sunset seemed close enough to touch. The jigsaw puzzle, as well as other essentials like binoculars, bird guides, flora and fauna life lists, and whatever books anyone happened to be reading, had been cleared off the table to make way for two of Gert's famous pies, strawberry rhubarb and black walnut; dark chocolate brownies—Amy's contribution; ice cream for the pies and brownies; plus a large fruit salad for Alexandra with a pitcher of crème anglaise, which she ignored, unlike the rest of the party.

"One of my patients made me a needlepoint pillow that said LIFE IS SHORT, EAT DESSERT FIRST," Ed Ricks said, digging into his full plate with relish. "I took it as a good sign—she was a clinically depressed individual who had made great progress over the years—but it also could have been a hint that the shrink should loosen up. Which I have." He laughed, and Amy said, "I think I'll make one of those for myself. Dessert really *is* the best part of a meal. Samantha should just have desserts at her reception. I know she'll have an awesome cake, but I'll bet the s'mores station will be the most popular."

"The what?" Alexandra seemed to be choking on a grape. Faith quickly poured her a glass of water, which the woman gulped down.

"S'mores," Amy said. "You must have made them in Girl Scouts or camp. You toast marshmallows over the campfire, or in this case little braziers, and eat them between two graham crackers and a slab of Hershey's chocolate."

"Of course, there will be many other offerings," Pix said rapidly, "and I meant to mention that the string quartet that will be playing during the reception before the dancing starts is performing at Kneisel Hall in Blue Hill next Sunday. It would be fun to get a group together to go."

Faith jumped in. Although her mind tended to wander during classical music just as it did at sermons by preachers other than Tom, she said, "Count us in."

"Me, too," Ed said.

Alexandra had regained her composure. "If we move the wedding to Boston, Yo-Yo would play," she said firmly. "I know what you're going to say, Sam. The plans are all set, even the marshmallow thingy, but just think of what a memorable wedding this could be."

"Oh, but it *will* be a memorable wedding." A familiar voice rang out from the doorway.

Sophie ran over and threw her arms around the woman standing there, flashing a kilowatt smile on everyone, in an outfit that rivaled Alexandra's.

It was Babs née numerous surnames, now Harrington, to the rescue.

"What have I missed? And I'm not talking about dinner, although I will have some of that lovely fruit, thank you. Oh, and Ed, bourbon and branch—you know where Ursula keeps it." Babs sat down next to Alexandra. "You must be Zach's mother. I believe we have friends in the city in common—the Auchinclosses? Connections of dear Louis—such a loss to literature and so much else. And if you don't mind a personal comment, you must have been a child bride! Of course, people are always saying that about me—just look at Sophie, a grown woman and married, but more like my sister."

Ed Ricks appeared with the drink and Babs paused to take a sip—and come up for air. It was a bravura performance, Sophie thought, and had the intended effect. Alexandra Kohn was speechless.

Babs was on a roll. "Yes, memorable nuptials. They were so lucky to book Edgewood Farm. It's in such demand. Didn't Travolta have an event there? He lives on Isleboro, you know. And Pix has done such a fabulous job lining up places for everyone to stay, because sweet as it is, Pix dear, your house would not stretch to anything resembling Mother Hubbard's shoe." She took another sip and sighed. "Heaven to be on the island. When I saw that no one was at The Birches, I figured you'd be over here. Now, let's talk plans. Lovely to have a new face! Today's Monday—and damn I missed Fishermen's Day! Ed—not this one, but my husband"—she addressed the remark to Alexandra—"has gone to Scotland to play golf but will be back in plenty of time for the wedding. Do you golf, Mrs. Kohn? Quite a nice little course here at the Island Country Club. Tennis is my game." She stretched her empty glass toward Ed, who took the hint.

Sophie thought it was time to let someone else get a word in edgewise, although she was enjoying the stun gun effect on the woman who was causing such problems for the Millers. "The weather is looking good for the rest of the week and I hear you had a good sail today, so we can definitely plan another soon. You might like to go down to Castine, which is a lovely historic spot. I think the garden tour may be this Thursday."

Ed had returned with a generous refill for Babs, who said, "This all sounds fine but we should do as much as we can early in the week—I for one want to go up to Bar Harbor and fill in a few wardrobe gaps." Sophie rolled her eyes at Faith. Babs had a closet at the house in Connecticut the size of many people's master bedrooms and had appropriated a small storage room on the top floor of The Birches for her Maine wardrobe.

"Our class starts Friday night, which doesn't give us much time. We'll be in memoir writing"— Babs shook her finger playfully at Alexandra—"and something tells me you have plenty of material, as do I. When we're finished, we can have a reading and everyone here can vote on whose is spicier!"

Alexandra was still looking dazed and a heavy dose of bewilderment was entering the picture. "What . . ." she started to say.

"Oh, of course, you have no idea what I'm talking about," Babs said merrily. "Such fun. Sophie told me she was enrolling in a fiction-writing program at Sanpere Shores, a beautiful resort here—we may never write a word, just enjoy the spa—and I went online to see what we gals could do. I've always preferred fact to fiction—so much juicer. When I called them, they had two spaces left in the memoir program. We'll be day students, like Sophie. Tomorrow we can move you over to The Birches. So much easier to commute together. I must say I'm very excited about it all. After we move you in, we can go up to Bar Harbor. Maybe stop in Seal Harbor to say hi to Martha. If you haven't seen it already, you'll love Skylands. She certainly has the touch." Babs leaned back, drained half her glass, and shot her daughter a cat-finishing-cream triumphal glance. She also gave Pix a warning glance that Sophie understood. Pix was too good and was apt to protest that Alexandra should stay where she was and only take the course if she wanted.

Sam was cutting himself another piece of pie and there was nothing but glee on *his* face. "Well then," he said. "This does sound like fun. Want to write my own memoirs someday."

Alexandra still had not uttered a single word. She appeared to be considering the prospect of both moving to a much larger space and hanging out with someone so obviously on her wavelength.

The choice was a forgone conclusion. Alexandra might as well have turned up at The Birches to start. The woman might be used to getting her own way, but Babs was a force of nature of substantially greater magnitude.

"Done and dusted," Tom whispered to his wife. "Now, let's get out of here."

Faith nodded, and as she went around saying good-bye, Ed Ricks said, "Come by for coffee? I haven't seen you much all summer."

"I'd love to," Faith said. "Tom and Amy are both working long hours, so I'm a free agent."

"How about tomorrow morning? Ten? You bring the baked goods, unless you want some admittedly old vanilla wafers."

"See you at ten and I'm sure I can drum up something a bit fresher."

The phone was ringing as the Fairchilds walked into the house. Amy grabbed it, a reflex inherent in all the teenagers Faith had ever known. "For you, Mom. Pix. I'm going to bed. Have to be at work early."

Kissing her, Faith took the phone. At first it was hard to make out what Pix was saying. "Could you speak up? I can't hear you. Is Alexandra right there?" Faith asked.

"No, she went straight to bed. But, Faith, I love Babs and I know she just wanted to help, but do you think she, well, railroaded Alexandra into all this? I feel a bit guilty, since it will be so much easier having her at The Birches and taking a course will keep her busy."

"And away from any wedding interference."

"Well, that, too."

Smiling, Faith said, "Now my best beloved friend, you have absolutely nothing to feel guilty about. Alexandra will be much more comfortable over at The Birches. There's plenty of room, and Babs redid the guest rooms last summer. The large one at the front has a gorgeous bath—you've seen it. It's not as if you're shunting her off to a shack with no indoor plumbing. And she'll love the Shores. Remember, you didn't invite her. She landed on you all by herself."

"But she's going to be family." Pix's protest did not sound all that strong.

Faith's answer *was*. "There's family and family. Once the wedding is over and she resumes her previous lifestyle, you won't see her. Not exactly family as in let's be sure to set a place for the holidays. Take her over to The Birches once she's packed up tomorrow and breathe a big sigh of relief. You've had enough stress this week to last for many summers to come."

"Mother said almost word for word what you just did."

Faith's smile broadened. She didn't mind being

the second opinion and second call—they had a longer drive home and Pix was bursting with the kind of inbred Yankee guilt that only an old Yankee mother could assuage.

"Go to sleep, or maybe not. Sam's leaving, and it could be a while before you two are together again."

"Faith!" Pix exclaimed, but her friend had already hung up.

Day camp at the Community Center took care of the mornings into the early afternoons. And it's not like it wasn't a great place. No, she didn't feel guilty at all. The timing worked, and at the end of the summer when camp was finished, there was preschool. But by then it wouldn't matter. She was going to stop, wasn't she? This was the last dose. So what if there were two refills? She wasn't going to use them. Maybe wouldn't even finish what was in this container.

The pain had been a nightmare. Both at the time of the accident and in the hospital before they treated it. Almost gone for a while except for an ache or two. No, it was a different pain. The one from trying to hold everything together. And being pretty much alone. All she had for neighbors out here were trees and water. Not like growing up off Main Street in Granville with people around all the time. People she knew and they knew her. It would *be okay to be where she was, except she didn't sign on to being with a guy she barely saw. She was proud of his job, sure—they were able to buy this place—but why did he have to work all the time? Yeah, he was the new kid compared to others, but what about her? What about dealing with all the stuff she had to do—the cooking, the cleaning, the garden they depended on to save money—and it all had to be done all over again the next day. Years from now she would be doing the same things, and when she thought about never being finished, never getting a break, she felt a kind of mist settle over her brain. If she was never going to finish, why not finish herself right now?*

Ed Ricks and Faith were sitting outdoors the following morning on his bluestone patio overlooking Penobscot Bay. Built some years ago in preparation for living year-round on the island, his home was similar to Philip Johnson's Glass House in New Canaan, Connecticut. Ed's privacy was protected by evergreens and the fact that the house sat high on a bluff. The result was to bring the outside in and the reverse. There was a separate guesthouse with more solid walls for friends from his former very urban life.

Fishing boats dotted the water at varying distances. By this time almost a full day's work was done. Ed's small boat, moored at his dock, was tossing in the wake—a wall of water—that had just been created by a large lobster boat as it sped on to pull the next trap.

"Same boat every day," Ed said. "Lets it out full throttle. Think he may be practicing for the races. If so, he's a contender." All summer long, starting with the first race in Boothbay Harbor, fishermen traveled up and down the coast for the Lobster Boat Races on Sundays. It was a rare chance to play, and the captains let loose, revving up to over sixty miles per hour while competing in a series of classes. The boats ranged from small dinghies with outboards to thirty-eight footers with very pricey engines; the sole stipulation was that the lobster boat had to be a working boat. No ringers who had never hauled a single trap but converted lobster boats to pleasure craft. Onlookers lined the courses onshore and in boats celebrating the tradition with a Down East version of tailgating. Freeman Hamilton, the Fairchilds' nearest neighbor, was still racing at seventy-five, even though his wife had insisted he retire from fishing a few years ago after what he called a "little episode" with his heart. He'd turned his boat, *Grandpa's Pride*, and the family's fishing territory over to his son, but not his place at the helm for the races. It was rare for Freeman to come in second in his class.

"Freeman told Tom he's entered again in Granville," Faith said. "He did well at Jonesport, and that's the toughest on the circuit. So much competition."

"Come on my boat to watch? Or are you and Tom already booked on someone else's?" Ed asked. "And I'm not just issuing the invitation because I know you'll bring your lobster rolls."

"We're not and I'd love to. Tell me how many people and I'll bring the whole picnic." Faith's lobster rolls were almost as famous as Freeman's legendary winning streaks. When it came to lobster rolls, Faith was a purist. No celery or other fillers. (See recipe, page 322.)

"I can supply the lobster if the catch gets better, otherwise I'll get them up at the Co-Op," Ed said as he pointed to his pot buoys, one on top of the boat, as required for identification. He'd told Faith he picked the colors—bright yellow with black stripes—so he could spot them easily. They were bobbing about like bumblebees in the wake's white spray. "I imagine as long as there have been men and boats, there have been races; but these didn't officially start until the 1930s, and I'm pretty sure it was because a lot of the skippers had souped up their boats as rum runners during Prohibition and wanted to keep going."

Faith laughed. "I'm getting a picture of all sorts of nautical contests, going back in history: Viking ships, Chinese junks, dugout canoes." She reached for another of the doughnut muffins she'd brought as Ed filled her cup with more coffee.

They'd covered last night's dinner—"Sophie was right. Alexandra could only have been out-maneuvered by Babs," Faith had observed—and Ed remarked that so many names were dropped there must be a number of new indentations in The Pines's living room floor today. They traded island gossip—Ed mentioned a possible split in his book group over bestsellers versus classics, and Faith said Nan and Freeman's niece from Massachusetts was living with them this summer, but Faith had yet to meet the young woman. She was a music major and singing at various spots on the peninsula. "We should go hear her," Ed said.

For a moment, they sat quietly and watched the activity on and above the water—boats, gulls, cormorants swooping down, even some porpoises breaking the surface. Faith was about to say she should get going when Ed started to speak.

"I don't think I ever mentioned that I first came to the island as a child. My parents had friends with a summer place that looked straight north out to Swan's Island. It had a small beach and plenty of trees to climb. I thought it was the most beautiful spot I'd ever seen. We came back only a few times more, but I never forgot it. When I was in medical school and thinking about the sorts of serious life questions a place like that engenders,

I decided Sanpere was where I wanted to be permanently, as in forever, and planned my life back from there. Before I bought the land for my house, I bought a plot in Hillside Cemetery." He grinned. "It's got a great view, and by now I know a lot of the neighbors."

"I like that notion," Faith said. "The one of picking a place or even a way of being and backtracking. Sanpere's become the same for Tom and me, but if you had ever told me when I was in my twenties that a spot like this was my ultimate goal, I would have thought you were crazy. I didn't ever want to leave Manhattan and only Tom could have made me."

Ed put his mug down. "I kind of knew you felt the way I do and I have to admit besides always enjoying your company I asked you to come by for another reason. Faith, I need your help. Tom's, too. All the talk I'm sure you've heard about the opioid crisis here isn't just talk. It's real and getting worse fast. I see it up much too close on almost every shift now."

Ed was a volunteer with the ambulance corps.

"Did you know that we carry NARCAN? And I keep extra gloves in my car to pick up syringes and other paraphernalia tossed along the roadside." He shook his head. "I was on duty when we took the young man you found to the hospital. It wasn't just the marks on his arms, but I could also tell by his teeth that he was a heavy user. Heroin causes dry mouth, and there's no saliva to wash away the bacteria. Users also tend to grind their teeth. He was probably into meth as well, which causes decay in a short amount of time."

"We are aware of it and talk a lot about what's happening," Faith said. "We've never locked our doors, but there have been so many break-ins that if both cars are out of the drive, we do now. From the kinds of things taken, you know it's not a ring of crooked antiques dealers like the thefts a few years ago. What we worry about losing are the computers, especially Tom's. Although, I was there when one of Ursula's neighbors told her he was locking his doors now, and her response was so strong, I didn't dare tell her we were also."

"I feel the same way," Ed said. "I don't want to have to do it, but I do have valuables here I wouldn't want to lose."

"Increasingly Tom finds himself helping people in the congregation cope with a family member's addiction. One of the main problems is the shame they feel. He's been trying hard to make them understand addiction is an illness, a terrible illness—has preached about it—but it's still a skeleton that most people want to keep shut up tight in the closet. The drug epidemic in Massachusetts is bad, and it affects all ages, all incomes; but I know it's worse in Maine."

"You're right. And the hushing-it-up problem is deeply embedded in the Mainer's 'we can do it ourselves' independent way of life, the belief that to get help, ask for it at all, is letting go of that. Plus, it's none of anybody's business. Like alcohol addiction, which has always been a major drug of choice here, there's also the notion that a person should be able to stop when he or she wants to and that not doing so is the person's own fault."

"Long winters," Faith said. "Maybe that's responsible for this crisis as well."

"I don't mean to give you a TED talk—although there are some good ones posted about all this—on such a beautiful Maine day, but it's not the winters. It's the lack of programs, structured support, rehab facilities, and most of all it's because of the overwhelming availably of the drugs. Heroin is cheaper than a pack of cigarettes. Prescribed pills like oxycodone, which started it all, are heroin in pill form. Commercial fishing is the most dangerous occupation in the country. Injuries and constant pain are a way of life. Starting in the 1990s the solution in pill form was, too. And it's not just the fishermen or young people who want the high, but also the elderly who were overprescribed pain medication and became dependent to the point where now that they can't get it from a doctor they're turning to the street, too. Impossible to contemplate.

Someone's grandmother meeting up with a dealer in Granville."

Ed got up and began pacing back and forth. "As a physician and more as a human being, I can't sit this one out and blame the politicians or whomever for not doing anything. A number of us on the island—people from here and people from away—are forming a group to try to do what we can in our corner of the world. Education, starting with elementary school kids—they see the signs up close more than anyone else, a parent who can't care for them. We need more doctors who are willing to treat the illness with Suboxone—they have to take special classes and many opioid users are uninsured. Treating addicts is grueling and depressing. I'm training to be a recovery coach and am encouraging others to do so. I could go on and on, Faith. There's no one magic solution. Addicts aren't criminals, no matter what anyone says. No one would say that about someone who was diabetic or had cancer. Relapses are part of the illness, just like other diseases, and they don't mean the individual is weak. The name 'Heroin' was a late-nineteenth-century trademark for the drug, because it made the patient feel 'heroic.' We never needed heroes more than now. One of the saddest facts I learned recently is the largest number of addicts on the island are mothers with small children, and of course they don't want to admit the problem for fear they will lose their children into care." He sat down and slumped forward. The lengthy, emotional outburst over, he looked exhausted. Faith reached for his hand.

"Sign us up, Ed. We'll do whatever we can. Talk to people you haven't—Sophie and her husband, the Millers."

"I'll tell you when we're next meeting. We're using social media. Facebook. Whatever reaches people."

They both stood up and Faith kissed his cheek. "You're a good man. A lot of people are and will be thankful to you."

"Not necessary. You see, it takes one to know one. I was a drunk for twenty years, Faith. High functioning, but a drunk. So, been there, done that, and don't want the tee shirt."

Amy was worried. Tonight Chef Dom had had to leave before all the guests were served. He'd asked Amy to make sure the orders were correct and pulled one of the servers from the dining room to help her before departing. The Shores was full, and to keep people happy while they waited for their food, the chef had also asked Cal Burke to get his guitar and play. The music filtered into the kitchen, not Cal's usual oldie favorites, but what Amy recognized from her parents' CDs as classical guitar. Cal really was a man of many talents and she wondered where he had learned to play so well. And where he grew up on the island. She was sure she must know where it was.

Cal came in for a glass of water. "Good job, kid. Looks like almost everybody has been served."

Amy nodded. "And the desserts are all made and plated in the fridge. Only the fruit crumble will need heating, and most people chose the Baileys cheesecake. I was thinking someone should check on the chef, see if he needs anything. Maybe you could do it during a break?" The chef and Cal shared a cabin that the Childses had deemed too far away from the main building and too small to refurbish, so it was used for staff who didn't live locally. Amy wasn't sure where it was and, in any case, didn't think it was appropriate for her to go check.

"Good idea. I can do it while dessert is being served," Cal said. "I'm sure he'll be fine by tomorrow."

"It's just that for the next two weeks we'll be having the most guests of the summer, so I hope he's completely better by Friday when they all arrive."

"I almost forgot," Cal said. "The scribblers and the number crunchers."

Amy smiled. "That's a good way to put it." She remembered that Sophie was taking one of the writing courses and now so were Sophie's mother, Babs, and Zach's mother. The other group, which was larger, was a team-building exercise for a national actuarial group. Fiction and faction, she thought and filed it away to tell her parents. It was the kind of joke they liked.

But what wasn't fiction was the chef's illness. Normally at this point in the day she would be feeling high at having spent time doing what she loved best and being where she knew she was meant to be. The chef had expressed surprise at her knife skills and overall culinary expertise. The rush of getting the food from raw ingredients to beautiful plating and the fun of thinking what they might make the next day and the next never paled. Tonight hadn't been like that. She went back to worrying.

"I'm taking the day off to spend it with my beautiful wife," Tom Fairchild said, rolling over in bed to pull said wife into a close embrace.

"Hmmm," she murmured. "This is nice."

"The work is going well, and this is one of those days the Lord hath made," Tom said, gesturing out the window. The sun was straight out of a kid's drawing, perfectly round and yellow, sending beams of light across the room. "Let's spend the day on the water. Maybe head out to Isle au Haut. We can stop at Green Island or one of the others where it's easy to tie up for lunch." Some years ago they had bought an eighteen-foot Grady-White powerboat, and Tom had been lamenting how little he'd been able to use it this summer.

"Besides," Tom said, "rabbit, rabbit—it's August first. We need to celebrate that." Faith's husband had never been able to explain this old New England custom—saying "rabbit, rabbit" upon awakening on the first of the month to ensure good luck and if one forgot, repeating it backward at bedtime, but Faith had adopted it. She murmured the phrase now. No point in taking any chances.

Last night after Amy had gone to bed, Faith and Tom had stayed up talking about what Ed Ricks had said. Faith had been restless since—thinking about it all. The idea of a day consisting only of keeping an eye out for harbor seals and avoiding pot buoys was a welcome one.

"We could ask Pix if you like," Tom added. "Zach's mother is over at The Birches now, right?"

"Yes," Faith answered, "but today Pix is going up to Bar Harbor with her and Babs. I tried to convince her that not only would she hate it—as you know, Pix would rather walk on a bed of nails than shop—but that they would probably have a nicer time without her. She's never been very good at hiding her feelings. But she feels she should make an effort to get to know Alexandra better."

"All right. Poor Pix. But just you and me, kid, is fine."

Faith got out of bed. "I'll pack the lunch. Chicken salad on sourdough? I can make deviled eggs, too."

"Fine." Tom smiled, not moving. "But what's the rush?"

The unusually intense heat of the past weeks had only slightly abated, but out on the water the temperatures always required layers. Faith had started out with a sleeveless tee and was up to a sweatshirt now. They'd passed close enough to the three-masted windjammer *Victory Chimes*, in full sail, for Faith to get what she hoped was a stunning picture. Lots of kayaks—or as the fishermen called them, "speed bumps"—were out as well as other pleasure boats, power and sail. And the working boats. Faith raised a hand in greeting to all. She'd learned from Freeman in her first days on the island that this greeting was a signal that all was well. She'd thought of it as a friendly gesture, waving heartily back each time. She still did, but now it was less energetic, one of a long-time sailor.

The sun was sending diamonds across the waves. There might not be as many lobsters at the moment as in years past, but Faith had never seen as many buoys, each with its distinctive markings and number. So far it had been a peaceful summer, no lobster wars. No one invading another person's territory to set traps. Retaliation was swift. First trap lines cut—and the loss of the trap and catch was a financial blow—and then maybe bait stuffed into a fuel tank, and finally shots fired across a bow. Fishing grounds were handed down from generation to generation and, unlike farmland, couldn't be fenced in. But those who fished it knew the boundaries, as did those trying to poach it.

Granville brought in more lobster than any port in the Northeast and close to more than anywhere in the country. It was a lucrative occupation, and as Faith looked at the fields of brightly colored buoys she thought about something else Ed had said. That Sanpere's dependency on lobster and tourists was new. In the past there had been granite, boat building, the cannery, sawmills, and ground fishing—all virtually gone now. The amount of money even a weak season for the crustaceans poured into the island was significant, and in recent years a lot of that money was going for drugs.

Faith looked back at the boat they had just passed. Two young guys were opening a trap, throwing some lobsters—shorts—back and others into the plastic bins on board. Both had raised a hand in greeting—the royal-blue thick rubber gloves the fishermen wore were more spots of color. There had been a letter to the editor in the *Island Crier* recently from a young fisherman detailing the prevalence of drugs the fishermen were using while hauling and calling for more public awareness. He pointed out that he didn't want his boat to get smashed into by someone who was high and unable to control his boat. The day after the paper had come out someone had left a dead gull on his front step with a tag bearing his name wrapped around its neck.

She shook her head to clear away the dark thoughts and concentrated on the view. The day was crystal clear, and Mount Desert Island seemed a mere hop away. She thought of Pix traipsing around Bar Harbor from boutique to boutique. She hoped she'd manage to get herself her favorite Moose Tracks ice cream at CJ's Big Dipper on Main Street. Alexandra wouldn't want the calories and Babs was usually on a diet, too, but Pix, and Samantha, too, never put on an ounce no matter how sinful the dish.

The image of one of those luscious scoops in a waffle cone made her realize she was hungry. Being on the water always created an appetite, and though there must be a scientific reason for it—salt air as an appetite stimulant?—she never remembered to look it up. She went back and sat in the second mate's chair. "Time for lunch? We can eat on the boat or pull in somewhere."

"Let's go to Green Island. It's close, and don't worry, I won't make you swim in the quarry."

The old quarry filled with fresh water from deep underground springs was a favorite swimming hole for locals. The one time Faith had been convinced to give it a try she was so cold she thought she wouldn't be able to swim the few strokes back to the rock she'd jumped off. "We can walk across to the little beach on the cove facing the Camden Hills," she said.

There were two kayaks tied securely to the iron stakes left from the days when the pink granite in this particular quarry was mined and prized. On a weekday the only people on Green Island would be vacationers. Two walls of the stone created a long, deep inlet, and the Grady-White just fit. Tom cut the engine and Faith tied the mooring lines to more spikes left in the rock all those years ago. Also years ago someone had attached a ladder up to the top of one wall.

They climbed up to the path, passing the quarry and the brave souls jumping in from the rocks, before crossing the top of the island. Low junipers spread on either side of a small trail that had been worn over time. The birds had eaten most of the blueberries and huckleberries, but the air still smelled of fruit. They scrambled down to the cove and Faith spread the checked oilcloth table covering she used for picnics on the sandiest rock-free spot she could find. Tom started to unpack the cooler, handing his wife one of the stainless-steel drinking bottles she'd filled with iced tea. He took the other and, unscrewing the cap, drank. "Ah, that tastes good. Now for a sandwich . . . oh, look, Faith—we'd better get that pot buoy."

A bright neon-orange buoy was protruding from the rocks off to the side, tangled lines anchoring it firmly. They'd drop it off at the harbor-master's office. If she didn't know whose it was by the color, she could look up the owner by the number stamped on it.

Faith stood up. "There's a trap floating farther out. The tide is coming in, which will make it easier to save."

"True, but sandwiches first," Tom agreed.

They made quick work of what Faith had packed, including ripe peaches and white chocolate chip cookies. She flung her pit overhand back to what little soil there was behind them. "Someday people will be here having a picnic under a peach tree and wonder how it got on the island. Heavy for a bird to drop."

She pulled her husband to his feet. He'd been packing up the remains in the cooler, muttering, "Leave only your footsteps . . ." She gave him a quick kiss. "Thank you for taking the day off. I've been missing you."

"I've been missing you, too," he said. "Let's

free the gear and head home. I'm thinking G and Ts on the deck."

They walked over to the buoy. It was bobbing freely in the water, and Tom grabbed the handle, rapidly pulling the green plastic trap onto the beach. "Must be full. Weighs a ton," he said. The reason was soon gruesomely clear. Pinned underneath was the body of a large man, faceup. He wasn't wearing either a survival suit or life vest of any kind, but too many fishermen didn't.

"Poor soul," Tom said softly. "He must have fallen in while hauling and drowned." Few fishermen could swim, many reasoning that the temperature of the water would kill you before you could take a stroke.

The body had been in the water awhile, Faith realized, noting the green tinge on the face and general overall loosening of skin. A series of waves, possibly the wake from a boat not that far off, moved the corpse and trap up onto the shore.

That's when Faith noticed there were no lobsters, crabs, or any other sea creatures in the trap. It was filled with stones.

And then she saw what was on the man's right forearm.

"Tom, I'm pretty sure I know who this is."

Six

"There's something very odd about this trap," Tom said. It appeared he hadn't taken in Faith's sentence.

Faith looked at her husband in shock and said, "Well, there *is* a corpse of a noncrustacean lashed to it." The sight of the dead man was making her giddy.

Tom straightened up. He'd been on his haunches close to, but not touching, the ghastly flotsam. "Wait, what do you mean you know who it is?" He *had* been listening.

"I think he's one of the motorcycle guys who were in the market with the deceased from the Lily Pond."

"But you weren't in the market, were you? I thought only Sophie was."

Now was not the time to mention the meeting with Earl and the photos he'd shown her. Instead, pointing to the trap, she asked, "What's odd about it?" The ploy worked. Tom crouched down again.

"The pot buoy is battered and has rockweed clinging to it, but the trap is brand-new. Look at the wire. This trap could have been bought yesterday. No signs of having been in the water at all. Same with the netting inside and the bait bag."

Tom was right. "And traps are weighted down with a few bricks," Faith said, "but not loaded with stones like these. They look as if someone picked them up on the shore."

Tom was checking his phone to see if he had service. "There's enough bars for me to call 911. They'll get in touch with the Marine Patrol." As Faith heard Tom describe the situation, the unreality of it all hit her hard. Two bodies in less than a week.

Two bodies with the same tattoo snaking up their lifeless arms.

It had been a long, very long day. Pix had joined Babs and Alexandra that morning, leaving her car at The Birches, taking Babs's Lexus. Alexandra had looked at the Millers' beloved—yes it was old—Subaru as if it were an oxcart.

Pix had no idea there were so many boutiques in Bar Harbor. She only went up once or maybe twice a season to meet friends passing through. The crowds and especially the sight of the behemoth cruise ships in the harbor were not her Maine.

They'd gone to Testa's on Main Street for lunch, and since they were eating late—Pix had been starving—got one of the upstairs tables with the view. Pix happily ordered the haddock Reuben with fries before the others predictably went for the Superfood Salad—kale, Brussels sprouts, sunflower seeds, and cranberries with dressing on the side of course and no, they didn't want bread. When the food arrived Pix's Reuben was delicious, and sloppy. Pix decided not to care and used her fries, every last one of them, to sop up the dressing and calories.

Ursula had called early this morning and said Gert would pick up the mail, so not to bother, stay away as long as she liked and have fun. Fun! The very long day had included precious little of that. Back at home now, Pix eased off her flats— not her usual comfy sandals in deference to the occasion—and took a long drink of the glass of lemonade she'd poured herself before heading out on her deck. There had been one very bright note today, however. Babs had convinced Alexandra that having the wedding on Sanpere was much more chic than what Alexandra was proposing. "So done, so yesterday," she'd said every time Alexandra mentioned the Taj or any similar ideas. Babs had followed up by reeling off A-listers who had had weddings similar to the proposed Sanpere plans, starting with Meghan Markle and Prince Harry's: "And if they could have pared it down even more they would have. I'm not suggesting a lemon and elderflower wedding cake—it must have had some secret significance for them, that Harry, such a rogue! But everything else Samantha and Zach have planned is straight from the royals' playbook."

It had worked, and knowing Babs, she'd have Alexandra opting for bare feet in the farm's meadow and daisies in jelly glasses for the table decorations.

Pix stretched out her legs and wiggled her toes in relief. *Bless Babs.* Later she'd call Samantha and tell her so she could relax, too, but right now Pix wanted to relish the peace of the late afternoon. With nobody to feed but herself, she didn't even have to plan dinner—she could have cornflakes if she wanted, her favorite fallback, much to Faith's horror. In fact, Faith thought Pix was joking when she'd revealed that cornflakes were what she had for dinner when alone. And when Pix added that Sam had been known to join her, Faith simply could not believe it. In any case, she didn't have to think about food for a while. She was still full from lunch and the ice-cream cone she'd sneaked away for when Babs and Alexandra were trying on endless tunic tops, most of which looked the same to Pix.

The tide was out and the air was still. It had been hot up in Bar Harbor, and in comparison it was blessedly cool here. A single great blue heron swept majestically past before landing in the mud-flats, its raucous cry at such odds with its beauty. Pix felt her eyes close and was soon drifting off to sleep.

"Not there! Over here!" A commanding voice startled her awake. A pair of clammers farther down the cove. She shaded her eyes and squinted. It was the Cranes. She should have recognized Cameron's voice immediately. She could see him motioning to his wife to join him. Drew was lugging a clam hoe and wooden roller and not making much progress. No rest for the wicked, Pix told herself. Clamming was backbreaking work, and the equipment, even empty, was heavy. The spot Cameron Crane had picked wasn't a good one. That end of the cove had been overclammed and they'd be lucky to get enough for an appetizer. It was also close to the turn of the tide, and the mud would be increasingly soupy. A good neighbor would walk along the shore and steer them toward better pickings. A good neighbor would tell them the best times of day for clamming.

A good neighbor? No thank you, she decided. Not today.

It hadn't taken the Marine Patrol—and it turned out to be Mike Brown on duty—long to get to Green Island. If Mike was startled at the grisly sight, he didn't show it. He asked the Fairchilds approximately when they had gotten to the spot and whether they had seen any boats in the area close to shore. They were getting ready to cross back over the island and leave when Earl arrived. After carefully examining the body, he made the same observation about the new trap that Tom had. "Unless somebody was replacing an old one. That's a possibility. We'll know when we run the ID number and find out who owns it." He walked over to Faith and said quietly, "You saw the tattoo?"

"Yes, it's the same I'm sure. I also think he was the man Sophie thought she recognized in one of the other photos you showed us. Same hair, beard, and the multicolored tattoos covering all but the one on his forearm. The Massachusetts police didn't recognize that single tattoo as gang related, right?"

Tom was looking askance at his wife and Faith

knew she'd have to explain it all to him later. Earl shook his head. "No. They'd never seen it before." He appeared lost in thought. "You found the other guy, LeBlanc, on Thursday. He hadn't been in the water long. This body hasn't been on dry land for at least a week, I'd say."

Faith knew what he was thinking. The tattoos were no coincidence and now possibly the times of their deaths weren't either. This time the letters in red script were clear: *L F D Y.*

Were there any more snake-tattooed bodies out there?

The return trip home was a speedy one, and after Faith secured the boat to their mooring and Tom shut the engine off, she was surprised that he didn't get up to disconnect the batteries and do the other things necessary before they could row the short distance to shore.

"We need to talk," he said, motioning her to the second mate's seat. Faith sat down. Male or female, no one ever wanted to hear those four words.

"This has got to stop. When we exchanged vows, I pledged 'with my body I thee worship' and I meant only two. Mine and yours. Not a count of other ones over the years that I don't even want to tally up. Other ones that were dead. Yes, you've been helpful—"

She interrupted. "Helpful! More than that, Tom. You're not being fair!"

"Fair! Do you think it's fair to put your life and yes, Faith, several times the lives of those near and dear, at risk?"

She had never seen him so angry. Not even when she'd had to confess she'd given his lucky Celtics sweatshirt to Goodwill. She had no idea what to say.

"Well?"

Apparently she was supposed to say something. "I don't go looking for them. Do admit."

He sighed heavily and raised the engine. "We'll go to the sheriff's office in Ellsworth tomorrow so you can view the photos with Sophie again. We'll sign a report or whatever about today. And then, Faith, that's it."

His voice was so stern it was scaring her. "You have no idea what you could be getting mixed up in. It's likely the men are drug dealers—and whatever they did to get themselves killed means those responsible are not going to play nice with someone poking around in their business, even if you are a good cook and kindhearted person."

"And pretty great-looking right?" She could see that Tom's mood was starting to change.

"Okay, great-looking." He drew her toward him, but just before he kissed her he stopped. "Promise me, Faith. Promise you won't get involved."

"I promise," she said, leaning in for the kiss. Yet her thoughts raced on: *She wasn't planning on detecting any further. Tom was the one who noticed the trap's age. She would look at the photos, not ask Earl any questions, and since they were in Ellsworth, they could have a nice lunch at Martha's Diner before they came home. Done and dusted. Wasn't that what her husband was always saying? Done and dusted.*

Her parents and Sophie were going up to Ellsworth for some reason, so Amy was dropped at Sanpere Shores early—even for the breakfast shift. She didn't see Darlene's car and then remembered Thursday was her day off. There were plenty of baked goods, and if the chef was still sick, Amy knew she could handle the breakfast requests. It was the turnaround day in any case. All the current guests had to be out by twelve so the cottages could be cleaned and readied for the two groups coming in tomorrow. Darlene and Amy had packed box lunches yesterday for those who wanted to take one along.

The back door was open and she was reaching for the handle on the screen door when angry voices within stopped her. She recognized Dr. Childs. She hadn't known they were here. Maybe they'd driven over for the turnaround and to welcome the new guests tomorrow, something they did often. She didn't mean to eavesdrop, but he was shouting. "No more slipups! You were supposed to keep an eye on him! If there's even a single one more, you know what will happen."

The voice that answered was lower, but Amy recognized it as Cal Burke's. She could just make out the words. "Hey, boss, it's been fine so far. Don't worry. He'll be okay by tomorrow. There's no dinner tonight, and the girl can handle breakfast and the box lunches."

Amy knew she couldn't walk in now. They were obviously talking about the chef's illness. It must be a chronic condition and Cal was supposed to keep him on his medication or some other treatment. She would have thought Dr. Childs would be more sympathetic. She backed away from the door and walked to the front of the lodge, entering there.

Cindy was at the desk. "Hi, Amy, thanks for coming in so early. We really need you today. Dom is still under the weather." She waved her toward the kitchen. "I forgot it was Darlene's day off and she has a doctor's appointment in Bangor, otherwise she said she would have come in. If you could begin breakfast service now for early risers and those leaving soon that would be great. I'll see if Cal is around—he can help before he has to pitch in on the turnaround."

Amy started to say that Cal was in the kitchen

but stopped herself. "No problem. There are plenty of pastries, and what we make to order for breakfast is easy."

"Maybe for you." Cindy smiled. "I can boil water for my tea and use a microwave. That's it."

The kitchen was completely empty and the only indication that there had been people in earlier were two empty Sanpere Shores mugs on a counter. It was too soon for the dishwasher to be in—and Amy hoped he would show, since he was new this week—so she unloaded the last load from the night before and put the mugs in before getting to work setting up the breakfast buffet.

She loved being in the kitchen alone. Solely in charge. Life didn't get any better than this.

Tom's swiftness at getting them in and out of the sheriff's office was almost embarrassing. No, it *was* embarrassing, Faith thought. She had been very much aware of every word that came—or didn't come—from her mouth. Fortunately, Sophie hadn't been subjected to the same talking-to and asked the questions Faith would have. She had called Sophie with the news of their discovery on Green Island as soon as Tom had left to get Amy the night before. Sophie had also leaped to the conclusion that the two men were killed around the same time and wondered whether the second man was also from Lowell. And she knew about the numbering system for pot buoys. It would be easy to find out who owned the trap. Happily, she asked the sheriff both questions.

"The second victim was living in Lowell," the sheriff said, "and may have grown up there. His last name was also LeBlanc. It appears the two men were cousins or maybe half brothers."

When Faith had heard this, she thought of the wake that would be held at some point down in Massachusetts. A family losing two members at once. No matter what the men had done or not done, it was still tragic.

The sheriff had appeared reluctant to answer Sophie's question about the pot buoy, saying only that it wasn't registered to anyone on the island or surrounding ones. Seeing that she wasn't satisfied with the answer, he added tersely, "It was from Gloucester, Mass." At that point, Tom had thanked the sheriff and walked toward the door. Faith had no choice but to follow.

The three stopped at Martha's Diner. It was the real deal. There was a Martha and first-timers as well as regulars got a warm welcome from her. The diner had opened in 2004, but the 1950s retro decor was no imitation. Faith thought Martha and her husband, Peter, must scour yard sales and eBay constantly for all the authentic memorabilia—Elvis, Lucy, *I Dream of Jeannie*. The diner opened at six in the morning and closed at two, six days a week. Although Peter's Greek heritage provided alternatives like his delicious spanakopita, you went to Martha's for all-day breakfast.

Settling herself into one of the booths with their red vinyl-covered seats and Formica tables, Sophie started to talk about what they'd just learned. "They didn't look alike, but they could have been cousins certainly, even half brothers."

Tom finished the coffee that had automatically appeared when they sat down and motioned to the server. "I'll have the Northwest Harbor omelet, steak as rare as possible, with sharp cheddar please. Faith, Sophie, are you having omelets, too, or something else?" They got the message.

"The spinach and feta, the Hancock one," Faith said quickly. "Your homemade bread for toast, thanks." It was extra for the bread but well worth it.

Sophie was scanning the menu fast. She didn't come here as often as the Fairchilds. "I'll have the Brewer—haven't had corned beef hash in a long time—Swiss, and the homemade bread, too. Also, some orange juice when you get a chance."

Tom was taking charge of the outing—timing *and* topics of conversation. "What did Babs have to say about her day out in Bar Harbor with Zach's mother? And is she looking forward to the memoir workshop?"

"They had a good day and came back loaded down with shopping bags. Alexandra did comment it was a wonder Pix wasn't as big as an elephant, given what she had for lunch and an ice-cream cone that had given itself away with a smudge of chocolate on Pix's lip," Sophie said. "Later Babs told me Alexandra grows on you. But she's used to people like that. I sometimes think my mother is a chameleon, adapting to whomever she's with. Thank goodness I know the real Babs and can laugh, or just be in awe of the other."

"Us, too," Faith said, happy to enter *this* conversation. She'd talk to Sophie when they were alone about the topic off-limits.

"As for the writing courses, I think we're all looking forward to them," Sophie said. "I've been procrastinating long enough and hope to get a short story that could be the bare bones of a novel done by the end." What she didn't say, but both Fairchilds knew, was that she also hoped the intensity of the writing would keep her mind off having a baby. "It will be interesting to see who's in mine. It was open to fiction writers at all levels of experience. And I guess for memoir you just have to be alive."

Faith shot her a warning look, and Sophie said, flustered, "I mean obviously you had to be alive. Have a life, I mean. Oh wow, here's our food."

Sophie looked around the room with interest the next evening at the writers with whom she would be spending quite a bit of time over the next two weeks. It was five o'clock and the Writers' Welcome, as specified in the booklet that had been sent out, was about to start in the largest room of the main lodge. Sophie had been here in the past, but the new owners had definitely opened up the space—floor-to-ceiling windows and a large outer deck now faced the view. In addition, the furniture was more comfortable, Arts and Crafts in style as opposed to the previous knotty pine midcentury-motel look that Sophie recalled. Sanpere Shores manager Cindy had urged the group to get a drink before she spoke, and as Sophie suspected, it was a group that needed no urging. Although the females outnumbered the males by far, they still seemed to regard imitating Fitzgerald's and Hemingway's alcohol consumption an authorship bona fides.

Watching a woman who looked about Ursula's age down a generous shot of Scotch before holding her glass out for another, Sophie wondered whether she was a memoirist or a fiction writer—from her Miss Marple appearance, possibly specializing in cozy mysteries with cats and more tea spilled than blood. Or she could be a mistress of bodice-ripper romances. One thing Sophie had learned, and not all that long ago, was you couldn't judge by appearances. Especially not books from their covers.

She leaned back, took a sip from the white wine she had asked for, and admired the way Cindy was skillfully herding everyone to the seats. Cindy introduced herself again—"Two hats, manager and head of housekeeping"—and went over a few rules: no smoking anywhere except in the designated area by the parking lot; meal hours; spa hours and services; and so forth. Sophie's mind began to wander. Back at The Birches, Babs and Alexandra had displayed all the attributes of kids before the first day of school, consulting each other on what to wear and whether to take laptops or just their phones for notes. Sophie felt quite maternal as she ushered them into the car. Maternal! Stop it! she told herself and then amended it—*she might as well get some practice in. It was going to happen . . .*

"And here is the most important person of all," Cindy was saying. "This is Cal Burke, the head of maintenance and all-around fix-it guy, including IT. If you have any problems with the plumbing, your Wi-Fi, or heaven forbid, an unwanted visitor in your cottage like a squirrel, Cal will sort you out."

Cal Burke looked to be in his mid to late thirties and was wearing Levi's and a well-pressed blue work shirt that exactly matched his Benedict Cumberbatch eyes. Sophie had no doubt he would fill many of the attendees' sorting-out needs. She looked across at Alexandra, who was tossing her hair back—she'd decided to go for casual and wear it down—and paying close attention. She caught her mother's eye, and Babs winked. If it came to that, a little flirtation would keep Alexandra busy, as well as possibly providing more fodder for her memoir.

It was the instructors' turn to speak next. Sophie tuned back in.

"Hi, I'm Patrick Leary, and while I have not yet written my memoirs, I teach a course in them," the first instructor said in a slight Irish accent. It was too hot for a tweed sport coat with leather elbow patches, but Sophie conjured one up for him. He looked to be about fifty and his wire-rimmed glasses had already slipped down his rather prominent nose, as she suspected must happen often. His baldness was camouflaged by a cut almost to the scalp and she applauded his choice as opposed to a comb-over.

After Leary finished telling his group when and where they would meet in the morning, it was the fiction writers' turn to meet their mentor. Sophie had thought the woman who stood up was one of the students, and an eccentric one at that. She was a dead ringer for Emma Thompson as Sybill Trelawney, the Divination teacher in the Harry Potter films—trailing multicolored scarves, owl-like glasses, the kind of hairdo achieved when one sticks a finger in a live electrical socket, and a caftan decorated with both beads and tiny mirrors. It was a look she had likely adopted in the late 1960s and never abandoned.

"Please call me Eloise. Professor Bartholomew is not only too long, but too open to amusement." She grinned. Sophie liked her immediately. Eloise ran down the schedule and further endeared herself to the students in her group by suggesting they all grab another drink and go sit on the deck. "The view is magnificent. No need to take notes. We can talk about how to avoid writing fiction that sounds like a travel or nature guide another time. For now, just go soak it up!"

They did not need any further urging. As Sophie passed her mother, Babs pulled her down and whispered in her ear, "I may have picked the wrong group!" Sophie took the hint and refilled her mother's glass before leaving. Alexandra was in a world of her own, striking a pose, her chin resting on one hand—future author photo?—as she sat facing the maintenance man, who was still in the room. As Sophie went to join her group she had second thoughts about Zach's mother's possible interest in the handsome employee. Could be tears before bedtime. But, she said to herself, Babs would be there to keep all in check. Although, glancing over her shoulder, Sophie saw that Babs was also looking at Cal. Babs, whose husband of the moment was far away in the land of golf and haggis.

Talk about all dressed up and nowhere to go! Tears of frustration streamed down her face, ruining the makeup she'd taken so long to apply. At the last minute he had to fill in for someone. Again. He'd make it up to them. They could go to the Fry next Friday.

No thank you! She'd been thinking about it all day. Going to the Café, the one restaurant they could afford. Friday's Fry, always crowded with people she knew, wasn't just a meal. It was a gathering. Seconds were free. She always went for the haddock and onion rings with plenty of coleslaw. Her mouth started to water. She hadn't felt hungry in a long time, but she could feel her stomach rumbling. Damn it! They had reservations—you had to on Fridays—and she'd have to call and cancel now.

Or did she? There was no law that said she couldn't go without him. The Café was more than kid friendly. On Fridays the kids often outnumbered the grown-ups. So big deal—there would be two instead of three. She didn't have to let them know. They could share a booth with friends.

It was hot, so no jackets. She looked out the window at the car parked in the yard. She hadn't been driving for a while. Didn't need to. Didn't want to. She closed her eyes, the panic starting. Her throat was closing up. In the pantry she was keeping a few pills in an old contact lens case buried at the bottom of her flour canister. Soon her hands were covered with flour. She didn't remember deciding, but she must have. Just one. Just to take the edge off. Just so she could breathe. She popped it, washed her hands, waited, and soon she was dancing out the door.

"Mommy's happy."

"Yes, Mommy's very happy." She laughed and buckled the car seat.

"Tree, Mommy!"

"Yes, honey, lots of trees."

The noise of the impact barely registered. The crying did.

It was dark when she woke up. She was on top of her bed and dressed. Not bedtime. Not in pajamas. She closed her eyes anyway and then sat bolt upright and ran into the other bedroom.

Thank you, God. Thank you, God, she prayed as she heard the soft steady breathing.

Thank you, God. She went outside and moved the car back to where it had been, backing ever so slightly into the alders to hide the smashed left rear light.

Thank you, God.

She went back inside and took another pill.

The Memoir Group had joined the others on the deck. Amy Fairchild and a young man, in the black pants–white shirt uniform that indicated a server, were bringing trays of hors d'oeuvres out in the approaching dusk. Amy was wearing a chef's white jacket and checked pants. She looked much as Sophie imagined Faith would have at that age. She went over to her. "Hi! This all looks delicious," she said and was delighted with the big hug Amy gave her. Still a kid.

"Try the seafood pot stickers—crab, lobster, and shrimp with a little chive. Oh, and the ham and cheese puffed pastry squares with Kozlik's sweet and smoky mustard. It's Mom's recipe. I taught the chef. You make it on a sheet pan in layers and then cut it up into little squares after it comes out of the oven. There's also a platter of cut-up veggies from King Hill farm in Penobscot with dipping sauces. And freshly baked breadsticks that we wrapped in slices of prosciutto."

"I'm going back to make dinner for Uncle Paul, but I can't resist some of these first," Sophie said, reaching for one of the breadsticks.

The cost for day students included lunch and dinner, but Sophie had the feeling she'd want to go home after a full day. Babs and Alexandra, social creatures that they were, would probably stay most nights, and in the future they should probably take two cars. She'd come back for them tonight unless they wanted to go back soon.

"I'll let you know when we're doing something special for dinner," Amy said. "Although most of them *are*. Tonight prime rib is one of the choices. Dessert is going to be on the beach. The Childses invited everyone to a bonfire once it's dark. We've got citronella torches to keep the bugs away. You might not want to miss it. Cal will be singing and telling jokes. It's fun, and the fire looks beautiful so close to the water."

"Don't tell me Alexandra is going to find out about s'mores!" Sophie laughed.

"Oh yes, and Darlene, who does most of the baking, made a ton of Whoopie Pies, too. Besides the Marshmallow Fluff–chocolate cake wicked good traditional ones, she also does maple filling and blueberry with lemon cake, in case someone doesn't like chocolate, which I cannot imagine! Did you know Whoopie Pies are the official Maine state treat? Like the state bird and other stuff."

"No, I did not," Sophie said in mock solemnity, "but if I'm ever on *Jeopardy*, this fact could come in handy." They both laughed. It was wonderful to see Amy so happy in her job.

"I have to go and finish the dinner prep," Amy said. "If you don't make it to the beach later, I'll send some of the pies back with your mom."

"Those two ladies won't have touched them I bet. Think of the carbs!" Sophie hugged Amy good-bye and decided to fill one of the small plates with the hors d'oeuvres. Paul liked to eat on the late side, and Sophie wanted a chance to check out the whole group further.

Why, she wondered, were there so many more women in classes like this than men? If you looked at bestseller lists, male authors outnumbered female significantly, so *some* men were writing. Maybe it was the whole notion of taking a class. Not a manly thing to do? Something you didn't need?

When they'd first gathered on the deck Eloise had announced that she was not a "Hello My Name Is name tag type," which did not surprise Sophie at all. "Mingle, mingle. Get to know each other without a label!"

Sophie had mingled and introduced herself to two women who looked to be somewhere in their sixties and had sat together during the orientation. She learned they were college roommates, Susan and Deborah, now living in New York and California. They had decided it was time to write the novels they'd never had time for before. "Of course, you always read about those authors who get up at four in the morning and write for two or more hours before their day jobs or taking care of their families. I'm afraid my muse didn't wake me," Deborah said. She revealed that she had four kids, a surprise set of twins filling out the roster at the end. The notes she'd been making for years on yellow legal pads had stayed in a drawer until now. Susan had much the same story, except it was aging parents living with them, added to the kids.

"We're the MacDonalds from Morristown, New Jersey," a lively-looking woman said as she pulled a man with a tolerant look on his face toward the group. Mrs. MacDonald was the outgoing partner, it seemed. "I'm Cynthia and he's Ross. We both took early retirement last year. I saw the ad for this online and it's perfect. Ross has been delving into our family trees, so he's going to write it all up as a memoir for our grandchildren, and I'm going to do the same, except make it fiction. Let them decide which ancestors they want!"

It was a novel idea, Sophie thought. She introduced herself and then made her way across the deck to speak to Babs and Alexandra.

As Sophie expected, the two women were the center of a group. "Isn't all memoir a kind of fiction?" Alexandra was saying. "What we remember is not always reliable."

"Especially at my age," said a man who could have been in his seventies but was definitely well preserved—thick slate-gray hair and the only wrinkles were laugh lines at his clear hazel eyes. Seeing

Sophie, Babs announced, "This is my daughter, Sophie. Sophie, this is Hans Richter, originally from Germany, and I'm sensing a major memoir. Sophie's in the fiction group. You can't tell from her accent, but she's a southerner now. Her irresistible husband lured her to Savannah, his hometown. But she's a New Englander at heart, since she has been on the island every summer of her life, as have I."

"I've only been here a few hours and I already plan to come back," declared a woman dressed much the same as Alexandra and Babs. Sophie followed Alexandra's glance and was sure she could read her thoughts—maybe the island wasn't as tacky and unfashionable as she'd first judged if people like this were raving about it.

Sophie leaned closer to her mother, who had looped her arm through her daughter's. "I'm going to take off now. I'm assuming you want to stay? I'll come back later to get you, and Amy has convinced me not to miss the bonfire."

"Yes, darling, we're going to stay." Babs lowered her voice. "You know why I was taking the course, but I'm glad now. Patrick is going to be a terrific teacher and I'm already inspired."

"And how about . . . ?" Sophie nodded toward Alexandra.

"I think she's even more excited than I am." Babs gave a little smile. "And such a good chance to make new friends." Alexandra was offering to get a tall good-looking gentleman who it seemed was in Sophie's class another drink.

"You're terrible." Sophie gave her mother's arm a squeeze. "See you later."

As she left she passed a new arrival—a pretty young woman Sophie judged to be her own age. As a whole, the group was older. The woman had paused in the doorway. Sophie stopped. "Hi, I'm Sophie Maxwell and taking the fiction course. Are you here for that—or the memoir one?"

There was no mistaking the relief on the woman's face. "Oh yes. I didn't know where I was supposed to go and I heard voices so . . . Oh, I'm Ellen Sinclair." She put out her hand. "And fiction. I mean I'm taking fiction." She blushed. Sophie shook her hand. It was small, in keeping with the woman's diminutive size. "I misjudged how long the drive would be. I'm from Burlington, Vermont."

"My family has a house here," Sophie said, "so I'm a day student. My mother and a friend are taking the memoir course. They're over there by the bar." She pointed. "I have to run, but I'm coming to the bonfire."

"Bonfire?" Ellen said.

Sophie laughed. "An old-fashioned camp-type one. Not *Fahrenheit 451*." She spied Eloise making her way toward them. "Here comes our instructor. Perfect timing."

Ellen gasped slightly. "She looks exactly like Sybill Trelawney, you know the . . ."

"Divination teacher," Sophie finished and patted Ellen on the shoulder. A kindred spirit.

The original owner of what was now Sanpere Shores had been a retired botany professor. He'd built a main lodge with several cabins in the 1950s, attracting like-minded naturalists who thought the spot, walks, and sails were an ideal vacation. He'd used the site well. The buildings were up high above the beach, a long curve on deep water. Sophie was glad for the outdoor lighting as she walked down the wide path, but also glad it had been turned off at the end as she stepped onto the sand. The fire was sending deep red and orange sparks into the night sky, and she could hear someone singing over the crackling flames. As she drew closer, she saw it was Cal, accompanying himself on the guitar. The two writers' groups numbered around twenty-five, Sophie knew, but the actuaries were double that. So it was a sizable crowd that was obviously enjoying the rich desserts and Maine sky.

Cal stopped playing as a man and woman emerged from the shadows to stand directly in front of the bonfire. Cal clapped his hands for silence and said, "It's my pleasure to introduce Dr. and Mrs. Childs, your hosts and my bosses."

Sophie was surprised at their appearance. As the owners of three such high-end resorts she had pictured a couple much like her mother and Ed. Dr. Childs looked like a pudgier, slightly taller version of Mr. Bean and wore round glasses with black frames. Mrs. Childs, also rotund, appeared twice his height and had a dark brown Dutch bob. The doctor was wearing a seersucker sport coat and his wife a shirtwaist dress reminiscent of June Cleaver. Maybe they had just arrived and hadn't had time to change into L.L. Bean–type clothes.

"Out of the three properties we are fortunate to have acquired, Sanpere Shores is our favorite. This is a very special island, and although you will be busy with tasks during the day, I hope you will get to explore a bit during your free time. Cindy, our manager, and Cal here can help you with suggestions. Cal can also provide transportation for those of you without vehicles."

He had an old-fashioned delivery, Sophie thought, but he wasn't that old—late forties at most. Same for his wife, who was echoing his advice. "Now, enough of us, enjoy!"

Cal proceeded to liven things up, starting a jazzy rendition of "Makin' Whoopee," presumably inspired, Sophie thought, by the Whoopie Pies going like hotcakes. "Another season, another reason for makin' whoopee . . ." He really had a great voice. He paused for a moment when a woman carrying a guitar walked onto the beach and went over to him. She picked up where he left off, their two voices complementing each other perfectly. At the end of the song, he nodded to her. She smiled and started singing "House of the Rising Sun" solo. She sounded like a young Joan Baez, that extraordinary range, the crystal notes. Sophie was spellbound and hoped she would keep on singing. She untied a pink bandanna, letting her long dark hair hang loose while shrugging off a black leather jacket, tossing both on the sand away from the heat of the fire. Sophie could see the back of the jacket clearly. A red rose, painted by an amateur hand.

The singer was the woman who had been with both LeBlancs in the market.

Seven

Sophie counted eleven people gathered in the Shores dining room the next morning, the tables cleared except for a small coffee and tea station by one window. There were four new faces, late arrivals last night she assumed—a man and a woman who had hitched their chairs close to one another, obviously a couple; a guy about her age wearing Diesel black jeans and a tight black tee, hair carefully spiked to appear casual; and finally a teenage boy dressed in tan work clothes, a bruised thumbnail that looked as if a hammer had landed wrong. If he had not had an open notebook, she would have assumed he was on the maintenance crew.

"Welcome, welcome! Hello everyone!" Eloise was clearly a morning person. Sophie was not and got up to refill her coffee mug before sitting back down.

"You've all come with differing expectations. The first thing you must do is discard them. The novel or short story you plan to write will not get finished. You will not learn any secrets about how to get published. In short, there aren't any, except to write a good book, and even then it's a long shot."

Sophie looked around the room at her fellow students, noting expressions ranging from shock to outright despair. The exception was the man her age, who looked smug. No doubt he thought he was the one who was going to make it— National Book Award, Pulitzer, Edgar, etc.

"But, as they say in the land of my birth, 'Don't get your knickers in a twist.'" *Ah*, Sophie thought, *Ms. Bartholomew was British. Emma Thompson's stand-in?*

"I'm not sure writing can be taught." Eloise seemed to be musing aloud. "I mean you have it or you don't. The itch. The talent." Finally noting the looks on most of the class's faces, she hastily amended, "But I can jump-start you *and* help make your results better. My mantra is 'Rewrite,

Rewrite, and Rewrite Again.'" She flung one of her scarves, turquoise with purple fringe, over her shoulder for emphasis.

"That sounds like Elmore Leonard," the man in black drawled in an accent Sophie found hard to place. Not southern, not anywhere distinctive. Very practiced, though.

"Ah yes, Elmore's rules. Miss him very much. If you want to look them up or any other's—I'm partial to Orwell's—go ahead, but I would highlight the one he shares with Mark Twain about avoiding weather. As in don't start with 'It was a dark and stormy night' unless it's satire. Twain left all the weather out of *The American Claimant*—'No weather will be found in this book.' And put it at the end in an appendix for those readers who absolutely had to have it. As for myself, I can safely tell you I have no rules or if I do offer some— avoiding adverbs totally for example—I'll tell you to break them, as I just have."

Sophie was enjoying herself. She'd read both Orwell's and Leonard's rules. Her favorite was Elmore Leonard's advice to "leave out the part that readers tend to skip." It occurred to her, however, that sticking to that could leave her with a very short book.

Eloise was continuing. "Now I said mingle last night and no name tags," Eloise continued, "but before we start this morning's exercise, please briefly introduce yourself, name and where you live will do. Leave out where you live or make up a name if you want, but I need something to call you. The class list didn't include mug shots."

This last brought somewhat nervous laughter from a corner of the room, but Sophie couldn't tell whether it was the couple or the woman she had already categorized as Miss Marple.

Louise Todd, "a Jersey Girl" she said proudly, went first, then Susan and Deborah introduced themselves. Susan was from La Jolla, California, and Deborah, Bronxville, New York. Sophie knew both places, and the women weren't going to have to rely on royalties to keep them in today's equivalent of typewriter ribbon. Miss Marple was Mrs. Joan Whittaker from Montreal, Canada, and as Sophie knew, Ellen Sinclair was from Burlington, Vermont. Sophie went next and mentioned both places of residence. The couple had different last names—she was Karen Mann and he was David Donaldson, both from Ohio, no specific town. The teen was George Finley from Portland, Maine, and a day student like Sophie. Last up was Jay Thomas, "from here, there, and everywhere," he smirked, adding, "published in—" But Eloise stopped him cold. "No prima donnas here. I don't care if you won the Nobel Prize for Literature or best editorial when you were in high school. This isn't a competition, and if it were, I'm pretty sure it would be an even playing field."

Ignoring the indignant look he shot her, Eloise said, "Now, let's get started with a seemingly simple exercise, but things are never what they seem." Sophie glanced over at Ellen Sinclair, who obviously shared the feeling that they were both in Divination class about to peer into a crystal ball. Sophie had to fight to stifle a giggle.

"*P-O-V*. Point of view. The ability as a writer to put yourself in another's shoes, or whole psyche, is key to developing voice. We'll get to that discussion this afternoon. Voice, I mean. Plots are an easy fix—usually. But only the writer himself or herself can supply voice." Eloise waved a small stack of index cards at the group. "I'm going to hand each of you a card with a character on it—a parent with a toddler, an alien visitor. You will have forty minutes—thirty plus ten to rewrite—to describe the place in which we are sitting from the point of view of what or who is written on your card. When we are finished, I will read each aloud and you will try to guess the character." She started passing them out. "Find a place where you can concentrate, outdoors if you like, and use the pads of paper that were in your course materials. No computers today. Too easy to cut, paste, employ a thesaurus, other tools. I want you to connect with the words directly, viscerally."

Someone let out an audible sigh of disgust, and it wasn't hard to tell who. Jay as in Jay K. Growling.

Pix was going to have to get over the feeling of foreboding that swept over her each time she woke up. Just the thought of the Cranes not so far from where her head rested on her pillow caused a knot in her stomach far removed from the nautical ones she was good at—learned from her father along with rowing a dinghy and hoisting the mainsail and jib.

She needed to get back to her old self. The pre-Crane self. It sounded like an epoch. Well, the way she felt placed her squarely in the Paleolithic. She got out of bed, relishing the metaphors. Faith would enjoy them. She'd call her and some other friends for a sail today. Maybe all women. A Girls' Sail Out.

It was quiet not only next door but also in the entire cove. Only the sudden arrival of a boisterous flock of crows jarred the peace as Pix sat on the deck enjoying her breakfast of homemade (not by her) granola, Greek yogurt, strawberries, and coffee. She was soon finished and made her calls. Everyone was busy today, but three, including Faith, were free tomorrow. When she hung up she was happy she'd arranged the outing. She was also due for drinks and dinner in Blue Hill at friends' tonight, so it wasn't that she didn't have things to do, but she missed Sam in a way she never had other summers. She'd always packed the kids up as soon as school ended and Sam came when he could, taking a long vacation in August. But that pattern had ended years ago when all three went off to camp for part of the summer and eventually whole summers elsewhere after college. She never minded being alone at the house. It was this summer that was out of sync somehow.

Concentrate on joy. She thought she'd seen it on a poster or maybe it was from one of Tom's sermons. She thought of Ed Ricks's LIFE IS SHORT, EAT DESSERT FIRST pillow and thought she'd do one with this reminder. Or at least put it on the top of her never-ending to-do list.

She washed her dishes and decided to go for it right now. Joy. The wedding. She would bring Arlene's matron of honor dress over for her to try on and drop off Kylie's flower girl outfit. Arlene was like another daughter, and the thought of seeing her expression when she saw the dress in person undid the knot in Pix's stomach, leaving only the knot her daughter was tying.

Who could it possibly be? Her mother had already been by as day camp chauffeur since the car was being repaired. It was drivable—only needed a new taillight and a little bodywork, but it wouldn't have been legal to drive it. If she'd heard that once, she'd heard it a hundred times, and how did it happen anyway? No one saw who backed into her in the market's parking lot? How was that possible? he kept asking. It was the busiest place on the island, especially at the time of day she said it happened— late afternoon, when the fishermen were heading home and stopping for beer, maybe pizza for dinner if they weren't married. Someone must have seen something. He'd asked around. She let him. What else could she do? It actually made her laugh.

But who was outside now? Coming toward the porch? The cabin wasn't a place you passed. You had to know the long dirt drive leading to it. For a moment she panicked. She'd been so careful not to let any of her off-island suppliers know that she even lived on Sanpere. And she didn't owe them money. Could it be Earl? Found out somehow? She raced to the window. No, it wasn't his patrol car or his personal one. She knew whose car it was and her heart sank.

Smile, Arlene, she said to herself. Smile—and get rid of your best friend's mother as fast as you can.

The variety in writing styles, and skill level, was noticeable, but Sophie was relieved that none of the pieces Eloise read aloud were duds. She credited the instructor with selecting a challenge that anyone could meet. She also was quite sure that Eloise had tailored the POV to each student, although how she could have known Sophie was surrounded by examples of the simple description on her card—"eighty-year-old person"—wasn't clear. Just eerie. Back to Divination.

Eloise read each without names, but Cynthia MacDonald had squealed, "Oh you're all going to hate this!" revealing herself as the author of an ant's point of view. Her piece was very funny, and Sophie decided that Mrs. MacDonald was much smarter than she let on. She wrote in first person and filled the space with Brobdingnagian creatures. The ant employed clever tactics to avoid getting squished. Sophie thought an expanded version would make a fun children's book.

Her own piece brought positive comments— although Eloise made it clear that if someone didn't have something good to say, a mouth should be kept shut. She was the only critic allowed. Sophie had imagined herself as an eighty-year-old woman who had come to dinner in this room, one she had not been in for fifty years. Most of it was a flashback—partly the room's appearance, originally heated only by the massive two-story fireplace still extant—but the rest recounted the woman's passion for her lover, as they secretly met here at the then old unoccupied hunting lodge for the last time, each unable to break their wedding vows. Sophie tried hard to keep it from being too sentimental, focusing instead on the wrenching nature of their choice. The last sentence returned the reader to the present and the woman's realization that her lover is there at the dinner. She hasn't recognized the old man nor he she. Or had they?

It was getting close to lunchtime, and Sophie saw Amy hovering at the kitchen door, peering out to see how the group was getting on. The memoirists were meeting in a large cabin up the hill, where the Childses stayed when they were on-island. The two groups would alternate spaces, and Eloise had also mentioned some off-site locations, specifically the Roland Howard Meeting Room at the Blue Hill Library with a side trip to E. B. White's lovely small hometown library in Brooklin.

So far all the guesses as to the identities of the names written on the cards had been close or spot-on. Eloise was now reading the last one. Glancing at her fellow scribblers, it did not take Sophie long to identify the writer. He was sprawled back in the leather Stickley-type armchair he had appropriated as soon as the group arrived this morning, and his eyes were half closed. She could see his thoughts clearly, like skywriting—"Words like jewels from the hand of a master."

And they weren't bad. He did have talent. Some. But they were so grim, so horrifying, that Sophie was afraid it might put the group off lunch. His last sentence, describing the final act of the card's "a killer—human or nonhuman," was doing it for her: "The adder's fangs like carefully honed shivs dripped crimson gore on the lifeless arm. His job was done."

Pix didn't see Arlene's car, but as she'd pulled up to the house she'd seen her face at the window. Carefully gathering the two garment bags with their precious contents in her arms, she went up the front steps. Arlene, Mike, and Kylie had moved into the log cabin a little over a year ago, and Mike was working on it when he had time. The steps had been replaced, she noticed, but Pix knew there was a lot to do inside. The former owners had bought it as a kit and only finished the shell.

Arlene was a passionate gardener—she was one of Ursula's acolytes—but Pix was surprised to see no sign of the blooms that had edged the front of the house last summer. Arlene must be concentrating on the vegetable garden in the rear. Mike had cleared enough trees to create a good-size sunny patch.

"Hi, Arlene?" she called. "It's Pix with your gorgeous finery!"

The door opened slightly more than a crack and Arlene said, "Hi, thanks. I'll take them and try mine on later. Kylie's at the Community Center day camp. She can try hers on when she gets home this afternoon."

Pix took a step forward. "I know she'll look adorable. Samantha sent you a picture, right? She's continuing the rose and ivory tones for the whole wedding party. Zach is wearing an off-white linen summer suit with a pale pink shirt and ivory bow tie. The ushers—Mark and Dan, his soon-to-be brothers-in-law—are wearing the same shirt with chinos and a pale green bow tie. The color of my dress." Pix knew she was babbling, but Arlene hadn't moved or said anything more. As the door opened a bit more, she added, "And of course Kylie's is pink, a tulle skirt and lacy top. Little Sam is going to be dressed like the ushers and best man, except Bermuda shorts, not chinos. And suspenders with little lobsters." She smiled but did not get one in return. "Samantha really needs you to try your dress on right away in case it needs to be altered . . ." Pix ran out of steam.

There was a brief silence. Arlene sighed. "You'd better come in."

The rooms had been partitioned off and a few walls were up. "We're going with 'open concept,'" Arlene said sarcastically. "Mike's never home to do any work and we can't afford to hire anyone. So our bedroom is closed in, but nothing else."

The house was tidy, but Pix imagined it might get depressing to live without a finished kitchen—just boards on sawhorses for counters, what looked like a hand-me-down stove and fridge plus no cabinets, only storage containers. Added to what must seem an overwhelming project was the fact that the cabin was in the middle of nowhere, even for the island, Pix reflected. No neighbors to commiserate with or lend a hand.

"Arlene, honey, is everything okay?" She chose her next words carefully. "You seem a little tired."

"I'm fine, absolutely fine. Why wouldn't I be? Let me take the dress into the other room and I'll try it on." She snatched the bag from Pix's hands.

"Samantha ordered shoes dyed to match from the same place she got all of ours, and she'll bring them when she comes up for the shower," Pix called after her. "And Susie Shepard is doing everyone's hair Saturday morning, plus she has a friend who will do mani/pedis." Pix looked at her hands. The last manicure she'd had was for her son Mark's wedding four summers ago.

Arlene didn't say anything, just walked out of the room and closed the only inside door. Firmly. Pix had known Arlene almost all of Arlene's life and had seen her in every stage of dress and undress. Well, she was a matron now. A matron of honor. It was fine if she didn't feel comfortable changing in front of Pix.

She was out almost immediately. Pix swallowed hard. "You look beautiful," she said softly. "The color is perfect for you and we just have to take a little tuck here and there." The suggestion was a huge understatement. The dress hung on Arlene like a tent. Arlene's arms, clearly visible extending from the short cap sleeves, were so thin her veins showed blue. She'd taken off her sneakers, and her bare ankles looked sharp enough to break through her skin. Pix had seen Arlene at the Fourth of July parade, but she'd been wearing a loose long-sleeved top and overalls. Pix remembered thinking Arlene must be roasting in the record heat. Now she knew it was so no one would notice how much weight she'd lost. It explained why she'd been dodging Samantha, too.

Pix couldn't help but walk over and hug the girl—she'd always think of the two as girls, these BFFs. Under the gown's beaded top she could feel nothing but bone—and a rapidly pounding heartbeat. "You know you can tell me anything. What's going on? You're so thin, darling."

Arlene pulled away. There were tears in her eyes—whether from sorrow or anger, maybe both, Pix couldn't tell. "I wanted to look good for the wedding, so I went on a diet. Leave the dress. I can take it in. Tell Samantha I love it and I'll see her soon. The shower is going to be great. I have to go weed the garden now."

It was a dismissal. Pix followed her out the back door and then detoured around the side of the house to her car. A quick look told her that there wasn't any garden to speak of—a few mounds of squash and a raised bed of what might have been lettuce before the deer got to it.

"Good-bye," she called over her shoulder.

There was no answer.

Samantha's shower! She had to do the shower. Invite people. Plan a menu. Who? What? For a moment she panicked. Then she remembered. Her aunt Gert was doing the food, and it was going to be at Samantha's grandmother's. She went back inside. The sunlight hurt her eyes. There was a stack of invitations on the table they used for everything—eating, paperwork, Kylie's art. She had stamped them with a heart stamp and she'd filled out the time, date, and place. She just had to address them. They could wait. There was plenty of time. Plenty of time now, too. She went into the bedroom and lay down on the quilt, wishing herself far away. And soon she was.

The two writers' groups ate lunch together. Sophie sat with her mother and Alexandra, both of whom were consuming a mound of salad greens, no dressing, and water. "You really should try the crab salad," Sophie said. "Amy told me it's made with a drop of lemon juice and scant amount of mayo. Very crabby. I know you won't go for it in the crab roll, but it's delicious." Sophie was savoring hers—the traditional flat-sided white bread hot dog roll had been grilled in butter, then stuffed with the crab mixture, no onion or celery fillers. It came with coleslaw and sweet potato fries, which she was also making short work of despite the looks both her mother and Alexandra were casting on the plate. "I'm drinking unsweetened tea," she said defensively.

"Darling girl, you're certainly old enough to decide what you want to eat," her mother said, eyeing the fries pointedly. "Now, tell us how your group is going? The instructor is certainly picturesque."

Sophie smiled. Trust her mother to assess Eloise by her wardrobe. She described the morning's exercise and said, "I think she's going to turn out—at least for me—to be excellent. We are each meeting with her individually after lunch. I like the others in the class, except for that guy over there all in black. I don't know why he would come to such an unknown program. Couldn't get into Iowa or Sewanee is my guess. His 'Too Cool for School' is already grating on me. What's your group like?"

Alexandra answered, "I'm not sure most of them would qualify when it comes to material for an interesting memoir, except perhaps Patrick. Married, by the way, even though he isn't wearing a ring. I heard him talking about his husband to Ross MacDonald." She turned her head away from the table quickly. Cal Burke had just walked into the room. Alexandra sat up straight. "There are other irons in the fire, so to speak," she said in what sounded to Sophie like a very adolescent sotto voce, then called out, "Cal, there's a place here." She patted the chair next to her.

Cal smiled back. "Sorry, ladies. I'm going to chow down fast in the kitchen. I have to get right back to work. That other group must be ditching old tax returns down the plumbing, judging from all the unplugging I'm doing. Another time." His smile, Sophie thought, really was pretty devastating. It crinkled his bright blue eyes and radiated across the room. She exchanged a look with her mother, who was watching Alexandra toss the scarf around her ponytail over one very smooth tan shoulder.

Babs picked up the thread. "Most of the people in our class have been doing research on the Internet about their ancestry and want to get it all down as a coherent story. Not really memoirs. Patrick is encouraging them to start with their own lives first. Childhood up to the present and then weave in the past or write it as a separate beginning or end."

Alexandra sniffed and continued to be derisive regarding her fellow classmates. "Take Ross for example. The man has sold insurance all his life. What kind of story is that going to make?"

"You never know," Babs answered smartly. "Didn't you ever see *Double Indemnity*? And come to think of it, Ross looks a little like Fred MacMurray."

Sophie swiftly changed the subject to Alexandra herself. "How about your memoir? I don't even want to think about Mom's. Possibly more of a list than a narrative," she teased.

"I don't know that I'll share it with anyone, except Patrick," Alexandra said. "We can opt out of having him read our works in progress." She shoved her half-eaten plate of salad aside. "It has been interesting to think back. Our first exercise was to write down our very earliest memory. Mine was very clear. I must have been only two or so, since my mother died when I was three. We had gone to a lake in northern New Jersey where relatives of hers had a summer place. The door from the living room onto the veranda had a bead curtain, strings of them hanging from the lintel. I suppose it was intended to keep flies from coming in. The room was dark, but it was a sunny day. I can still recall the sensation of that bright warmth as I pushed through and the way the light made rainbows of the jewel-like beads. I think that's why I've always been drawn to beautiful things." She stretched out her left hand. No wedding band, but a large square-cut emerald surrounded by small diamonds that would not have been out of place in the Tower of London's collection. "I like to rotate my rings and other baubles," she said complacently. "Today seemed like a green day. All these pine trees."

"What a beautiful memory," Babs said. "I'm afraid mine was quite prosaic. And I wasn't as young. We were at my grandmother's and I was bored, so I snuck out of the room and down into her preserves pantry in the basement. I did write about how cool it was—stifling upstairs and maybe the company, too. Anyway, I opened up at least ten jam jars, stuck my finger in to see which I liked best, and knocked over a whole shelf of watermelon pickles before anyone missed me. Every time there was a family gathering after that, someone was sure to ask me if I wanted jam or a pickle."

Sophie laughed. "Did you get punished?"

"Of course. Those were 'spare the rod and spoil the child' days. My grandmother was pretty handy with a switch. I never did anything to provoke her again. Sadly she was gone before you were born and I'm sorry you never got to know each other." Babs sighed. "I'm afraid she wouldn't have thought much of my serial nuptials. I'm sorry to hear you lost your mother when you were so young, Alexandra. I was eleven when my mother died."

Sophie knew this and had often wondered

whether Babs's adolescence spent in boarding school with a loving but absent father had caused her to seek so many "forever" partners. It also explained why Babs had been so close to her late aunt Priscilla, uncle Paul, and The Birches. The sole sureties in her life. Who had been there for Alexandra?

"People, people, I mean *my* people," Eloise said, standing up at her table and clapping her hands together. "Finish up please, and look at the list I've left with Cindy indicating times this afternoon for each of you to meet with me. And I've left you another exercise that should be both a challenge and fun."

Knowing that Sophie and George Finley were day students, Eloise had thoughtfully scheduled them early. First George and then Sophie. During the break before lunch, Sophie had spoken briefly to him. He worked as an elementary school custodian in Yarmouth, outside Portland, and lived in South Portland, he'd told her. He was attending night classes at Southern Maine, working toward a BA in English with enough education courses so he could teach high school someday. His dream was to support himself as a writer, but he was realistic about his chances and figured "I'll always have to have a day job." He'd enrolled in the Sanpere Shores class to get feedback on a detective novel he'd been working on, the first he hoped in a series. "People like a series. I do anyway. Watch the main character change, but also deep down stay the same guy."

He'd found a good deal on a studio Airbnb in Granville and was enjoying living on the island. He looked about fifteen—freckles and a carrot top— but he told her he'd graduated from high school two years ago, so that made him nineteen at least. When he came to tell her Eloise was ready for her, he grinned. "Don't worry. She was gentle." Sophie laughed. He called after her, "Does she look like that teacher in the Harry Potter movies to you? Maybe she can predict my future as a writer."

"What do you hope to get from me? From these two weeks," Eloise asked Sophie. They were sitting down on the beach. Eloise had spread out a woven mat and offered Sophie water or juices from a cooler. A large package of Oreos had already been opened. Eloise pointed to the cookies. "I always get very hungry when I write and assume other writers do, too. When we meet bring your snack and tipple of choice. Oreos and lemonade are mine, but you may have other preferences."

"I'm not a writer," Sophie said, "but a lawyer, and as for a tipple I'm afraid I drink way too much Diet Coke. I live in Savannah, Georgia, most of the year and it's a food town, but when I grab a snack it's a yogurt from the firm's fridge. My husband is trying to change my ways, though. He's introduced me to pimento cheese sandwiches, my new favorite."

They talked a bit about Sophie's background—Sophie stuck to the expurgated version, omitting her resignation from a high-powered New York law firm and her heartbreak in London. This wasn't memoir—or therapy. Instead she sketched out her idea for a short story set in Savannah during the time of the Underground Railroad.

"When I moved there I began to learn about the signals—hanging patchwork quilts with certain blocks whose names indicated a safe house on fences and the escape tunnels under the city, remnants of which remain. But what was most evocative for me was visiting the First African Baptist Church, the oldest African-American congregation in the country and a stop on the railroad. There are twenty-six sets of apparently random holes drilled in the pine floor in what is now the lower part of the church that provided ventilation for the men, women, and children who hid there. The pattern wasn't random. It was a Kongolese cosmogram symbolizing the four movements of the sun and the journey of the body from the physical to the spiritual world. So a sign of hope. I thought I could try to imagine myself as one of the people huddled there. Perhaps a mother with a small child . . ." Sophie's voice trailed off.

"Are you a mother?" Eloise asked.

"No," Sophie said. She started to add "not yet" but stopped and just said "no" again.

"Go for it. I love your idea." Eloise nodded her head firmly.

The exercise Eloise had assigned was an intriguing one. It was a bit like a menu that asked you to choose one from Column A and one from Column B. The instructor had listed a number of first lines and an equal number of last lines. The task was to select one of each and fill in the part in between. No word count was specified. Sophie took her laptop, permitted now, out to the deck where several others from both groups were at work. She was relieved that the rule of silence was in effect and no one did more than nod in her direction.

She sat taking in the view for a few minutes. The cove was a large one, and the land that marked it on either side was heavily wooded above the sloping granite ledges. And the beach itself was a single sandy crescent with few of the stony outcroppings common to others on Sanpere. Sophie imagined what a haven this sheltered landing spot would have made for the Abenaki, the original settlers on the island or, more correctly, the original summer people, traveling from the north to spend the months in the comparatively warm clime fishing and storing up essential foodstuffs for the winter.

She examined the list. One of the last lines was simply, "The End." She liked Eloise's sense of humor and decided to go with that choice. The first line was harder. What to write about? As she stared at the beach, the white sand seemed to be moving in front of her eyes, but she knew it was the effect of the harsh sunlight. The scene came first—the canoes landing, the occupants setting up summer quarters. No lightweight North Face dome tents. They'd have to first venture into the woods, much denser than now, to find saplings, strip the leaves and bark, bend them to support the animal skin coverings they'd packed. She looked at the first lines again. "Her tired face betrayed her words." And there she was on the beach: an exhausted woman, how old? Reassuring someone, a man? Another woman? That she was fine and could keep working.

Sophie's fingers flew across the keyboard and when she looked up, Sophie was surprised to see that only two people remained on the deck—Ellen and Jay. She glanced at the time on the screen. She'd been working for over an hour. So this is what writing could be like. She'd experienced the same intensity working on briefs, and it occurred to her that the process was the same. Eloise had said, "Good writing is good writing, whether it's fiction, nonfiction, a letter to your mother, or a report for your boss."

Sophie stood up and stretched. She did a few yoga poses—"tree" seemed a natural—to get the kinks out. She saw someone—no, it was two people—heading up the path at the end of the parking lot. Cal Burke was easy to spot. And so was the young woman with him. The red rose on her jacket a dead giveaway.

"Mom, you have to make her stop!" Samantha's voice over the phone was close to a shriek.

"Of course I will, just as soon as you tell me who it is and what's she doing to you? From the sound of it, pulling your hair out one strand at a time?" Pix thought a little humor was in order. She was pretty sure this had something to do with the wedding, but it couldn't be Zach's mother. That was all settled and she was far from Boston, plus from the sound of it she was deeply involved in her Shores class while enjoying The Birches's guest quarters.

Pix was wrong. The future in-law's tentacles were far reaching.

"I get like ten links a minute to items on wedding websites for the most ridiculous stuff you can imagine with demands that I choose at once or they won't be shipped in time!"

"Can't you just politely write back that everything's under control and already ordered?"

"I did, but she wanted to know what they were and what our theme is. She's suggesting 'Modern Glam' or 'Beach Chic,'" Samantha said glumly.

"Theme? The theme is 'Getting Married.'" Pix had to stifle a giggle. Samantha was seldom this upset.

"Matchbooks, packets of tissues, Tic Tacs, pens, lip balm. Refrigerator magnets, golf balls—golf balls, Mom!—cocktail shakers, glassware, bride and groom rubber duckies, 'Measure Up Some Love' measuring tapes, fans! And all with our names or initials, the date. She knows I'm keeping my name and also not going to be a 'Mrs.,' but she's already sent us terry cloth robes with 'Mrs. Zachary Cohen' on mine and 'I'm the Groom' on Zach's."

"The fans might not be such a bad idea," Pix said. "It could be hot. And you don't have a terry cloth robe."

"Mom!!!"

"I know, sweetheart. Just trying to lighten things up. I'm assuming Zach has tried to get her to stop?"

"Total failure. And even worse, she hates what he's picked out for his best man and the ushers. 'Tacky,' she said."

"Remind me what they are?"

"Zach's best man is as much of a geek as Zach is, and he found some very cool circuit board cuff links and a matching belt buckle. The ushers are getting belts with monogrammed buckles. How could you call that tacky?"

"Sounds elegant," Pix reassured her, "and the computer whatever is a very personal touch."

"Alexandra wants Zach to get the buckles in sterling. Even if we could afford that, we already have them in their sizes—the guys will be wearing them for the wedding. And speaking of tacky, she wants to order toilet paper with little stick figure brides and grooms on the rolls!"

"Surely she was joking. That doesn't exist, does it? I take that back. I'm sure it—and more like it—does. As for the belt buckles, I honestly don't think your brothers either care or could tell the difference between sterling silver and whatever you picked. They're just happy to be part of it all. I'll have a word with Babs—she can deal with Alexandra—but for now why don't you give in on a few items?"

After a pause, Samantha said reluctantly, "Okay, the fans. You seem really big on those."

"Exactly. Your grandmother is bringing one of hers anyway, and now we'll have plenty to go around need be. But I think you have to choose a few more items."

"She's picked out reusable water bottles, too. So fans, the bottles, and I don't know. The ducks?"

Pix did start laughing now. Samantha was still her little girl. Rubber duckies! "Go for them! Suggest date and initials on the other two and that way you avoid any Ms./Mrs. conflict."

"I love you, Mom," Samantha said in a voice now several octaves lower and unruffled.

"I love you, too, darling, and it's going to be a wonderful wedding. Can't wait!"

"That makes two of us. Gotta go. Another email coming in. Maybe you could do something to her computer?"

"I'll tell Babs instead. Way more effective. Bye."

Pix knew Babs would still be over at the Shores with Alexandra, and she certainly wasn't going to leave a message on the machine for anyone, that is, Alexandra, to overhear, so she'd wait until she could get Babs alone either on the phone or in person. In a way she hated to take away the fun Alexandra was obviously having searching out all these favors—the measuring tape could come in handy—and maybe the solution was to have her send the suggestions to Pix, explaining Samantha was in a crunch time at work, which was true.

The tide was right and the air was warm. Time for a swim. The Cranes were in residence, so that meant a bathing suit. She didn't want them trying to have her arrested for indecent exposure. Her skinny dips would have to be on moonless nights.

Chef Dom told Amy to take a break after lunch, so she had walked the Barred Island trail the Island Heritage Trust had created in the woods on one side of the beach. It felt good to be outdoors.

The kitchen was empty when she returned and she was surprised that the chef wasn't there starting dinner preparations. Saturday night was prime rib with traditional sides, as well as grilled halibut and a tofu veggie stir-fry option. She got out the veggies from the walk-in and started to cut them up. The creamed spinach was done and just needed warming, but after she finished the veggies she'd better start getting the potatoes ready for baking.

The whole lodge was quiet. Amy put down the knife and went through into the main area. Cindy wasn't at reception and no one was inside, although she could see a few of the writers with their laptops out on the deck. Sophie wasn't one of them. She must have gone back to The Birches already. Amy went back to the kitchen and was relieved to see Chef Dom come in through the outside door.

"Oh hi, Chef, I've started some of the prep work," she said. Chef Dom sat down unsteadily on a stool. His face was ashen and his eyes were half closed.

Her relief became short-lived. Alarmed, she asked, "Could I get you some water, Chef?" He didn't respond, but Amy poured a large glass from the pitcher of ice water they kept in the smaller fridge anyway and tried to hand it to him. He didn't reach out to take it, so she left it on the counter where he could reach it easily.

"Chef, would you like me to start on the desserts? The meringues are made, so they just need some of the Ice Cream Lady's strawberry ice cream and fresh berries. We were going to do grapenut pudding with whipped cream, but I think we'd better do that tomorrow and maybe tonight just offer ice cream sundaes with various toppings." She could hear her words rush together in a long, agitated stream.

Chef Dom slumped over and Amy ran to keep him from falling, bracing him against the counter. He opened his eyes wide, but he didn't seem to recognize her. His pupils were huge, and she realized he was sweating, even in the cool kitchen.

"Chef, I think you need to see a doctor. I don't want to leave you alone, but I have to go find someone to take you to the medical center."

The words seemed to rouse him from his stupor. "No doctor," he shouted, straightening up.

Amy backed away, frightened. She slid her hand in her pocket to feel for her phone. She pulled it out and turned away, punching her mother's number on the favorites list. But before the call was answered, she heard a crash and whirled back around. The chef was on the floor, eyes closed. She could tell he was breathing from the rapid rise and fall of his chest. She ran over. "Chef, Chef Dom!"

He didn't answer, but her mother did.

"Mom, Chef Dom may be in some kind of a coma. He fell off the stool onto the floor and isn't responding to me! I'm calling 911."

"And I'm on my way."

Eight

He wasn't dead. Amy repeated the fact to herself several times. She knew the ambulance corps would be here soon, very soon if one of the volunteers lived nearby. Help would come in time. He wasn't dead . . .

She knew there were people on the deck, but unless one of them happened to be a physician she didn't want to alarm them nor leave Chef Dom alone. His face had lost all its color and his eyes were shut tight. She felt his pulse but had no idea what the rate meant other than that he had one.

The door to the dining room opened. It must be the dishwasher, she thought, but it was one of the students in Sophie's class. The guy who looked really young.

The sight of the chef cut off whatever he was starting to say and he instantly went over. "I'm an EMT. What's happened? You called 911, right?"

"Yes. He just came in and sat down, didn't say anything except when I suggested he go to the medical center he got mad and said 'no doctor.'"

"From the look of it, he's had a heart attack. I'm going to start CPR. Why don't you go outside and tell whoever comes where he is? My name is George, George Finley."

"I'm Amy Fairchild. He's been kind of sick all week. Even before that. He has bad allergies," Amy said, pushing open the screen door and swiftly heading for the drive. It felt good to be able to do something.

She had barely reached it when the ambulance sped in. "This way!" she called and waved toward the door. "In the kitchen! It's the chef. He's—" The EMTs pushed past her.

Cal Burke came running from the conference center. "Who's been injured? What's going on?"

"It's the chef. He—" Cal didn't wait to hear whatever Amy was about to say but raced into the kitchen. She hesitated, not knowing whether she should follow or not. Then she saw her mother's car pull into the parking area and ran to it. As Faith opened the driver's door, Amy blurted out,

"Oh, Mom, I don't know if he's going to be all right. He just fell over and he looked so bad when he came in. Not like himself!"

"Hush, sweetheart," Faith said, gathering her daughter into her arms. "They'll get him over to Blue Hill Hospital immediately. You did the right thing, calling so quickly." Over Amy's shoulder Faith could see the ambulance crew loading what appeared to be a very large man on a stretcher into the ambulance. They were giving him oxygen. A young man and another older one, neither of whom she recognized, were following close behind. She kept Amy nestled tight. This was not a scene she needed to see.

The ambulance took off in seconds, leaving the two men standing by the lodge. Both stood still for a moment and then the older man darted around to the front door and went in. The younger man looked over to where Faith and her daughter were standing. Amy pulled away from Faith, running toward him. "George! What did they say? Is he going to be all right?"

Faith followed and said, "Hello, I'm Amy's mom, Faith Fairchild."

"I'm George Finley. I'm taking one of the courses here and I happened to go into the kitchen for some water right after your daughter called 911. I work in an elementary school and we're all certified EMTs."

"What grade do you teach?" Faith asked.

"All of them," he said. "I'm the school custodian."

Faith knew why he said that. The custodians at Ben's and Amy's schools in Aleford knew the kids better than anyone, and yes, they had lessons to impart.

George put a hand on Amy's shoulder. "Your chef will make it, but he's not going to be cooking for a while. I wouldn't want to give any kind of false diagnosis, but he was carrying a lot of extra weight. I'm sure the hospital will be in touch with Cindy." He looked at Faith. "She's the manager here. She'll be able to tell you more when she hears." He turned back to Amy. "This must be hard for you, since you've been working with him all summer, right?"

Amy nodded and Faith realized there were tears in her daughter's eyes. "He was an amazing teacher. Let me try new things. Treated me like a future chef."

George dropped his hand. "Well, future chef, at the moment you are the only chef. I'm pretty handy with the basics like scrambled eggs—except nothing more complicated. But if you tell me what to do, I might be able to help with dinner, and I'm sure the Shores will have a replacement by tomorrow."

What a prince, Faith thought to herself, perhaps

though a prince in cloud cuckoo land. There was no way the owners of Sanpere Shores were going to find a replacement for the chef at the height of the summer season, especially as the resort/conference center promoted its gourmet cuisine as one of its attractions.

She looked at Amy. Amy was looking at her. "Mom . . ." "Amy . . ." Their words overlapped. Amy's prevailed. "You could fill in at least tonight, right, Mom? Dad has been working late. You don't have to be anywhere, do you?"

George looked puzzled, and Amy said, "My mom is a caterer. A pretty famous one in Massachusetts and New York City before that. But we might need your help, too. Almost nothing is ready yet. The chef said he would do it all this afternoon and told me to take a long walk." Amy started off in the direction of the kitchen.

Faith sighed to herself. What was she getting into? Motherhood meant a lot of things, but showing up when needed had to be number one. "Okay, let's go see what we have to do."

As soon as they entered the kitchen, they could hear loud angry voices from the dining room. Faith didn't recognize them, but George quickly said, "Amy, maybe you'd better tell Cal and Cindy tonight's dinner solution." As she pushed the door open, Faith could hear the woman saying, "This is totally your fault. If you think I'm covering for you, you have another think coming. Or like a few hundred. And you call. Oh hi, Amy." Her tone changed markedly. The door swung shut behind Amy, muffling the rest of her words.

Amy was back a few minutes later. "This is pretty bad timing," she said. "We are fully booked and the actuary group is an important client of Dr. and Mrs. Childs. Cal is calling the two of them about what happened, but Cindy doesn't think it will be easy to find a chef for at least a few days and definitely not one close to here."

"Let's just get through tonight," George said. "I mean, who doesn't love a good rare prime rib? Doesn't need fancy sauces, so pretty simple. Shouldn't the servers be coming soon to set the tables? And there's a dishwasher, right? I talked to him last night while he was putting in the final load. I'm kind of a night owl. Good habit for a writer. Anyway, he's a good guy and will pitch in. And what about that lady who has added pounds to my body with all her baked goodies? Maybe she can work extra hours for the next couple of days?"

Faith looked at the young man. A prince didn't come close. George Finley should be bottled.

Even though Pix knew Sam wasn't coming this weekend, she'd kept listening for his car in the drive. He'd be here by Friday and would stay until after the wedding. Like shrinks, it seemed lawyers disappeared for most of August. Faith had called earlier and explained she wouldn't be able to go sailing today. "Or maybe not for the foreseeable future. The chef at Sanpere Shores is out of commission. Maybe a heart attack. It all happened yesterday afternoon. Amy and I handled dinner."

Pix had expressed her regret, but there would be other sailing days. "Be careful, Faith," she'd warned. "They will try to get you to take the job. I can't imagine where they'll be able to find an experienced chef at this time of year."

The other two women were still on for sailing, but with an hour to kill before going out, Pix decided to walk to the other side of the Point. She didn't know where all this nervous energy was coming from, but she found herself inventing tasks and outings for herself. It must be the wedding, she thought. Wedding jitters.

She took the long way around—the opposite direction from the Cranes' house—strolling through the remnants of an apple orchard. The Point had been home to several farmhouses, but aside from the Hamiltons', they were barely discernible cellar holes. When the children were young, they'd thought of them as buried treasure chests—digging up pieces of china and occasionally a deep cobalt medicine bottle. Mark had found a coin silver spoon once, and it now reposed in a case at the Historical Society with his name as donor.

A stand of slender birches was so beautiful, the trunks strokes of white against a backdrop of greens, that Pix stood still for a while. It was Sunday, after all, and this was as much a church as any. More, perhaps. Sunlight filtered through the branches, making patterns on the moss and pine needles below—a kind of stained glass window. She said a brief prayer of thanksgiving and, whether it was that or the surroundings, felt her previous unrest melt away.

"Hey! Is that you, Pix?"

It was Nan Hamilton, and Pix circled round the trees to where the woman stood, a basket on her arm. "I thought I'd find some chanterelles. This is usually the best spot, but it's been too dry. Instead I've found a large patch of wild strawberries. If you have time to help me pick, we'll drop some off at your house. Ever since Faith taught me how to make that Italian pudding with these strawberries on top, Freeman can't get enough!"

Pix laughed. The "Italian pudding" was panna cotta and so easy that even she could make it once Faith walked her through the steps.

"I'd love to help you, but with just me at the house now, you keep them all for yourselves." There was something very satisfying about picking any kind of berries, Pix thought as she crouched down to pluck the tiny ruby-colored fruits from their stems. Blueberries were best, especially when the can was empty and they made that *plunk* sound. "How have you been? I haven't seen much of you this summer," she asked.

"We've been fine. Freeman is ornery because his doctor won't let him smoke cigars anymore or eat pork rinds, but it's lobster boat racing season, so he's plenty busy. He's raced in Jonesport and is only going to race here besides, but he and the boys have been going to all the others. They're up to Winter Harbor this weekend."

Pix smiled to herself at the mental image of the "boys"—Freeman and his buddies were in their late seventies and beyond—cutting loose on the Schoodic Peninsula.

They picked in contented silence until Nan said, "It has been a little hard this past month what with Freeman's niece Jenny living with us. You may have heard. That she's with us, not that it's been hard."

Nan wasn't given to personal revelations like this. Pix *had* heard that the niece, whom she remembered visiting as a younger girl, was there. But nothing else. "She used to come up during the summers, right? Remind me where she lives the rest of the year?"

"In Massachusetts. She's Freeman's youngest brother Harry's girl. They lost her mother to cancer a few years ago and Harry remarried this winter, but Jenny and her stepmother don't get along. No blame on either side. Just oil and water. Maybe Harry spoiled the girl—she wouldn't remember a time when her mother wasn't sick, and I guess he thought he could make up for that."

"How old is she now?"

"Just turned nineteen and she's some smart. Going to the University of Massachusetts near where they live in Lowell. Music major. She wants to teach, but she could make a pretty good living singing. Voice like an angel. I still get goose bumps remembering how she sang 'Ave Maria' at her mother's funeral. Don't know how she got through it. I was crying like a baby. Freeman, too."

"So she's here to get a break from her home situation?"

Nan nodded. "She's no trouble. Helps out—even hauling traps with her cousin, always was handy on the water, could pilot the boat before she was twelve—but I worry about her on land. She's out at night a lot, singing at various places. Freeman fixed up that VW bug he found in Uncle Henry's for her to use while she's here." Pix smiled. Like many men, including her own husband, Freeman was devoted to Uncle Henry's weekly classified swap or sell guide.

Nan stopped picking. "Sometimes she's not back until early morning. I know because I lie awake until she's in. Of course, Bar Harbor, that's one of the places she goes to perform, is far; but Sanpere Shores is almost around the corner."

Having spent sleepless nights for all three children, Pix was sympathetic and gave her friend a hug. "Poor Nan. You must have thought you wouldn't have to cope with a teenager, especially a teenaged girl, again."

Nan gave her a sharp look. "My girls are all growed, and most of my grandchildren, but you know you're never done coping or raising, however you want to put it. Not until they're all tearful at your wake."

"Truer words never spoken," Pix agreed and added, "Why don't you tell her that you're worried and would appreciate knowing when she expects to be home? And why don't we go hear her? Maybe we can hire her to do a few songs at the wedding if she is still here?"

Nan looked a bit more cheerful. "Well, I'll ask her when she'll be singing at the Shores next. She goes over to the open mic nights at Tinder Hearth in Brooksville, too."

"Now let's get the berries to your house and I have to get ready for a sail this afternoon. Why don't you come with us? Elizabeth, my friend in Sedgwick, is coming, and Marcia Klein—you've met her. She's a friend in Massachusetts and rents here in August."

"Another day. Without Freeman underfoot, I'm getting so much done. Enjoy your sail—perfect weather for it."

"How about your niece? She might enjoy coming."

Nan looked straight at Pix. "She might, but I have no idea where she is today. Never do."

Dr. and Mrs. Childs drove up to Blue Hill, hired a private ambulance, and moved Chef Dom to a health facility in Massachusetts. They spent Saturday night at the Shores and early Sunday morning. Dr. Childs called Faith to ask if he and his wife could meet with her.

"Sure," she said. "But I know what you're going to ask and the answer is no. We have a family wedding coming up at the end of the month"—well, if the Millers weren't family, who was?—"and I can't commit to a full-time job as chef for the Shores."

"Would you please just talk to us for a few minutes? We'll come to your house if that's easier," he'd pleaded.

His wife had taken the phone at that point and Faith had realized from her brisk manner who was in charge. "Mrs. Fairchild, if Amy were over eighteen we'd hire her in a heartbeat. She's an extraordinarily talented young chef—and a lovely young lady."

Faith had felt herself softening. It was all true. "Okay, I'll come for a brief chat. I'm driving Amy over now anyway. After yesterday's shock, we wanted her to sleep in, and I was sure Darlene's handling breakfast fine on her own with your manager and the servers."

Which is how Faith found herself sitting on the deck at the Shores with Dr. Childs, who looked a bit like a Teletubby, and Mrs. Childs, who had the tubby part down, but was an amazon. She towered over him, and Faith, too. As she shook each hand Faith noticed the contrast there as well. The doctor's grip was limp and flabby; his wife's could break a brick. Dr. Childs was wearing a dark suit; Mrs. had the kind of dress that Faith associated with old black-and-white TV shows. Where did one buy this garb now? Vintage stores? It had what she knew was called a Peter Pan collar, but there was nothing that wasn't very grown-up about both Childses. Their teeth, of course, were perfect.

All the way over to the Shores, Amy had begged her mother to take the job. "A week, tops? Less. They'll find someone soon. You don't have to do anything for Samantha's wedding until way closer to the time. Gert Prescott and Arlene are doing the food for the shower."

Then she delivered the coup de grace. "I'll be

going away to college in another year. This would be a special time for us to be together doing what we love. A time we'd look back on all our lives, Mom!"

Hence Faith had given in before she took a single step onto the deck, where Darlene had placed a carafe of coffee, cups, milk, sugar, and a basket of mixed berry muffins on one of the tables. She kept the fact that she was going to take the job—for a short time—to herself and let the couple urge her, offering an extremely good wage and making promises to search the whole country as fast as possible to find a replacement. She negotiated a raise for Amy, whom she'd sent off to the kitchen—"My daughter will be acting as sous chef"—and endured final handshakes.

Before she left, Amy gave her a tour of the kitchen—it was impressive—and showed her the menus she and the chef had drawn up for this session. Also impressive. Faith left with the menus and lists of suppliers, and steeled herself for Tom's reaction.

She was very pleasantly surprised.

"That's great, honey," Tom said. "Gives you a chance to spend quality time with Amy." Faith was suddenly thrust back to the days when that phrase meant reading *If You Give a Mouse a Cookie.* Tom continued, "I know it's been lonely for you here without any of us and I like that I can think of you two in the Shores kitchen making people happy with your great food."

You don't fool me for a minute, Thomas Preston Fairchild, Faith thought. You want me tucked safely away stirring pots instead of stirring up trouble, that is, bodies.

When Pix pulled into the drive at The Pines, she was surprised to see that Gert Prescott's car was still there. Her first thought was that something must be wrong. When Pix rushed in, she found Gert sitting at the kitchen table reading the *Ellsworth American.* "Your mother was resting, but she must have heard the car. I can hear her walking about."

"Is she okay? Just tired? Or . . . ?"

"More okay than almost anyone I know," Gert answered. "I knew you'd be along soon, so I stayed to ask you if you knew what happened to the shower invitations. No one I know has gotten one. I thought Arlène was sending them out, but she said Samantha or you were. I called her to talk about the food as well, but she had to run. Take Kylie someplace."

Pix frowned and sat down next to Gert after putting the groceries on the counter. "I'm pretty certain Samantha said Arlene was taking care of them. I know she gave her a list of names and addresses, because she gave me a copy, too. Most on the island, of course, but Samantha also wanted to invite some of her Wellesley friends who are coming to the wedding even though they probably wouldn't be able to make both."

"I asked the postmistress and she said she would have noticed them going out or in—the envelopes are blue with a big silver wedding cake sticker on the flap. And they have those LOVE stamps on them. Well, it's a mystery. That's what it is."

Ursula came into the room. "What's a mystery? Or maybe what isn't?"

Pix laughed. Her mother was in a good mood, well rested, and there was nothing to worry about. In the long scheme of things, missing wedding shower invitations were a mere sprinkle.

Gert told her about the invitations, and of course Ursula had the solution. "No one will care if she ends up with two invitations. You have the list, Pix. Go to Blue Hill tomorrow morning. I'll bet The Meadow has dandy ones, and we can call on Thursday to get the RSVPs unless they come in. Besides, it's only people off-island who haven't had it on the calendar all summer. Now, Gertrude Prescott, what are you still doing here? Go home and put your feet up! Unless you want to stay and have a drink with us. Paul will be over."

"You know very well I haven't had any alcohol since my friend Margie and I mixed ourselves a concoction from her grandfather's liquor cabinet that had us sick as dogs for days. Can't abide even the smell of the stuff."

"This is the first time I've heard about your wild youth and I'm shocked," Pix teased.

Gert walked toward the door, turning back to say, "I said I didn't drink, but Margie and I were devils in other ways—she started driving when she wasn't but fourteen and there were always rowboats we could 'borrow' and go out to Green Island for midnight swims."

After she left, Pix mixed drinks—gin and tonic for herself and martinis for Ursula and Paul, arranging crackers and cheese on a wooden bread board either Mark or Dan had made in shop in the shape of a fish. She and her mother went out onto the porch to enjoy the cool of the early evening. Paul would know where they were.

"What do you think happened to the invitations?" Pix asked.

"I don't want to think, so I'm not," Ursula answered. "We'll have a fine time. Gert has the food all set. You'll get new invitations out. Concentrate on that. Maybe go up to Ellsworth after you send them—won't matter if they are mailed from Sanpere or Blue Hill—and get some decorations. Some foolish-type favors, too."

Her mother may not want to think, but her thoughts were way ahead of Pix's.

By Thursday, Sophie was totally immersed in her characters—and the characters around her. After her initial visit to First African Baptist Church with her Savannah neighbor Lydia Scriven, who was a member and also a guide, Sophie had gone back often. Sometimes for services—the music *much* livelier than the Maxwell family's praises to the Lord—but often to simply sit and feel the events of those years, tangible echoes in her mind. She was drawing on these memories now for the story and found that even when she wasn't putting words down, she was thinking them during the day. Seeing scenes, hearing voices.

As for the other characters—her fellow students—they were providing mostly entertaining distractions, breaks when she came up for air—or in, as she had claimed a quiet spot out of the way on the deck to work. Eloise had not assigned any more group assignments but individual ones. She asked Sophie to write a full description of her main character—appearance, personality, background, and so forth—explaining that these were not necessarily words that would appear in Sophie's finished piece but would inform it. It had taken Sophie hours, and then, dissatisfied, she'd started it all over again. Not trying to alter what she had written—heeding Eloise's cut-and-paste admonition—but starting from scratch. She felt a bit as if she were cooking and maybe that was what writing was—assembling ingredients. She was even more pleased with the instructor as time went on, writing down some of Eloise's advice: "If you want to be a writer, you have to like to be alone and indoors." And the most important: "You have to write every day. Not intend to write, but write. Something, no matter how short."

As she had first thought, Ellen was a kindred spirit and Sophie already knew the two would keep in touch once the course was over. Ellen didn't share what she was working on and Sophie didn't ask. She also liked George Finley, who was the opposite and entertained them with updates on his progress and possible plot twists in what seemed to Sophie a very complicated suspense novel. The three had formed the habit of eating lunch together.

The college friends, Susan and Deborah, had explained to Sophie they'd set themselves a word total each day and once reached, they wanted to enjoy this all too seldom time away from responsibilities. They'd told her the Shores spa was great, which Babs had also mentioned. Sophie kept her nails short and did her own manicures, but a facial, or even better, a massage, sounded like a fine idea.

Cynthia MacDonald was having fun fictionalizing the family tree, as evidenced by the occasional bursts of laughter while she typed. It occurred to Sophie that husband Ross might not find the anecdotes his wife was dreaming up quite so amusing. Babs had mentioned that he was taking his memoir very seriously and had not agreed with Patrick's suggestion that he include his personal reminiscences, but was sticking to the facts, ma'am, only the facts.

The Ohio couple had announced that they were collaborating on a romantic suspense novella and after Eloise greeted the group each morning, they retreated to their cottage to work—or "work." Several times Sophie had seen them drive off before lunch, and perhaps they wanted to explore the area for inspiration. They'd been very open about their plan, adding that they'd decided to set the tale on an island in Maine. They already had a title: *Tides of Love*. Now they just had to write it.

Joan Whittaker, the woman from Montreal, was also writing a mystery. She'd revealed this when Jay Thomas told the group he was working on one. "Me, too," Joan had said brightly, and the look he'd given her was appropriately poisonous. "I doubt they'll have much in common. I do 'noir,'" he'd said.

Eloise had jumped in at that point, interrupting Jay before he could describe his magnum opus.

"I'm not surprised by the group's choices. Genre fiction"—Jay made a face that bordered on indecent, which she ignored, continuing firmly—"genre fiction is easier to sell, and market, than literary fiction, that coming-of-age breakthrough debut novel every writer has in the back of his or her head. Joan is writing a traditional mystery, and as he has said, Jay is going for noir. Big difference. Traditional mysteries end with the restoration of order. Noir sees the world, or universe, as chaotic. Impossible to fix. I enjoy both, all forms in the genre—I have catholic tastes, which is one of the reasons I enjoy teaching. I never know what someone will be writing. And romantic suspense has always been popular. I often think of those books as cinematic, like du Maurier's *Rebecca*. So we are running the full gamut here—humor, historical, several kinds of mysteries—George has me on the edge of my seat with his chapters." She laughed and told them to get to work, ignoring Jay's scornful glance at George.

Before she got to work, Sophie went into the kitchen to talk to Faith. It was a bonus to have her friend so close by. As predicted, the Childses had not found a replacement chef, but Faith told Sophie she was getting regular texts telling her how hard they were searching. Faith and Sophie had laughed at the skepticism reflected on each other's face.

"Always smells great in here," Sophie said now. "What's for lunch?"

"Cobb salads—I know your mother and Alexandra will modify theirs—then, since I am cooking bacon, a lobster BLT, plus a quinoa bowl with edamame and other good stuff. What you're smelling is the biscuits in the oven for old-fashioned strawberry shortcake, one of tonight's desserts."

"*Real* strawberry shortcake, you mean. I remember the first time I ordered it in New York and it came on a sponge round. Ugh!" Sophie looked around the empty kitchen. "Where's Amy?"

"Chef Dom had the foresight to plant an herb garden when he arrived in June and she's picking basil for us to make pesto."

Sophie gave Faith a little poke. "You're happy that things turned out this way, aren't you? And the longer the Childses take to find a replacement the better. Admit it."

"I do. For two reasons," Faith said. "The most important is that I'm having fun cooking professionally with my daughter. We've cooked at home often, but this is very different. I haven't changed my mind about her college choice—I still want her to get a liberal arts education first—but I also have no doubt she's going to be a great chef. Far too few women in the profession. Just think of those competitions on the food networks and the most well-known restaurants chefs—all very heavy on the testosterone."

"Try lawyering," Sophie said. "Although that has changed since I started. But you said two reasons. What's the other?"

"I think something's wrong here." Faith frowned and stepped past Sophie to take the first batch of biscuits from the oven.

"As in?"

"I'm sure you wouldn't, but please don't let on to Tom or talk to me about it in front of him or Amy either. I'm uneasy. And it has nothing to do with what happened earlier, although I guess I'm kind of on high alert. I never met the chef, but from Amy's description of his behavior prior to his collapse, I'd say he was heavily into cocaine. She told me he kept a giant box of tissues in the half bath over there because of his allergies. He was leaving more and more of the food prep to her while he took a 'nap.' And his herb garden has a large, healthy crop of marijuana—yes, it's legal, but I'm not sure for as much as is there. I saw it when Amy showed me around Sunday. She's so naive, she had no idea what it was. It was gone Monday when I went to cut some parsley. Not that smoking weed would produce his symptoms or behavior, but it's another indication that something may be going on among the staff."

"I've heard that restaurant workers are often

drug users. The pace, the intensity, and some kind of macho gonzo chef thing."

"Exactly, but I wouldn't have expected it in a place like this—at a conference center essentially. I've asked both Cal and Cindy separately how the chef is doing, telling them Amy is worried, and both said he's fine. Had become overtired and his weight put a strain on his heart. They both looked away when they were speaking—the way Ben always did when he told me he hadn't touched the layer cake on the counter with a slice missing."

Sophie had told Faith about seeing the girl who had been with Dwayne LeBlanc and the others at the market at the bonfire that first night. Now she recalled she hadn't mentioned that she'd seen her go off with Cal the other day. She did now.

"And you said she sang like a professional, right? I wonder if she could be Jenny Hamilton, Freeman's niece who is living with them this summer. Nan told Pix she sang 'like an angel.'"

"That's a good description," Sophie said.

Faith stopped taking the biscuits off the baking sheet. "Pix also said she was having family issues—new unwanted stepmother, having lost her own mother to cancer. And Sophie, Jenny lives in Lowell."

After Sophie left, Faith kept thinking about the vibe she was getting from Sanpere Shores. Cal

Burke had crossed off a number of the suppliers that had been on the chef's list, telling her that Cindy thought they were being overcharged and was finding new sources. At the time, Faith hadn't given it much thought. She got along with both Cal and Cindy, but she wished they would stay out of the kitchen more. It seemed they were in for coffee or a cold drink every time she turned around.

And she'd started to wonder about Cal in particular. She knew he was from the island and had left when he was either just out of or still in high school. Why did he come back? And she never heard him refer to any family members, even when she asked. The island was so interconnected that his answer—"No one around anymore"—didn't ring true.

Today Cal had asked Faith to prepare a range of snacks for a storytelling and sing-along tonight in the Annex, which had a lounge where there was a full bar. "We'll be showing a short film about the island on the big TV, then I have a few tales up my sleeve to convince them they really are Down East. After that we'll have some live music," he'd said. It was her daughter who asked the question Faith couldn't—she wasn't supposed to have heard of Jenny Hamilton. "Cal, is that lady who sang at the bonfire coming again? She was amazing."

"Jenny? Yup, I'm sure Jenny will show up."

After Cal left, Faith slipped around the lodge to the back steps that led to the corner of the deck where she'd seen Sophie working. On the way she passed a large covered woodpile and some other sheds. The smell of pot from behind one of them was so strong, Faith picked up her pace to avoid a contact high. Over her shoulder she caught a glimpse of someone dressed in a black shirt and jeans and another person, a woman, or at least someone with long hair down the back. She went up the stairs quickly and tapped Sophie on the shoulder, startling her.

"Sorry to break your concentration. I know how writers are."

"Not this one. I'm beginning to think that even though I have a good story to tell, I don't have the skill. But you're right, it is engrossing and I didn't hear you come up behind me. What's up?"

"You may want to stay for dinner tonight, or come back afterward. Jenny Hamilton is going to be singing."

"I will definitely be there," Sophie said. "Let's hope she wears a sleeveless top." Faith had told her about clearly seeing the tattoo letters dripping from the adder's fangs on the second body at Green Island. L F D Y. They had both recognized the pop culture initials representing the phrase, a credo: "Live Fast Die Young."

Faith had to shoo Amy out of the kitchen when Tom came to pick her up. "Two of the servers are staying on, and there's the bartender—you couldn't help there anyway. As soon as the program starts and I'm sure the food is covered, I'll leave, too. We're both tired."

Amy put up one more feeble token protest and left. They were working a long day. If she hadn't wanted to hear—and see—Jenny Hamilton, Faith would have left the last of the work for the others. The food was prepared—bar snacks: small Cubano sandwiches, nachos, pigs in a blanket, thin and thick pretzel sticks with various mustard dips, cheddar popcorn, and a mix Faith had created: roasted chickpeas with some cayenne for kick, mini corn chips, golden raisins, sesame sticks, and honey roasted peanuts. A sweet, salty, spicy combo for every taste. Having seen the way both the scribblers and number crunchers were going through the wine and beer plus mixed drinks before, during, and after dinner, she wanted more than enough food to soak up the alcohol.

She walked over to the center and slipped in next to Sophie, who had saved her a seat. The film was about life on the water—a day with a lobster fisherman. "Good thing this isn't smell-o-vision,"

Sophie whispered. "Will went out with Ed Ricks and it was only a few traps, but the bait got to him, and he was pea green for the rest of the day!"

When the lights went up, Faith looked around. Babs and Alexandra were in the front row, literally at Cal Burke's feet. The place was packed, whether from lack of alternatives or the open bar, Faith wasn't sure. Cal was telling a few stories Faith knew he'd cribbed from Bert and I, the original Down East yarns that Marshall Dodge and Bob Bryan had recorded so many years ago, but familiar to all Maineacs. The Fairchilds' friends Steve and Roberta Johnson had even named their lobster boat tours "Bert and I Charters," although Faith suspected the "Bert" part was also a nod to the lovely second mate.

"Are there many from your group here?" she asked Sophie softly.

"Some," Sophie answered. "I don't see my friend Ellen, but her shyness would have kept her from a gathering like this. I also didn't see Jay, the obnoxious literary enfant terrible I told you about. This wouldn't have been his thing either, but for a different reason. What amounts to home movies, tired jokes, and a sing-along? I don't think so."

Cal had worked his way through "You can't get there from here" and was finishing with the "You're up in a balloon, you damn fool" answer to the "Where am I?" question from someone from away in a Montgolfier hot-air balloon from the Maine codger in the field below.

Faith yawned. "I don't think I càn stay awake much longer. You check Jenny out and let me know. Everyone will be hitting the bar now for a while before the music. I'm going to be sure there's still enough food and leave."

"No worries. I'll move up next to Mom and try to keep Alexandra from throwing her panties at Cal."

Faith laughed and went over to the buffet they'd set out. The servers had been keeping the platters filled and assured her there was plenty more. She also spoke to the bartender, as Cindy was nowhere in sight. It was the manager's job to remind him to cut anyone off who had had too much, watering the margaritas or whatever the drink was before it got to that point, but since she didn't see her, Faith took it on herself. It was all fine. "That guy over there has been happily drinking lime seltzer in a glass with a salt rim for an hour, and that lady"—he nodded in another direction, at a woman who looked like a member of Ursula's sewing circle—"has been steadily imbibing OJ and seltzer 'mimosas.'" Faith thanked him and headed for her car in the employees' parking lot up the hill past the larger lot for guests and visitors.

A darkened pickup truck was parked almost

next to her car. As Faith got closer, the driver's-side window rolled down and a head wearing a gimme cap turned to see who was coming. She paused, not sure what to do. She was very aware how far away from the lodge she was. Before she could decide, the passenger door opened. Someone jumped out, slammed it shut, and sprinted for the woods. The truck backed up, narrowly avoiding Faith, and screeched off down the road.

Shaking slightly, she walked to her car. There was something on the ground. Something that had been tossed out of the truck when the door opened.

It was an empty syringe.

Faith called Earl's home number. He told her not to touch the syringe and he'd be there right away. He also told her to get in her car and lock the doors. "Faith, I'm afraid finding these is becoming more and more common."

When he arrived, she started to tell him what Ed Ricks had talked to her about, but he cut her off. "We'll talk soon. Right now you need to get home and get some rest. If you remember anything distinctive about the truck or the people let me know, but don't stress yourself out." He patted her shoulder, the equivalent of a bear hug—Earl was not demonstrative.

"Thanks," she said and left him to his task. He'd put on gloves and was placing the syringe in a plastic evidence bag, shining his flashlight over the entire area.

As she drove down the long road from the Shores to Route 15, she tried to think about possible details. There had been nothing distinctive about the pickup. Black or navy. Not tricked out with loud mufflers. Not new. She was pretty sure about that. And the two men—if they had been men; she couldn't be sure of that either—were like cats in the night.

An hour later she got a long text from Sophie. "Long-sleeve peasant blouse and yes, incredible voice. More tomorrow, but during a break I accidentally spilled red wine on her right sleeve, rushed her to bar for club soda despite protests. No snake. But same letters L F D Y plus ♥."

Pix knew Sam was leaving work Friday as soon as he could get away. Samantha was coming with him for Saturday's shower. So after she made a run to Madelyn's for a haddock burger to go, extra tartar, she put on a well-worn pair of pajamas and sat at the kitchen table with a bag of salt and vinegar potato chips, the burger, and a beer. She propped the latest Mary Kay Andrews open and felt utterly content. Her near and dear would arrive in fewer than twenty-four hours. All was well with the world.

"Surprise!" Her near and dear were here now!

"Don't worry, Mom, we stopped at Madelyn's, too. Don't you think we know what you get up to when you're on your own?"

Pix wasn't thinking anything except how good it felt to have Sam's arms around her, then Samantha's. She was, however, very glad they had brought their own provisions. Otherwise it would have been a cornflakes night.

"Honey, do you smell something?" Sam was shaking his wife's shoulder.

"Hmmm?" she said sleepily.

He shook harder. "Wake up! I smell smoke."

Nine

Pix was awake instantly. She sat up, and sniffed. "It's not here," she said, starting to lie down again.

"But I think it's near," Sam said. "I'm going outside to check. Stupid kids may have set off firecrackers at the end of the Point again, and it's been so dry."

Samantha was at their door. "Do you smell that smoke? I'm heading down the road to check."

Pix was alarmed now, too. She shoved her shoes on, quickly following her husband and daughter downstairs and out the door.

"It's coming from the Cranes' house!" Sam said

as soon as he stepped onto the deck. "Call 911. I'm going over there."

"No need. Listen," Samantha cried. "Sirens."

All three took off toward the next-door neighbors', using the shortcut—very short, since the clear-cutting.

"Thank goodness," Pix said, emerging into the field. "It's not the house."

They circled to the front. The fire was contained to the shed, threatening a few pines next to it. Cameron held a dripping garden hose, his wife a household fire extinguisher. Her hands were black with soot as was her face. In contrast, Cameron looked spotless. Apparently, Drew had been the one to attack the flames.

The volunteer firefighters immediately went to work, training hoses on the structure. Cameron dashed over to the Millers, followed closely by Drew. But it was Drew who started screaming at them first. The woman who had been silent in their presence before had plenty to say now. Arm outstretched, with her finger pointed at Sam, she said, "I saw you!! You're not going to get away with this! The glue was one thing, but trying to burn us in our beds is attempted murder!!"

"What the hell!" Sam said. "I haven't been here! You think I set this?"

Cameron's voice was only a few decibels lower

than his wife's. "You're denying it? We both saw you drive past early this evening. My wife has trouble sleeping and she saw you run away from the shed from our bedroom window!" Before an astonished Sam could say anything, Cameron went back to the almost extinguished blaze and began talking to one of the firefighters, gesturing toward the Millers.

"Come on, let's go home," Sam said. "This is more lunacy. I don't believe it. These are very sick people."

Drew had started to move away to join her husband, but hearing the last remark, she stopped. "*We're* sick? Take a good look in the mirror. I don't care what kind of fancy lawyer you think you are. You're not getting away with arson!"

"Come on, Dad," Samantha said. She pulled him in the direction of their house. Before they had taken more than a few steps, Seth Marshall, one of the volunteer firefighters, approached. The fire had been reduced to smoldering ashes; it had been a small shed, and the fire hadn't had much to feed on, no dry grass and even the nearby pines hadn't caught. It was a windless night. The Cranes had been lucky—in that respect.

"Hi, Sam, Pix, Samantha—good to see you, although not under these circumstances." Seth held something out toward them. "The couple found this by the side of the shed when they came to douse the fire."

It was a single glove, heavy-duty striped thick cotton with a leather palm and fingertips. It was charred, but you could clearly see MILLER written on the wristband.

"One of yours?" Seth asked.

"Obviously," Sam snapped. "Too big for Pix or Samantha. Have no idea how it got here unless I left a pair when I was helping Ed clear brush. I buy them in bulk from Barton's, keep them in the barn to lend out when we have roadside cleanup days."

The Cranes had come up behind Seth. "The house was totally empty, the shed, too, when we bought the place. No glove," Cameron hissed. "I knew you'd try to wiggle out of this! Not so smart, counselor! You left evidence!"

"I can swear that my husband has been home since he arrived last night and he hasn't been wearing or carrying gloves!" Pix said, her face drained of color in marked contrast to those of the enraged couple confronting them. "And it doesn't matter. Why on earth would he want to burn your shed down?"

"You know very well why and I'm sure you were with him. Probably lit the match. Just can't deal with our cutting a few twigs!" Cameron spat the words out.

Seth was looking more and more uncomfortable. "We'll stay for a while more. Be sure nothing more ignites. All fires get reported to the sheriff's office and they can deal with any suspicions you may or may not have. Did you store anything combustible in the shed? Gas for a mower?"

"That has nothing to do with what happened," Cameron said. "I might have known you'd stick up for your friends. Thought this was supposed to be a friendly place. More like friendly only for some. Good old Sam help you out of a spot or something?" he asked snidely.

"Now just a minute . . ." Seth was a big guy and not someone you wanted to antagonize.

Pix slipped between the two men. "It's time we all went home. Mr. Crane, I'm sure you will be calling the sheriff yourself. I'm sorry your property has been damaged and it must have been quite frightening when you saw the fire, but we came over to help. We won't make that mistake again."

The Millers left by the drive, stopping to say hello to the volunteer crew, all of whom they did in fact know. Out on the road, Samantha said, "Good job, Mom. 'I am woman, hear me roar!'"

Pix smiled weakly. "More like 'I am woman, hear me snore'—I'm exhausted."

Sam put his arm around his wife. "Me, too. Arson is tiring work." He put his other arm around

240

his daughter. "Guess we won't be inviting them to the wedding, eh?"

The sheriff's office had called early. Pix felt as if she had just gotten to sleep when the phone rang. The Cranes had wasted no time in reporting the crime, and two officers were coming to inspect the damage, which the fire department had reported, and "talk"—that was the word used—to the Millers. She waited until a more decent hour and called Faith. "I'm not going to be able to meet you for coffee," Pix said. "Sam and I have to wait for someone from the sheriff's office."

As Pix related the early morning events to a very surprised Faith—"Sheriff's office!"—she had gasped, and they took on an even more surreal aspect than when they'd occurred, which had been bizarre enough.

"Obviously he was storing something flammable in the shed," Faith said, "and I'll bet he's a smoker. Left a butt that ignited a drip. He can't honestly believe Sam would do this. He has to have someone to blame other than himself to collect the insurance. And his wife is in on it. Just 'happened' to look out the window and see her neighbor. I am so sorry, Pix. I wish there was something I could do. Slashing tires, keying their car might make me feel better, but ten to one they'd think it was you. Call me after the police leave. I want to get some things for the Shores at the farmers' market and then I'll be home until around eleven. After that you can reach me at the Shores kitchen."

Pix had smiled at her friend's indignant proposed actions. Feeling better for the imagery, she said, "Thanks, Faith. It's been a lot to take in. The whole summer has been out of kilter."

"Well, some unexpected stuff, but eyes on the wedding, starting with the shower tomorrow! I've arranged for a Saturday night clambake on the beach for dinner here at the Shores, so not much prep. The weather is cooperating. And Amy is coming to the shower, too. Samantha has been like a big sister all these years. Hard to believe she's all grown up and getting married!"

"You're going to make me cry," Pix said. "Now what does one wear for grilling by police?"

"Avoid stripes and all will be well," Faith advised.

Earl accompanied the other officers, which was a relief to Pix. But he, and they, were all business. "The Cranes have leveled a very serious charge: arson with intent to harm, bodily harm. Mrs. Crane did admit she couldn't make out your face from her window, but she described an individual your size, and then there's that glove."

Pix flinched, thinking of a different infamous glove.

So far Sam had kept quiet, but Pix could see it was a struggle. "I know you've had issues with the Cranes this summer over trees and they did violate the shorefront regulations," Earl continued. "They swear you destroyed a chain saw to protest what they claim was their right to do as they wished on their own property."

"That's correct," Sam said, addressing all three. "Correct that this is what they claimed. Incorrect in that I had nothing to do with that or any other destruction of their property. I believe that the tree cutting is being dealt with by the town Code Enforcement officer and we have deliberately kept out of it. We have planted new trees well within our property line and may put up some sort of a fence for further privacy. The only contact we've had with the Cranes was our initial protest over the clear-cutting. I've been in Boston all summer except for a day here and there. Last night was the start of my vacation."

Pix reached for his hand as she thought, *Some vacation.*

One of the other officers was shaking her head. "We've called in the state arson specialist and secured the area around the shed. Without a positive ID, all we have is a glove that may or may not have been there before last night. Could you write out a statement regarding your activities last night? You, too, Mrs. Miller. Sign and date it, then we'll be on our way. I should tell you that we have heard from the Cranes' attorney, and he's pressing to have you arrested."

Sam gave a hollow laugh. "Of course he is. Make it a criminal case, so they'll be able to sue us in civil court."

"I'm going to pretend no one in this room heard that," Earl said.

That's when Pix began to really worry.

Sophie came into the kitchen just before lunch. She'd just met with Eloise, who continued to be supportive and offer constructive criticism. Sophie wasn't ready for the instructor to read any of it to the group, but she was getting close. Several in the course had given permission and the instructor had read them during the morning meetings before they separated to work or meet individually with her. Sophie had been surprised by the quality of Joan Whittaker's mystery. The Canadian woman had hooked her with the character, possibly some kind of vicarious self-portrait—Persis Gray, a foul-mouthed, tough elderly spinster with a black belt and fondness for Jack Daniel's. Sophie was even more surprised by the Ohio couple's romantic suspense work in progress. She hadn't taken them seriously, making the false assumption that they were sneaking off for a dirty two weeks away from possibly a wife and husband.

She pushed the thoughts of her fellow would-be writers away—she had more important things on her mind—and said, "I don't want to get in your way, but wanted to say hi." She gave a nod toward the door to the outside.

Faith took the hint. "Amy, sweetie, I'm going to cut some lemon thyme to add to the vinaigrette for the grilled chicken salad. I'll be back in a minute."

The herb garden was in a sunny spot not far from the spa and pool. "Have to fit in time for the amenities," Sophie said, pointing. "There's a sauna in there as well."

"Definitely with you! Now tell me about last night," Faith said.

"Jenny could definitely go pro. She has the voice, the looks, and made an instant connection with the audience without a lot of superficial patter. Some of what she sang, solo and with Cal, were her own compositions. And yes, she has the tattoo. The lettering style was the same, but what does it mean? That she knew the LeBlancs or just happened to go to the same tattoo parlor in Lowell? There were a few people in the audience I hadn't seen at the Shores—I think she has a following—but none of them looked like bikers, and the person I saw her with afterward when things were breaking up was Jay Thomas. The annoying guy in my writing group I told you wasn't there. But he came in just before the singing and stayed. Afterward I saw them leave together looking very much *together*."

"Hmm, that's interesting," Faith said. "Doubtful she would have known him before—but I guess he's not bad looking under all that gloomy garb."

"I thought she might be with Cal when I saw them sing together at the bonfire. They played up the steamier songs to the hilt, but that could have been part of their act. He's attractive, but too old for her," Sophie said.

"I'm not sure age matters. From what Nan Hamilton said, Jenny is calling her own tune, and it's one that worries Nan," Faith said. "I told you she said Jenny stays out into the wee hours, so she's with someone, or with a group. Nothing here or across the bridge is open late, so has to be outdoors or someone's house. Nan would be even more upset if she knew Jenny was with those guys at the market."

Thinking of the fertility superstition Marge Foster had mentioned, Sophie had been idly picking some parsley while listening to Faith. She dropped the bunch. "Guys who are dead now."

She'd only had a few hours' sleep on Friday night. It was hot and the fan was broken. The sheets on her side of the bed were soaked with sweat. He'd promised to pick up a new fan at Home Depot, but of course forgot.

Today was the shower. She told him she had to go over early to help Gert get everything ready. He could drop Kylie off at his sister's on his way. No men at the shower, but he'd told Ursula he'd help Sam and Tom Fairchild set the mooring for her son Arnie's boat, make sure all the equipment on board was working. Arnie was a doctor, she remembered suddenly. She couldn't recall what kind, but he might have a blank pad he'd leave lying around. You never knew.

The shower wasn't working, only a small stream of lukewarm water. He could go help Ursula—and Arnie was rich, could afford to pay someone to do all this for him—but he couldn't use his day off to do what was needed at his own house. She felt her anger rise until it felt as if it would tear holes through her skin. Her whole body ached lately.

She threw on some clothes, not bothering to dress up. Samantha wouldn't care. She paused a moment. But the others would. Gert. Her mother. She changed into a loose bright pink top but kept her jeans on—the skinny ones, the only ones that fit. Kylie called the top "Mommy's Princess Shirt" because it had bands of silver thread woven around the neck and cuffs.

She'd told Gert she would be there at noon. Plenty of time for the start of the party at one. And plenty of time to get to the Walgreens in Ellsworth for a refill and back. She had two more. And after this one she'd be stopping. She might see someone she knew in Ellsworth, but there wasn't time to go anyplace farther. She could always say she was picking stuff up for the shower.

"So, did you have a wedding shower?" Amy asked Faith. They were hanging a sparkling BRIDE TO BE banner on top of the door between the living room and the porch. Honeycomb white bells were suspended from wall sconces and the beams on the porch. The buffet table was swathed in white tulle, and Amy had scattered paper rose petals on almost every surface.

"Yes, I had a shower. My friend Emma—you've met her—gave it at her mother's very nice house in Manhattan." Poppy Morris's town house had been more than nice, but the shower had taken an unexpected turn that Faith was not going to mention now or ever to her daughter. Her future sister-in-law had slipped Faith a mickey. The two eventually became close, but Faith kept a curtain tightly drawn over that nightmare shower.

Gert came in with a platter of what she called "fancy sandwiches"—chicken and egg salad, crab and tinted layers of cream cheese, crustless, most cut in bell shapes. "I don't know what's keeping Arlene. I've called the house and there's no answer. Mike said she was going to leave right after he did. She had something for Samantha she wanted to wrap."

"I'm sure she'll be here soon," Sophie said. "If she's had car trouble we'd have heard. Probably decided we needed more juice for the mimosas or something like that."

Island time meant if you were invited for one o'clock, you arrived at one o'clock. Maybe even quarter to. The living room and porch were soon filled with women oohing and aahing over the decorations and the food. Amy and Faith had made cupcakes, piping wedding rings, bridal bouquets, and bells on top of the icings. Marge Foster made her layered cherry Jell-O, cream cheese, and graham cracker mold shaped like a wedding cake with three tiers. "Got it from the Internet," she announced proudly, making the last word sound like an actual destination akin to another planet. "My nephew is a whiz with a computer, and when I told him what I wanted he found it and it was at the post office two days later."

Besides the mimosas, Gert had made strawberry shrub—"my grandmother's recipe." (See recipe, page 326.) Faith was familiar with the tangy fruit drink, which dated back to the days before refrigeration, when vinegar was used as a preservative. The combination of macerated fresh fruit, sugar, and cider or white vinegar boiled and strained had a long shelf life. She was tempted to tell Gert that her grandmother's recipe had become the new happening menu item, especially when combined with alcohol, at upscale New York restaurants. It would be the only thing on the buffet that would meet with Alexandra's approval. Samantha's future mother-in-law had already cast her eye on the decorations and had been about to say something when Babs whisked her out to the porch to meet Samantha's godmother, whose last name revealed very blue blood. The two were soon playing the "Who Do We Know in Common?" game—Samantha's godmother was a good sport and knew exactly what Babs was doing, having heard from Pix about Zach's mother.

Sophie had told Samantha about Jenny Hamilton's performance and she'd invited her to come to the shower with Nan, mentioning the possibility of singing at the wedding. Jenny had accepted the invitation and said she'd bring her guitar and stay afterward to talk about what Samantha might want. She was going over to Brooksville at five and could leave from The Pines.

Amy excitedly pushed a button on her phone as Samantha walked through the door, filling the room with the strains of Mendelssohn's "Wedding March." Ursula, who seemed more excited than anyone, popped a fascinator she'd made on Samantha's head—a headband with white silk blossoms and wisps of lace—crying out, "Here comes the bride!" The party was officially in full gear.

The asshole pharmacist wouldn't fill the prescription! Said it was too soon and pointed to the date. Also questioned her ID. Same thing at Walmart and the Rite Aid. At Walmart the pharmacist told her to wait while he went to check, but something told her not to stay and she was out of there.

She had trouble opening the car and people in the parking lot were looking at her funny. "What's your problem?" she yelled at one woman, slamming the door as she got behind the steering wheel. She could feel tears on her cheeks. She didn't have anything. Not a single pill. Nothing. Her heart was pounding. She couldn't breathe. She was going to die.

Sleep. Maybe she could get some sleep. A little nap, and when she woke up she'd figure out what to do. Where to go. She had to score.

Not on the island. Not on the island. Suddenly she was wide awake. Her phone had service here. And she knew who to call. A name. She laughed. It was Mike who had told her their former classmate had been arrested for possession. Even if she was clean, she'd know where to score. She made the call. There were a gazillion missed ones, but she ignored them. They made arrangements, and it wouldn't take long.

Lucky. She was in luck. She started the car and headed for Denny's.

It was going to cost her more cash than she had, but she could give her the watch. A Christmas present from Mike. It had real diamond chips around the face. She only wore it for special occasions.

And this was a special occasion.

By four o'clock the guests had all left. No one commented on the absence of the hostess, but as soon as the last car pulled away, Arlene's mother, Marilyn, began to cry. "Something's happened to her! Mike, call the police!"

The men had finished their nautical tasks and turned up half an hour ago, assuming correctly that there would be food left.

Mike went over to his mother-in-law and sat next to her on the couch. "I would have heard if there'd been an accident. She's been so touchy lately that if I do something like call around she'll get upset. Her phone must be off or she's where it doesn't get service. Maybe she took a nap before she left the house and lost track of time. She's been awful tired lately. She's going to feel terrible about missing this and I'll bet she walks through the door soon."

Soon was a half hour later and she didn't so much walk through the door as fly. "Party! Let's party!

This is for the bride!!" She rushed over to Samantha and thrust a bouquet of gas station flowers at her. "Come on, everybody. Let's have some music. We want to dance!!" She began to spin around and collapsed on the couch onto her husband's lap.

No one else had said a word and then Alexandra stood up. "This is your matron of honor?" she said scathingly to Samantha. "She's drunk or . . ."

Ursula stood up, too. "Hush. The child is sick." She looked around the room. "We need to take care of her. Marilyn, did you know?"

Arlene's mother had stopped crying. "I've been suspecting, but I can't believe my daughter would ever get involved with drugs."

Mike looked stunned. "What are you talking about? Arlene on something? That's crazy! I'm taking her home now. My sister can keep Kylie overnight."

Arlene jumped off his lap. Her face was flushed, and Faith could see that her pupils were pinpricks. Before she could say anything, Arlene did. "Prezzie, I have a prezzie for my BFF. Here in my purse." She began to dig into her bag, throwing things onto the floor—a juice box, tissues, makeup, one of Kylie's small stuffed animals, her phone, her car keys, receipts, and a pill container. She got down on her knees to sort through it all. Jenny and Samantha got down with her. "Don't worry about it, Arlene, you can give it to me later," Samantha said, covering the keys with her hand and pushing them under the couch.

Jenny was looking at the pill container. Empty. She picked up one of the pieces of paper. Faith was watching and saw a look of surprise cross the girl's face. She also saw her put both in the pocket of her denim skirt. "I'm very sorry, Samantha. We can talk about music for the wedding another time." She picked up her guitar case. "I have to be at a gig off-island soon."

Every eye was focused on Arlene as Jenny left—except Faith's. She followed the girl out the back door. "I saw you take the container and a paper off the floor," she said.

Jenny started to run toward the VW Freeman had loaned her. "Not now, Mrs. Fairchild."

Faith ran, too. "Yes, now! What do you know about all this?"

Jenny stopped at the car. "Nothing. But I'm going to find out." Seconds later she was driving off.

"Nobody in our family has ever had a problem like this," Marilyn was saying firmly when Faith came back inside. "You know the doctor gave her pain pills after the accident. It was all legal and she needed them! Maybe she kept a couple and took them today. She's been nervous about the shower and the wedding."

Arlene was lying on the floor, her eyes closed. "I can hear you," she said. "I can hear every single word. Your good little girl would never do anything wrong, right, Mom? And I'm married to a cop, so I *really* wouldn't do anything illegal? I'm just going to relax like this a minute and we can all go home."

"Help me take her upstairs, Samantha," Ursula said. "She can stay here tonight."

"I'll sit with her," Gert said. "Things will be better in the morning."

Tom spoke up. "Actually, they won't. Arlene is going to need all of us. Need us to know what has been happening and not judge"—he directed a steely glance at Alexandra, who looked as if she had been sucking lemons. "And she needs to go into a rehab facility now. Come off what she's on, which since she was prescribed pain medication, we can assume is an opioid. It has to be done under supervision, and once she's through it comes the even harder part—support counseling for Arlene, the whole family, and her friends."

Mike was crying now. "She didn't want to move out of town. I was the one who pushed for the place in the woods. It was cheap because it wasn't finished. And I wanted Kylie to grow up away from some of the influences in Granville. And here it was under my nose. I'll never forgive myself for doing this to her. I love her, I love her so much . . ."

"We know, son. Come on out to the porch," Tom said. "We'll talk if you feel like it. But I'll tell you right now that you're not to blame. Nobody here is, least of all your wife. And in your heart, you know that, too. Any one of us could be in the situation Arlene is in now. She's not a criminal. She has a disease."

"I'll call Ed Ricks to come over if that's all right with everyone," Faith offered. "I don't think any of us want to be alone right now. Marilyn, you don't know him well, but he and some others have been working to educate and treat what is an epidemic. In every part of the country. It may help you to hear what he has to say."

Pix sat down close to Marilyn. "We've known each other and been friends a long time, since the girls were toddlers. Arlene has always been like a daughter to me, and I know Samantha is for you. But I can't think of any other way to put this except as one mother to another. I don't want to see her picture in the paper with 'died suddenly' in an obituary."

The room was quiet and then Marilyn took Pix's hand and nodded. "Whatever it takes to prevent that. I'll do it. Our whole family will. Faith, call Dr. Ricks."

Ursula's living room filled up quickly after that. Marilyn called her husband to come. Arlene's brother and his wife lived in southern Maine, but Mike called his parents, too. After a few words, Ed had praised them all for responding so quickly. "What Arlene will need most now is the support of her family and friends. You need to expect that she'll be doing fine and then most likely relapse. It will be hard to keep going—for her and you— but we have some wonderful individuals here on Sanpere and across the bridge who have trained as recovery coaches. Many of them have been through the cycle themselves. They are here to help her, and you. More and more people are stepping forward to be trained, or just involved, as word spreads. We already have a group that meets at the Community Center Wednesday nights for support and education."

Upstairs, with Gert at her side, Arlene slept. Tom and Mike had come in from the porch. Samantha and Sophie were making coffee.

"I should have guessed," Samantha said. "She's been avoiding me all summer—no even earlier, during Memorial Day weekend, too. And when Mom brought the dress over she told me how thin she was." Samantha's voice caught.

Sophie put her arm around her. "You couldn't have known. Addicts are very good at hiding what's going on. Arlene is a very smart cookie, and just as she was good at everything she did, she was a good liar. Having to be good at everything has probably played a part in all this. She couldn't admit any weakness. Samantha, you've known people with addiction problems I'm sure. Alcohol or drugs."

"Or both," Samantha said. "When I was working in Manhattan I tried not to know, but the pressures at work were horrendous. Must have been the same for you at your law firm."

Sophie nodded. "If you admitted to getting a full night's sleep, you were a failure. The creep I followed to London thinking he was the love of my life did me a favor getting me off the corner office/partner track."

"What's going to happen now?" Samantha sounded very young, Sophie thought. She and Arlene were both still so young.

"Well, judging from the amount of time Tom and Ed have each spent on the phone," she said, "I imagine they'll get her a spot at an excellent detox facility that will transition to a longer stay there or someplace else. It may be in Massachusetts or here in Maine. Let's bring in the coffee. Mugs, not cups and saucers. People want something to hold."

On their way back in, Alexandra pushed past them. "Sorry, must dash. Clambake on the beach tonight and I don't want to miss it. Babs is staying here."

It didn't escape Sophie's notice that Samantha's

future in-law had carefully redone her makeup and hair. After the door closed, she said to Samantha, "Remind me to tell you about my mother-in-law, actually Will's stepmother. Alexandra will seem like a prize."

"The question is 'prize what?'" The two stifled a giggle. Comic relief.

When they finally got home, Pix was surprised to find an envelope with her name on it stuck under her car's windshield wiper. They had all gone to the shower in Sam's car. Pix picked up the envelope and opened it. Inside was a single sheet of paper. "I need to talk to you. I'll be at the coffee place in Sanpere Village tomorrow at 9:00 A.M. Drew."

Could life get any more complicated? Pix wondered and started after her husband and daughter to show them the note.

"Maybe she wants to apologize," Samantha said after Pix read it to them.

"I doubt that," Sam said. "And I don't want you going. Looks like a setup to me."

"But what kind?" Pix asked her husband, overlooking his preemptory "I don't want you." "What more can the Cranes do? I think Samantha is right, maybe she's going to say she's sorry and tell me they're calling the whole thing off. That it was an accident."

Sam shook his head. "I love you both to pieces, but not everyone is as nice as you are—nor as gullible. At least let me come with you."

"But she specifically put the note on my car. I think she wants to talk woman to woman."

"Woman to harpy is more like it." Sam shook his head.

There were several messages on the answering machine. Freeman, who hated the "durn things," coughed and said, "Be at the dock at eight." Sam looked at Pix. "You forgot tomorrow is Granville's Lobster Boat Race day. We'll be out on their other son's boat with Nan and about a hundred other Hamiltons to watch Freeman tear up the competition. His brother Harry is coming up from Massachusetts special. So I'm afraid you won't be able to keep your date." He sounded pleased.

"I have the feeling Drew doesn't want Cameron to know," Pix said, "so I'll leave word at the Café. They open at seven." She was tempted to stick her tongue out and say, "So there," but the next message quelled the impulse. It was from the sheriff's office, advising them to get a lawyer.

Even though she knew they'd prepared everything for the clambake, Faith decided to stop by the Shores after leaving The Pines and make sure all was going well. They should have reached dessert at this point, and afterward it was movie night in the conference center with popcorn and a craft beer tasting. She'd been astonished to discover how many local beers there were—all with names appropriate to the region, like "Rising Tide."

She parked in the guest/visitor lot, having no desire for a repeat of the pickup truck incident. Which brought her thoughts to Arlene. Faith had known Arlene ever since the Fairchilds had started coming to Sanpere. Amy hadn't been born, so it was at least eighteen years. More. Arlene was a chubby little girl, playing at the Millers' when Samantha wasn't playing at the Prescotts'. She and Samantha worked summer jobs together on the island and were indeed best friends. Before she was married, Arlene often came down to Aleford or to New York to visit Samantha. When Kylie was born, Samantha was almost as excited as the loving new mom. Faith thought about the pain the young woman must have been in these last months since that accident. Physical and psychological pain. Mike was right. The location of the new—and very unfinished—house had isolated her from contact with friends and family in Granville. Support she had needed. People might think it ridiculous to think of the few miles as an impediment, but they were.

She wondered where Arlene had been getting the pills and then chided herself. Everything she'd been hearing this summer and last had indicated the availability of just about anything in just about every part of the island and peninsula. Arlene wasn't shooting up. At least not on her arms. The sleeves on her shirt had been rolled up this afternoon—she must have been feeling warm—and there wasn't a single mark. But addicts found other places in order to escape notice, even between their toes.

As Faith walked down to the back of the lodge and kitchen door, she passed a steady stream of guests heading for movie night or beer night, depending on one's interest. Maybe both. She was happy to see some of the maintenance crew pushing the oversize cart they used for beach events, fully loaded, toward the trash area. Another close behind was piled with cookware and other remnants of the feast headed for the kitchen. Cal followed the carts looking tired, but content.

"Hi," Faith said. "Looks like it all went well, from the smiles on the guests' faces."

He grinned at her. "Thanks to your organization. I don't know what we'd be doing without you, Mrs. Fairchild—and your daughter."

Faith gave a quick thought to what Amy had just experienced at the shower and was glad the job would be a distraction for the rest of the summer. Tom was planning to take her night kayaking in the double kayak, and Faith knew they would talk.

"Call me Faith, please. I'm glad I could help. Is everything off the beach?"

"Yes, I doused the fire myself. The tide's coming in, too, so even if there is a hot spot that will take care of it. We spread out the rockweed we used to steam the bake to be sure there weren't any embers."

"Great. I'll just check the kitchen. Maybe we can salvage any leftovers for lobster salad or quiche for tomorrow's lunch." As Faith moved away she noticed Alexandra coming from the front door of the lodge. She was about to ask her how she'd liked the clambake, but Alexandra wasn't looking at her. "Hey, Mr. Cal," she called out. "I believe we have a movie date."

Cal winked at Faith. "I believe we do. I picked the films myself. Hope you like Bruce Willis. We're having a *Die Hard* marathon."

Alexandra flinched visibly, but Faith had to give her recovery credit. "Bruce Willis? Oh but of course. Adore him. So, so—masculine."

The two went off toward the conference center and Faith indulged in audible laughter.

Faith let the crew go, maintenance and kitchen. It was a Saturday night after all. She definitely wanted to hold on to all of them, especially the dishwasher who had shown up for work every day and, more important, stayed. Without help, it

263

took time to pick the lobsters and finish cleaning before she locked up and headed for her car.

As she looked up at the sky, the author Henry Beston's words from *The Outermost House*—words she knew by heart as one of Tom's favorite quotations—came to mind:

For a moment of night we have a glimpse of ourselves and of our world islanded in its stream of stars—pilgrims of mortality, voyaging between horizons across the eternal seas of space and time.

Tom and Amy would still be on the water. Faith could see the white curve of the beach beckoning. It was the perfect spot to sit, think over the day, and appreciate Beston's words, which put things into perspective as sharply as if she had a telescope to focus on all that was above and around her.

It was warm, and she had no need of a sweater. Walking down the steep drive that led to the sandy crescent, she could smell the beach roses, *Rosa rugosa*. The only sounds were night sounds—crickets, the swoosh of a bird. Everyone was either away from the Shores or enjoying tonight's entertainment—not Bruce Willis she was sure. Something more like *Mamma Mia! Here We Go Again*, or the first *Mamma Mia!* Something with music.

She was sorry to miss the Lobster Boat Races tomorrow, since she and Amy would be working. She wouldn't have been on Ed's boat in any case.

He'd called to tell her he would be driving Arlene to a placement he'd arranged outside Boston. He'd added it had been difficult to persuade Arlene to go. She finally gave in when he mentioned Kylie's name, which triggered what amounted to hysterics and Arlene told him she had hit a tree when Kylie was in the car. Mike and her mother wanted to go with her, but she asked Gert to come. Only Gert. "Steady as a clock," Ed had said, and Faith had to agree.

It had been a long day. The Shores beach was one of the only pure sandy ones on the island. Faith slipped her sandals off and felt the grains like silk on her bare feet. She walked a short way and sat on a log, a huge timber that had washed up during some storm and had served as a convenient resting place ever since. The moon was bright, its beams rippling across the incoming tide. Far out she heard the sound of a boat. It was coming closer and going fast. She thought of the one she'd seen at Ed's when they'd had coffee. A week ago? Two weeks? Time was collapsing this summer.

The boat's captain must be practicing for tomorrow, running his craft at full throttle. Even though it was far off, the wake was churning up the water, sending waves of foam toward the beach. The cove was deep water here and supposed to be one of the spots where the Abenaki summered.

Faith had read the short piece Sophie had written imagining those first people and heard about the longer one she was working on. She hoped Sophie would finish the project, and it had already served its purpose. Sophie's mood had changed and she was no longer obsessing about an empty cradle. She'd told Faith that Ursula had asked her a question no one else had. "Do you and Will want to reproduce yourselves or raise a child together?" She'd emphasized that a yes to either question was perfectly understandable. Trust Ursula, Faith thought. Sophie had gone on to tell her she'd called Will right away and he'd responded, "With my gene pool? And you don't know the half of it—for example, great-great-grandfather Aloysius Maxwell was a notorious swindler and a crook. His name is even scratched out in the family Bible!" Their plan now was to begin an adoption process in the fall. "I've been so stupid, Faith," Sophie had said. "Approaching the whole thing the way I had to get a high score on my LSATs."

The log was a nice perch but hard, and Faith decided to head for home. The lobster boat was coming closer and closer at full speed and she wondered why. The race wasn't an obstacle course, so it wasn't practicing maneuvers. Just a straight shot like bats out of hell toward the finish.

She was only a short way up the drive when she heard a scream. It was coming from behind, not in front of her. She ran back to the beach where she could make out a person—or two people?—at the far end. The boat was heading just as fast, maybe faster, away from the cove now, the wake lapping the shore almost up to the high-tide mark.

Faith sped through the sand as fast as she could, grateful for the moonlight illuminating her path. The scream had given way to a loud wailing sound.

Two people, not one. Two people Faith knew. Alexandra had her arms around Cal Burke. It was not a romantic gesture. The water from the boat's wake was swirling about them. It was red. From the size of the gash on the maintenance man's skull, there was no question he was dead.

A husband about to be charged with arson; her future in-law who was not only found clutching a dead man but also the only person in sight who could have killed him.

Pix was not going to be happy.

Ten

Seeing Faith stopped Alexandra's piercing cries. She let go of the corpse in her arms.

Faith crouched down and put her hand on the body. Cal Burke was still warm, but there was no sign of even a faint pulse at his wrist. Despite the blood—bright red in the moonlight, sticky, oozing over his face, puddling at the neck—Faith pressed her fingers on his neck. Nothing. His eyes were wide open, but they were sightless.

She looked for signs of anyone on the beach or in the nearby woods. No one. She couldn't leave Alexandra, and Alexandra was in no shape to go get help. The woman was moving as far away as she could, backing away from the water, scuttling like a crab. She'd started screaming again. Faith understood why people like Alexandra were always getting slapped across the face in old movies. Instead of acting on the impulse, she said forcibly, "Stop it! Shut up!" This produced lower-volume moans. Faith was able to catch the words "I didn't do it. It just happened."

It was then that Faith noticed where Alexandra was heading. A tartan picnic blanket—probably Barbour—was spread out on the sand. A large leather tote was off to one side, and the necks of two bottles of extremely expensive champagne were clearly visible. The scenario was clear. There certainly were crashing waves at this point. A cinematic tryst—a reenactment of Deborah Kerr and Burt Lancaster in *From Here to Eternity*—only something had gone very, very wrong.

Faith eyed the tote again. "Your phone. Do you have it? Is it in your bag?"

Alexandra nodded.

"Get it," Faith ordered. It was then that she realized the reason for the woman's odd choice of movement. Her legs were shaking so hard she couldn't stand. She tried and collapsed back onto the ground.

"Never mind. I will. Stay where you are."

Over the years, Faith had memorized Earl's home number and punched it in instead of 911.

Earl answered, clearly puzzled by the caller ID. "Mrs. Kohn?"

"No, it's me. Faith. I'm with her. Cal Burke has been murdered. We're at the far end of the Shores beach. However he was killed, I'm sure it's just happened."

"Okay. I'll be there soon. Tide's going to be a high one tonight and it's coming in. Try not to move him much, but you may have to. Aside from Mrs. Kohn, anybody else there?"

"No, but there was a boat, a lobster boat that came in fast and near to the shore. Caused a huge wake. Other than that, nobody on the beach or on the water."

"What's that noise? Sounds like a coyote. Could he have been attacked by one? Lots around this summer."

"I doubt it. What you hear is Alexandra Kohn."

Faith hung up and considered her options; the water *was* coming in fast and the waves had already obliterated possible evidence. She looked at the body more carefully. His clothes were soaking wet and torn in places. She didn't think it was a result of an act of passion. Switching the phone to camera, she took several photos, particularly of what had been revealed on his right forearm: a tattoo of a realistic green adder snaking up to the elbow, its fangs dripping blood, a few Gothic letters in red. *L F D Y.*

"Live Fast Die Young." But Cal had messed up

when it came to the rest of the credo: "and leave a good-looking corpse."

Alexandra was sobbing softly. Faith sat down next to her, putting an arm around the woman's shoulders—a woman barely recognizable as the figure of the last month. Proving there is no such thing as waterproof mascara, her face, red and puffy from crying, sported black rivulets, and her hair was a mess. There was blood on her white lace camisole and more on her hands.

"Valium, I need some Valium," Alexandra said.

"I'm sorry, but I don't have any. Try taking deep breaths," Faith answered.

"There's some in my bag. Get it!"

Interested as she was to see what else might be in the bag, Faith knew to leave that for Earl or some other officer of the law. She'd already had to take out the phone. She repeated her breathing suggestion and Alexandra hiccupped several times and then got quiet.

"Can you tell me what happened?" Faith said.

"I don't *know* what happened!!" she whimpered. "We'd arranged to meet here after the program was over. He suggested we wait an hour. Make sure we wouldn't be disturbed. I told him I'd bring a midnight picnic. When I got to the beach, he wasn't waiting like he usually was." Faith filed that admission away for later, letting Alexandra continue.

"I spread the blanket out, and it was such a beautiful night, I lay down to look at the stars. I must have dropped off. This has been a very stressful day."

"Yes, we're all concerned about Arlene," Faith said.

"Arlene? Oh, that girl at Samantha's shower. No, my dressmaker called and she hasn't been able to get confirmation that the fabric I'm having woven in Italy for my wedding outfit will arrive in time for her to finish it. She has the toile and my measurements never change, but . . ."

Faith almost *did* slap her now. She took a breath herself. "Okay, so you fell asleep and then what?"

"I heard a noise. Like some kind of engine. Cal was nowhere to be seen. I looked at my watch. He was two hours late. Well, I thought, I'm not going to be treated like that by some hired help and I stood up to pack all the things away. And then I saw him." She gulped for air. "I saw him in the water. I thought he was drowning. Huge waves pushing him back and forth into shore. I ran down to pull him in and there was all this blood." She shivered and stopped speaking for a moment. Collecting herself, she said, "I thought he must have gone for a swim when he saw I was asleep and banged his head on a rock or something. Except why wouldn't he have just woken me up?"

"Was there anyone on the beach or over at the sides, near the woods or ledges?"

"No. I looked, because I needed help. I don't know how to do any of that rescue stuff. CRV or whatever. I turned him over on his side and saw . . ." Alexandra closed her eyes. Clearly she didn't want to recall what she had seen and she clearly also didn't want to talk about it anymore.

But Faith did. "So you have no idea how he was killed?"

Alexandra's eyes snapped open and she said briskly, "Well, it's obvious, isn't it? They killed him on that boat and threw him in the water. I'd like to leave now, Faith. You can tell the police whatever you want."

Mrs. Kohn's return to the guest room at The Birches wasn't quite as speedy as she wished, but after she'd been questioned by both Earl and the state police homicide officers who'd arrived soon after, Faith—who had also told them what little she knew—drove her back. The kitchen lights were on, and both Babs and Sophie were waiting up. Faith had called with a brief account of the events. She had also called Tom and explained why she would be late, emphasizing that someone else, *not* Faith herself, had found the body this time.

At The Birches, Babs took charge of Alexandra. "I've drawn a nice soothing bath for you—lavender salts and here's something to start on," she said, handing Alexandra a glass of chardonnay and shepherding her out of the kitchen. "You poor dear. What a horrible thing."

"It was! And the police have taken all my things, including my Fendi leather tote! They're probably swigging down the champagne I put in it right now! Dom Pérignon!"

As soon as they were out of earshot, Faith filled Sophie in with more details. Shocked, Sophie said, "I can't believe it! Cal Burke had that snake tattoo? That makes three of them! No coincidence, but how do you think he was connected to the other two?"

Faith had been wondering the same thing ever since seeing the image on Cal's lifeless arm. "He's from here originally, but has been living all over the place apparently and worked in both of the Childses' other conference centers, near enough to Lowell to have formed some sort of connection. He was older, but maybe they were all bikers?" It didn't sound very plausible to Faith, and Sophie said dubiously as well, "I guess that's possible . . ."

Faith thought of something else. "Cindy went to tell everyone still up in the bar that there had been an accident and not to be alarmed if they heard sirens. I was there on the beach when she came down with one of the officers. I wonder if there was something going on between them? She was crying almost as hysterically as Alexandra had been—an extreme reaction for just a coworker?" Faith shook her head, trying to put her thoughts in order. "One thing is clear—the Childses are losing staff by the minute, and this staff member needs to get some sleep or I may end up confusing sugar with salt tomorrow—or rather today."

She was almost at her car when she realized she hadn't told Sophie about seeing Jenny Hamilton take the pill container and a piece of paper from the items that had spilled out of Arlene's bag. Jenny Hamilton, Cal Burke's singing partner. She went back and described what had happened. "I confronted her, but she wouldn't say anything. Only that she had to find something out. Wait, I just had an idea. Why don't you take my place on the Hamiltons' son's boat tomorrow for the races? Jenny is bound to be on it. Amy and I have to keep the kitchen going at the Shores, especially after tonight. People are going to be understandably nervous. And that means comfort food, plenty of it."

"I was going to skip the races and get some writing done, but I'll call Nan in the morning and see if there's still room. Oh, Faith, this was supposed to be a carefree wedding summer . . ."

Faith gave her a hug. "Try to get some sleep." Sophie hugged her back. "My cell will work on the water, so if I have anything to tell you, I'll text."

"Totally unrelated topic that just occurred to me," Faith said as she let herself out once again. "How are Babs's and Alexandra's memoirs going? Have you read them?"

"Mom is being very secretive but said she was surprising herself—how much she remembered about growing up and then later all the husbands. She also said that Alexandra was working sporadically, taking frequent breaks—we now know the reason—but that she'd read a passage to the group about growing up rich."

"Kind of 'Poor Little Rich Girl'?"

"That's what I was expecting. An only child lacking for nothing but love. Losing her mother when she was young."

"It would explain a lot," Faith said sympathetically.

"Except she wasn't! All she remembered about her mother was the smell of her perfume. A silver spoon childhood that was as happy as a clam at low tide! And more sunny days to follow apparently. Talk about mixed metaphors!" Sophie said. "Anyway, Mom reported Alexandra told them very seriously that it *was* possible to have it all."

"Are we happy to hear this or . . . ?"

"Not." Sophie laughed.

Faith said with mock gravitas, "I'm beginning to

think Samantha's mother-in-law-to-be has hidden shallows."

It was hard telling Amy about Cal Burke. As with the chef, she had worked with him all summer and liked him. Faith described the death as some kind of accident, which was all she knew in any case. She also made a brief call to the Millers, and clearly Pix was as baffled as Faith about any role Alexandra might have played.

Hanging up she went back to Tom and Amy. Amy, although upset about Cal, was determined to do her best to keep the Shores' kitchen operational. "We can't let the Childses down—or the guests," she said. Thinking back to some similar situations in her own culinary career, Faith realized that there might be something in her DNA that she had passed down to her daughter. A version of "The Show Must Go On"—"The Meals Must Be Prepared."

Sunday the island awoke to fog, but old-timers like Freeman Hamilton were not dismayed. "It'll burn off," he told Sam Miller when Sam called to see whether the races were canceled. And by the time the Millers plus Sophie boarded Roy Hamilton's lobster boat, the fog was gone, replaced by crystal clear sunshine.

Roy's boat was filled with people ready to

cheer their favorites—and coolers packed with comestibles and drinks of all kinds. Pix had barbecued chicken yesterday morning before the shower and also made a vat of Faith's coleslaw (see recipe, page 323), the old-fashioned kind but with red and green cabbage and carrots for color. The enthusiasm of the crowd—those getting into boats to watch from the water and those staying on the pier—was contagious.

Sophie smiled at Pix. "I feel a little bit as if I've been on that ride at the Blue Hill Fair, the Tilt-A-Whirl, and despite all that happened at the shower and hearing about Cal Burke, I'm happy to be here, and the only thing on my mind is Freeman winning again."

"I know exactly what you mean. Whirling events. On the way I had to stop to leave a message for Drew Crane of all people at the coffee shop in Sanpere Village. She left a note on my windshield sometime yesterday when I was at The Pines saying she wanted to meet me there today at nine."

"Any indication why?"

"None—both Sam and Samantha think I should ignore it, but I didn't agree. The message I left said I'd be at the races. It's up to her now to get in touch again, or not."

"I'll bet she wants to apologize for her husband and tell you they're dropping the whole thing," Sophie said.

"That's exactly what I said. My family told me if I believed that, the next time we had a rainbow I should get in the car and find the pot of gold at the end."

"Don't pay any attention to them," Sophie said, glancing at Sam, who was helping Roy cast off. "I'm a tiger in the courtroom, but a lamb outside—according to Will—so I'm with you."

Sophie had watched Jenny Hamilton get on board. Her long dark hair was tied off her face with the pink bandanna Sophie recognized from the market and the campfire, but she wasn't wearing the leather jacket. She greeted everyone warmly, and it seemed she didn't have a care in the world. Sophie thought the engine noise would preclude any private conversation for now, but she intended to keep a sharp eye on the girl.

The boatload watched several contests and started in on the food and drink. Freeman's class was the last to race. Sophie realized there was plenty of time to decide how to approach Jenny. The races were an all-day affair.

After a while, Roy turned the wheel over to his cousin Norman. "I think she's pulling to the right. No problem when I hauled yesterday, but I could swear something went wrong overnight. See what you think while I grab some of that chicken before it's gone."

"You don't mean you think someone was on

your boat last night?" Norman asked. His face registered more than dismay. Using—even stepping onto—another person's boat without permission was tantamount to a crime.

Roy shook his head. "I don't think so. Doesn't make sense. She was moored the same. Just have a funny feeling that's all."

"I'll check it out," Norman said. A few minutes later he called over his shoulder, "Seems all right to me. How about the fuel gauge? You'd know if she'd been taken for a spin."

Roy shook his head. "It read the same as when I left her."

The conversation ended as a tight race began to unfold between two friends of the Hamiltons. As most of the group loudly encouraged one or the other captains, Sophie took the opportunity to sit next to Jenny, who was sitting apart up on the bow. The captain had cut the engine.

"I was sorry to hear about Cal Burke," Sophie said. "I'm taking the writing class at Sanpere Shores and it was a pleasure to hear the two of you sing."

Jenny looked wistful. "It's hard to believe I won't be doing any more duets with him. I met him down in Massachusetts at an open mic night near where I go to school. Somehow we ended up doing gigs together when he didn't have to work. It was a coincidence that he was coming up here to Sanpere when I was. I hadn't even known he was from Maine." She looked away when she said this last, and Sophie wished Babs were on board with her innate "Can you look me straight in the eye and say that" skill.

"He was older than you, right?"

Jenny looked her straight in the eye. "Yes, why do you ask?" Her tone was cool. She didn't wait for an answer and stood up. "I'm going to get some lemonade. You want anything?"

A lot, Sophie said to herself—and I'm not getting it from you. Not yet anyway.

"Nothing like a day on the water to make a man feel full of good cheer," Sam said as they pulled into the drive.

"And also possibly because of the number of Sam Adams Summer Ales you imbibed," Pix teased.

"Had to keep my throat lubricated so I could yell loud enough. Freeman was happy as a dog with two tails. His best time ever."

They had all been thrilled when Freeman crossed the finish line well ahead of his archrival. Pix's throat was a little hoarse, too. It had been a lovely day. She was sorry Faith, Amy, and Samantha, who had set out for Boston that morning, had missed this year, but Tom videoed much of it. Samantha and Zach could at least get a feel for what had been a perfect Maine day.

The food was all gone and Pix felt a secret satisfaction. One disastrous year she had experimented with the recipe, glazing the chicken with her version of hoisin sauce. It was so salty that only Sam ate any—not from loyalty, but because he'd eat anything.

"How about I make Americanos and we sit outside?" Sam suggested. They had developed a taste for the Campari, sweet vermouth, and seltzer drink with an orange slice in Italy two years ago, and it was now a summer favorite. Although unlike James Bond, the Millers did not insist on using Perrier, but whatever club soda was at hand.

"*Grazie.* I'll clean the cooler and put the containers to soak while you make them," she said. Neither her mother nor Gert would be peering over her shoulder at leaving the dirty dishes for later, and Sam certainly wouldn't care.

Pix was feeling pretty cheerful herself. Even after she spied the same kind of envelope under her windshield wiper as yesterday, it didn't quash her spirit. If anything it made her feel even better. Drew Crane had replied. Pix was right to be optimistic.

She tore the envelope open to find a brief message. "Could you meet me at the small park by the Mill Pond at five today? I'll be there and wait thirty minutes."

Sometimes the planets align and what drops

into your lap is more than serendipitous. "Sorry, honey, we're out of oranges," Sam called from the kitchen. "Gin or vodka tonics it is."

"Oh, Sam, I was craving an Americano. I haven't had one since you were here for the Fourth. I'll go to the market and be back before you know it."

"Are you sure you want to bother?"

"Definitely."

"Okay, I'll stretch out in the hammock until you get back."

This was even better news than the lack of citrus fruit. Sam would fall asleep before her car was out of the drive. She had plenty of time now.

She made a lightning-fast stop for the navel oranges and was at the bench by the pond a little before five. Drew was already there. There was no question that the woman looked nervous. And pale. She was picking at a cuticle and dropped her hand when she saw Pix.

"You'd never believe I had a manicure every week before we came here. And a pedicure. Even if there was a place on the island I could get one, look at my hands." She stretched her fingers out, and yes, Pix could see that a few nails were cracked and several fingers had cuts.

It seemed unlikely that all this subterfuge was to get Pix to look at Mrs. Crane's hands, however. "I'm assuming you had something to say to me alone. Not my husband?"

"And not mine. He thinks I'm at the market."

"Mine, too." Pix smiled. The ice was broken.

"I don't know where to start," Drew said. She looked down at the previously displayed hands, which she was twisting in her lap, then looked up and burst out, "I never wanted to buy the place. When Cameron started talking about a vacation home in Maine I assumed it would be southern Maine. Someplace like Boothbay or Kennebunkport. Not on a damn island away from everything!"

Normally Pix would leap to defend her beloved Sanpere, but she kept listening.

"He bought it on the spot one weekend on what he called a 'scouting' trip when I was at my sister's. At Winnipesaukee. Right on the lake," Drew said bitterly. "I never saw this place except for some photos he took—and it looked kind of cute—until we arrived. I certainly had no idea how far away it was or that from the moment I set foot here I'd be slaving away, clearing brush, chopping trees, digging clams, laying new flooring, painting the inside, and now Cameron's ready to stain the outside—after we treat it with some kind of stuff you have to push between the cracks in the logs by hand. I tell you, Mrs. Miller, I am exhausted!"

Still wondering where this was going, Pix gave her what she hoped was a supportive look and said, "Well, summer houses can be a lot of work."

Drew shook her head, sending her red curls bobbing in the slight breeze. "Not for this girl. Not anymore . . ." She stopped abruptly and lowered her voice. "I did it. All of it. The glue and the fire. I took the glove from a stack in your barn."

Pix was stunned. "Wait a minute! You're telling me you destroyed your own property to get back at us for complaining about the trees?"

"No, no. I'm sorry about the trees, but Cameron wanted a better view, and as you've discovered, he can be pretty obstinate. When I saw how things were developing between us I realized how I could get him to leave. And he is. The house is going on the market tomorrow. He's had it with the island—no one has been sympathetic, he says. He's sure everyone, including the authorities, are biased against us. So, and it's a quote, 'I'm out of here.'"

"But what about the arson charge?" Pix could hardly believe what she was hearing.

"Once we're gone he'll have some new project. I'll give our lawyer a call soon, instructing it be dropped. I handle our legal stuff and finances, too. I was a CPA before I retired. Kept the books for his business and got some nice jewelry out of it."

She couldn't help it. Pix started to laugh hysterically.

"Are you all right?" Drew asked anxiously.

Pix gasped, swallowed, and replied, "Never

better. We'd better get home from the market."
It seemed appropriate to shake hands, so she extended hers. She could almost see Mrs. Crane as a friend in some other context. Or maybe not.

"Can't wait to get to a nail salon," Drew murmured as they headed for their cars.

Walking over the grass to wake Sam up, clutching one of the oranges, Pix knew he would be angry when he heard the tale—might want to take some kind of action—but she couldn't be. It was all over now, and even though Drew hadn't said she was sorry directly, Pix recognized a woman driven to the breaking point. She vowed to keep her secret, except for Sam and Faith—and also vowed to get on the phone to the Realtor first thing in the morning and buy the place. She and Sam should have bought the property to begin with, although now it would be a bargain, what with the fire damage and lack of privacy. She felt herself starting to laugh again.

Hearing her, Sam woke up. "I must have dropped off. Meet anyone at the market?"

"Not today, but I did find that pot of gold you and Samantha were so sure I wouldn't."

Dr. and Mrs. Childs arrived at the Shores Monday morning dressed in black clothes suggestive of what Queen Victoria donned for Albert. Faith noticed that even Mrs. Childs's slip, which was hanging slightly below the hem of her dress, was black edged in somber black trim. They came into the kitchen just as Faith and Amy were starting lunch preparations.

"A terrible thing," Dr. Childs said soberly. His wife nodded, too overcome for words. "We've known Cal since he was a young man. What kind of monster would do such a thing?" He pumped his little fist in the air for emphasis. "The goal now is to keep the Shores moving along normally. We've finally found a very well-regarded chef. He's been working at one of these new luxury camping re-sorts, which is shutting down for the season, since so many schools open early. He'll be arriving Thurs-day. You will be able to stay until then won't you?"

Faith finished drying her hands, which she had just washed. Mrs. Childs interpreted the gesture as hesitation and quickly jumped in. "We'll pay double time for the hours."

Faith had been planning to agree before the offer but was glad she hadn't opened her mouth. "I can stay through dinner Wednesday."

Amy piped up, "And I'll come early Thursday to show the new chef where everything is. It's the end of this session, so no dinner and just box lunches for those who want to take them along."

Both Childses appeared relieved. "Thank you both. We'll be leaving tonight. We are working with the authorities about notifying any family.

So far as we knew he didn't have anyone—or at least people he was in touch with. We will see to all the necessaries, in any case."

Why didn't they just say "burial"? Faith thought. All these overblown euphemisms.

"He grew up on the island, Mom," Amy said. "I'll bet the Hamiltons will know if there's anyone here who's a relative."

"I can give them a call," Faith said. "Good idea, although Earl has probably already looked into it."

"Well then, Mrs. Childs and I will be on our way. We want a word with Cindy, who is of course distraught, as she knew him almost as long as we did. And then we have to see to packing up his quarters to make ready for the new occupant."

At that moment, Sophie came into the kitchen. Faith quickly said, "Did you want a glass of water? I believe you met Dr. and Mrs. Childs at the start of your course."

Sophie stayed where she was. "Yes, good to see you again, although I wish it were not under such sad circumstances. My class has been wonderful and I'm sorry it's ending so soon."

"We have always been fortunate to find gifted teachers," Mrs. Childs said. "Patrick's courses fill up immediately."

Dr. Childs added, "We were happy to discover Eloise this season and she, too, has been equally popular at all our locations.

With those pronouncements, they left. Necessaries to see to, Faith thought ironically.

When she was sure the door had shut behind them, Sophie said, "I'll take that water, but I have to get right back and find out what we're doing the rest of the day. We spent the morning rewriting and this afternoon Eloise is meeting with us individually."

Sophie gave a slight nod toward Amy, and Faith picked up on it. "Sweetheart, could you see if we need more supplies at the coffee station?" One serving tea as well had been set up in the main lodge for the students.

As soon as she left, Sophie said, "Early this morning I stopped by the Hamiltons' to see if Jenny wanted to get together later—come to The Birches for a drink maybe or go off-island—but she wasn't there. Nan said she'd left just after dawn but didn't say where."

"Maybe you could drop back after you finish today?" Faith suggested.

"That's what I planned."

"Did Alexandra come today?" Faith had almost forgotten to ask.

"Oh yes. Not grieving. A new bright blue outfit, or at least new to me, and she's sitting next to—and rather close to—Hans Richter. The woman is incorrigible!"

After Sophie left, Faith took Amy's suggestion and called Nan to ask about any family Cal might have had.

"I'll tell you what I told Earl, too," Nan said. "Calvin Burke left the island when he was a teenager. Didn't wait to go to graduation, and I hadn't heard a word about him since until he turned up last summer working at the Shores and singing with Jenny. His family wasn't from here. Aroostook County I believe. His father came to work in the shipyard and his mother stayed at home. Not very sociable, and only had the one child. But his father was one of those men who never growed up. Out on his motorcycle, off with drinking buddies in Belfast. Course he went off the road one night, leaving her a widow, and once Cal took off, his mother did, too. Probably up north. Earl is checking."

"Roy is about Cal's age right? What does he remember about him?"

"I asked him early this summer when Jenny started singing with him and he told me he couldn't say anything bad about him. Couldn't say anything good. Restless, but not wild like his father. Mother spoiled him wicked, Roy said. Whatever he wanted. Fancy guitar, new car for getting his license. He liked money that was for sure. Worked as a caretaker for summer people, so probably did all right."

"Jenny must be upset," Faith said.

"You know something? She hasn't shed a tear." She sounded puzzled. "And now she's gone home. Classes start soon. When I asked her if she was all right, she told me she didn't really know him, and from the look on her face I could tell the subject was closed. Now, wasn't that some great about Freeman winning?"

Faith knew the other subject was closed so far as Nan was concerned, too. After chatting a bit more about the victory, she hung up and concentrated on getting a lobster quiche in the oven.

Sophie meant what she had said to the Childses. The course had been wonderful, and she knew she would finish her story once she got back to Savannah. She wanted to keep writing and thought finding a writers' group would motivate her.

She looked around the room as her fellow scribblers settled in. She'd become used to, and attached to, this group. And was still learning things about some of the members. The biggest surprise had been that Jay and Ellen were a couple now—or at least headed that way. Sophie prided herself on her powers of observation, but she had not picked up even the smallest hint. They didn't sit or eat together. Whatever went on was after

Sophie left for the day. Ellen herself had shyly revealed the attachment to Sophie and also that Jay was in fact a gifted writer. Ellen was even more so. She'd finally shared some of her work with Sophie. She certainly didn't need this class. Sophie hoped that Jay's hubris didn't overshadow Ellen, an obviously adoring acolyte. How many women writers married to male ones had seen their own promising careers eclipsed? Women artists, too.

"Time is always fleeting during this course," Eloise was saying. "Only three more days together. I've written a schedule of our afternoon conferences and I'll pass it around. I must say that this has been an impressive group. Both your dedication and your skill. Cynthia, your factitious family history has made me laugh out loud often, but you never went for cheap shots. You made the various relatives both likable and funny."

"Once I started," Cynthia said, "I found I was remembering real anecdotes that I knew Ross would leave out. There's some embellishment, but not a lot."

"Everyone else is well on the way to a manuscript that could get you an agent or be published in a literary magazine in the case of the short stories. Sophie, your piece is both moving and an important historical contribution. I'm sure any journal, especially one devoted to African-American history, would be glad to look at it. And, George, if you don't end up with an Edgar from the Mystery Writers of America, I'll be very surprised."

Eloise looked straight at Jay. "And you, too, if you're willing to cut some of what you've fallen in love with—it's too long. I have to admit, though, that my favorite in the mystery genre is Joan's Persis Gray. Again award potential—an Agatha. I've been called a bit quirky myself, and we're both of a certain age. Elderly sleuths bring knowledge the young ones can't hope to imitate." She glanced over her shoulder. "Oh dear, they're putting lunch out. I'll talk about the rest of you at tomorrow's morning gathering."

Sophie looked at the schedule. She wasn't scheduled to meet with the instructor for a few hours. Through the glass door in the manager's office she could see Cindy with Dr. and Mrs. Childs. Their plates piled high with food, they were sitting and seemed to be going over a ledger, with Cindy taking notes on an iPad with a keyboard. They'd be there awhile, and this gave her the chance to do what she had been mulling over.

The police would have thoroughly searched the cabin Cal shared with the chef, so it was doubtful there was anything left to find. But Sophie kept thinking about Jenny and wondering about that relationship—and the significance of Jenny's tattoo. One that partially matched the others, specifically Cal's.

"I need some fresh air," Sophie told her mother as the groups broke for lunch. "I had a big breakfast, so I'm not really hungry. See you later."

"Alexandra is eating with Hans and for *some* reason doesn't seem to want me at her table," Babs said. "I'll join the MacDonalds. Cynthia and Ross are quite a delight together. Polar opposites, but devoted. Kind of like Ed and me."

"Glad to hear it," Sophie said to her mother. It was time that Barbara Proctor Maxwell Rothenstein Williams Harrington found the One.

Sophie quickly made her way up the path to Cal and the chef's cabin, which was distant from the other updated ones. She hoped the door was open. It wasn't.

Walking around the outside, she decided the only choice was to break a window, unlock it, and carefully make her way in. There was a low one at the rear that already had a crack. She picked up a rock and heaved it. The whole pane fell into the cabin in pieces and she unlocked the window, lifting it up. Glad that she was wearing jeans not shorts, she stepped over the sill and was in.

The cabin was small with one room housing a kitchenette, table, chairs, and a sofa in front of a woodstove. She checked this immediately. No ashes with partially burned letters as clues. Then she opened the few drawers and cabinets. The contents revealed that no one had been doing much cooking—or eating—here. Next, she went into the tiny bathroom, where she searched the medicine cabinet—empty—and the cabinet under the sink. It contained a few towels, a plunger, and nothing else. She shook out the towels, hastily folding them back. The stall shower contained a bar of Irish Spring and Axe shampoo. Any other toiletries, even a toothbrush, were missing.

The bedroom had two twin beds, neatly made. Remembering Chef Dom's size, Sophie wondered how he possibly could have fit in one. A closet covered by a curtain was empty. Where were Cal's clothes? Taken by the police? No suitcase or backpack left, nothing personal from either man. The two nightstands had a drawer each, also empty. Sophie pulled them out and turned them upside down. Nothing taped to the bottom.

Ready to give up, she thought she'd give the old "under the mattress" hiding place a try. She was impressed by the Shores housekeeping. Not a single dust bunny. Each mattress rested on broad wooden slats, not springs. Methodically she slid her hand on top of each, getting a splinter from the first bed for her effort. Nothing. She turned to the other and close to the foot felt something.

Excited, she pulled out a small rectangular notepad. She sat back and turned it over. Excitement built to elation. It was a prescription pad! Each page had been carefully filled out for a wide range of opioid types, strengths, and amounts. The patient's name was left blank. What wasn't left blank was the doctor's information and signature. Dr. Sidney Childs D.D.S.

"What are you doing here? And what's that in your hand?"

For a big woman, Pamela Childs had a very soft step.

Sophie jumped up. "I wanted someplace quiet to think about my writing," she improvised hastily, "and remembered this cabin. I knew it wouldn't be occupied. I'm just jotting down some ideas."

Heavy footsteps in the other room indicated the good dentist was with his wife. "Sidney, get in here. We have a problem."

"What is it, my dear?" he said, out of breath and coming into the room. He was red faced and sweating. Not used to hiking in the woods. "What is she doing here? Isn't she in Eloise's class? Don't tell me she's another of Cal's conquests?"

"No," his wife said grimly. She snatched the prescription pad from Sophie's hand. "She's been nosing around, and look what she found. Cal was so careless."

The doctor glanced at the pad and his usually benign expression switched to Hyde—pure evil.

Sophie edged toward the door, but Pamela blocked the way. "Give me your handkerchief, Sidney," she barked. "And your belt." Useless to protest—or reason—with them. Sophie realized her only chance was to get to the front door. She aimed a swift kick at Mrs. Childs's kneecap and was rewarded with a howl of pain. The doctor was cowering on the other side of the room. Apparently violence was not his thing. Just hiring people to do his dirty work.

She ducked past the woman, who was screaming, "Don't let her get away, Sidney, you fool! Shoot her!"

Dr. Childs had a gun.

Before Sophie could get to the front door, which they had closed behind them, a bullet whistled very close to her head. She stopped.

Mrs. Childs, enraged, grabbed her and stuffed the handkerchief in her mouth, painfully tying Sophie's arms at the wrists behind her back with the belt. "We can't leave her here, Sidney. She'd be found eventually." Sophie felt a twinge of hope.

"I say we deal with her like the others," Dr. Childs said. "My bag is in the other room. I'll just get a syringe."

Hope died and Sophie felt herself start to faint. She struggled to stay upright.

"No, we don't want to do anything suspicious. We really only need her on ice for an hour or so. More if we want to be sure she isn't found until we reach the border." Pamela appeared to be considering alternatives.

"Not keep her on ice, my dear. Something warmer."

Which is how Sophie found herself in the spa's soundproof sauna with the heat on full blast, after being frog-marched securely between the two down the path she had come up and whisked behind several outbuildings to the back door.

"You should have minded your own business," Pamela Childs chided. "I'm hanging the OUT OF ORDER sign on the door, so you won't be disturbed. Good-bye."

The doctor had some parting words, too. "I want my belt back. It's my Tom Ford, remember, darling." Sophie was positive this last did not refer to her. As soon as he'd freed her hands, she'd pulled the gag from her mouth and flung it at him. "You may keep that as a souvenir," he sneered and shut the door firmly.

She collapsed onto the cedar bench. As a place to stash her while the couple made their way to Canada, the windowless sauna was diabolically perfect. With the sign and the out-of-the-way location, by the time Sophie was found extreme dehydration would have killed her.

The three resort conference centers. What perfect covers for drug distribution. And the same staff, so well versed, rotating among the three, setting up operations. Plus the Lowell connection.

The tattoo must have been the biker-dealers' own private one, Cal their leader.

The Childses and any accomplices were obviously pulling the plug on the entire operation. Somehow Cal's death had triggered it. Cindy and Chef Dom, if he was still alive, were in on it, too.

The wooden bucket that held water to pour on the hot rocks was empty. Sophie didn't know whether it made more sense to strip down or keep her clothes on, keeping moisture in. She was burning up and her head was starting to spin. She started to lie down across the bench but sat up immediately and started pacing the room. She couldn't let herself fall into a coma.

Doctors and motorcycle gangs. She recalled reading about a New Jersey doctor running a similar scheme, caught only when he had one of his nonmedical associates kill his wife.

Jenny. What did she know and how involved was she? The pill container and the slip of paper in Arlene's purse must have been from Dr. Childs. That's what Jenny had seen. What did she plan to do? Or was she in on it? As soon as she got out of here, Sophie intended to find out. No, wait. *If* she got out of here.

That's when she started to sob. Will! Would she ever see her husband again?

299

"I'm sorry to disturb you. I know you must be busy, but I'm looking for Sophie Maxwell. She's a friend of yours isn't she?"

"Yes she is and no, I haven't seen her since before lunch," Faith said. She hadn't seen the writing instructor up close yet and she was every bit as eccentrically dressed as Sophie had described: today, a bright persimmon linen caftan belted with a plum-colored Japanese obi. Large hoop earrings with tiny bells hanging in each and chains of the same bells around her neck reached below her waist. Somehow it worked.

"It's just that Sophie didn't turn up for her appointment with me, which isn't like her. I've taken the others after her and had a look around. I know she's a day student, so perhaps she went home, but I'm quite sure she would have left word. And she isn't answering her phone."

This *wasn't* like Sophie. Faith took her apron off. "Amy, honey, I'm going to find Sophie. If she comes here, tell her to wait. We're in good shape for dinner."

"No prob," Amy said, concentrating on turning out millimeter-thick radish slices for a rose-shaped garnish.

Sophie's car was in the guest parking lot. Faith touched the hood. "Cold. She hasn't been anywhere recently."

"I hate to be an alarmist, but I don't have a good feeling about this," Eloise said. Given that the woman was a dead ringer for the Divination professor in the Harry Potter movies, Faith had to agree. Besides, she was feeling the same way.

Just then Faith's phone rang. Sanpere Shores had the best service on the island. Her heart leaped, but the ID said "Unidentified Caller."

"Hello?"

"Faith, it's Earl. A heads-up. Don't be alarmed, but all hell is going to break loose there in a few minutes. The state police and DEA are raiding the place. I want you and Amy to stay put together in the lodge living room. Sophie, too. And tell no one else."

He ended the call before Faith could respond.

"News about Sophie?" Eloise asked.

"Nooo, just a friend. But I need to go back and help my daughter with dinner. If Sophie is there or turns up soon, I'll tell her you're concerned."

With that, Faith took off almost at a run, leaving a bewildered Eloise standing by the cars.

She wasn't wearing a watch, so she had no idea how long she'd been cooking in the sauna. Her phone was in her bag, which the Childses had taken from her. It was probably in Penobscot Bay by now, flung from the bridge as they made their escape. Sophie had succumbed to the fatigue and was lying down. She'd also taken off her jeans, which felt as if they had melted onto her.

At first she wasn't sure whether she was hearing things or not. Someone was pounding on the door! Using both fists she pounded back. She yelled, too. There was a brief return knock and then silence. Her heart sank. Whoever it was had gone. She kept knocking until her hands were raw. After what seemed like hours, the door opened and she tottered out, determined to hug her rescuer to bits. Which was quite appropriate.

It was Babs.

Mom!

"However did you manage to get yourself trapped in there, Sophie? It could have been very dangerous. Good thing I decided to come for a nice sweat. Getting rid of all those toxins. I was about to leave because of the sign on the door, but I could tell the sauna was on from the gauge outside. You know how people are. Selfish at times. I figured it was someone who wanted it all to themselves. Then I heard the knocking. Fortunately, the key was at the desk."

"Mom," Sophie said, still clinging to Babs tightly. "It's a long story, but we have to call 911 and every police force in the state. The Childses are major drug dealers and on their way to Canada. They put me in here."

"The dentist? And that enormous wife of his? Well, as I've often told you, darling, people are seldom what they seem. Now drink this water. I'll make the calls. And do put your pants on."

Stepping outside, the two women could scarcely see the woods for the police vehicles. Calling in the troops wasn't necessary. Someone already had.

Uncle Freeman was a sweetheart. He hadn't said a word when Jenny asked to use the car to drive back to Massachusetts. "I'll return it soon," she'd promised. "Keep it as long as you need it, de-ah," he'd said.

She'd thought they were dealing only weed, maybe some coke. She didn't do any of it, so never paid much attention. Stupid. Or worse. The LeBlanc brothers were fun to be with, and Jenny had never been the frat boy type. She'd always preferred Harleys to Vespas. Her tattoo was a thumb of the nose at the wimpy butterfly ones. And it had been a kick hanging out with Cal, especially once they started singing together. She felt free for the first time since her mother died.

She couldn't go back to Lowell. She'd told her father the day of the Lobster Boat Races and she'd also apologized for being such a brat about her stepmother, who really wasn't all that bad. Just not Mom. Nobody could be. She'd told him she was going to transfer to the University of Southern Maine's music school. The Portland music scene was great and she wanted to be closer to the island.

It was seeing Arlene that had opened Jenny's eyes. Seeing the result of what they were doing to people up close. Saturday night on her cousin's boat—she'd "borrowed" it more than once, carefully replacing the fuel—she'd confronted him with the bottle and prescription. The doctor's name. She'd hoped Cal would deny any part in it, but he'd laughed and started bragging. How rich it had made him. "And what about the Le-Blancs?" Jenny had asked. She hadn't heard they were dead until then. She thought they'd gone back to Lowell. "Collateral damage," he'd said. "Got careless. Started using themselves. A big no-no. Chef, too, but we need him. He's in rehab."

"I thought all of them were your friends," she'd protested, and his response made her sick. "Friends? Guys like me don't have friends, little girl, and the sooner you learn what the world is really like the better." He'd put his arm around her, a gesture she'd always liked. It had made her feel wanted. That night, she felt her skin crawl.

"You take over. Need to take a leak," he'd said and moved toward the stern.

She was ready.

A long drive never bothered the operative. Just as the wildly different postings didn't. It was a second career. A radically new chapter. She liked to think of herself as a Mrs. Pollifax, the fictional amateur spy for the CIA.

Only she was very real.

It had been a near thing this time. She should have been keeping an even closer eye on them in Maine. Sophie Maxwell could have been injured— or worse. It was over now. Her part. Time for a new look for the next case. She could stop at the outlets in Freeport. Maybe L.L. Bean outdoorsy woman? Or preppy Ralph Lauren? A Talbots lady who lunched? She'd make pillows out of all those *ridiculous* scarves and caftans. But what to do with all those little bells?

Usually Faith's eyes stayed dry at weddings, no matter the size of the lump in her throat. Not this time. She'd started dabbing at her eyes the moment Kylie Brown came down the mown path in Edgewood Farm's meadow, past the seated guests, enthusiastically scattering rose petals from her basket with a huge grin. She stopped to give her father a kiss, then continued on, closely followed by Sam Eaton, who was as serious as a preacher, clutching the little satin pillow with two gold rings embroidered on it that Ursula had spent hours making. Faith realized Samantha was right when she'd said the kids would steal the show.

Zach, his best man, and Tom in his robes were waiting in the gazebo under an arch that Mary Cevasco had made from what seemed like all the flowers in her garden. Samantha followed the children, her mother and father on either side. She'd told Arlene, who had moved from the facility in Boston to a center near Portland, that a year from now she and Zach would renew their vows on the dock at The Birches with Arlene as matron of honor, and even Kylie and Sam in their roles all over again. The Miller clan was always up for a party, so the suggestion was heartily approved by all.

Pix took Samantha's bouquet and sat down between her mother and husband, her heart filled with joy. The weather was perfect. Not a hint of a nor'easter. She looked at her boys and daughter-in-law, Rebecca. Becca hadn't wanted any coffee since she'd arrived at Sanpere and had ducked out of the kitchen when the aroma filled the room. Pix was hoping they might have news. But all in good time.

She caught the eye of her brother, Arnie, and beamed at him and his family. Son Dana had grown a foot it seemed since last summer. Arnie gave a slight nod at their mother, resplendent in her gold dress. Pix knew he was sharing her thought, thankfulness for Ursula's good health and the hope it would continue so for many years.

Stunning as she looked, Ursula was outdone by Millicent Revere McKinley, who was wearing a turquoise-blue silk sheath and jacket, selected with Samantha's help one afternoon in town, followed by tea at the Copley. Millicent had also been to her safe-deposit box; her mother's long rope of pearls was luminescent. But it was the art deco diamond brooch, sending rainbows over the guests, that had caused surprised gasps. Who knew? If Pix had given any thought as to what might be stored safe and sound at Cambridge Trust she would have put her money on a brooch made from the hair of dearly beloved departeds and perhaps the secret recipe for the potent Revere family gunpowder punch.

Tom had included the seven traditional Hebrew blessings and the couple had read short vows they'd written to each other. Samantha, no veil, her shining chestnut hair crowned with a wreath of flowers, was breathtakingly lovely.

And now—"With this ring . . ." Pix reached for Sam's hand and squeezed it tight.

"What a beautiful wedding," Sophie said. "It makes me want to get married all over again."

"To Will, I assume," Faith joked. The couple had been inseparable since Will had flown up immediately after Sophie's escape from the sauna.

"You assume correctly." The two had grabbed a small table away from the rest of the wedding guests, kicked off their shoes, and were drinking champagne. Their husbands, and others, had settled into party mode—ties loosened or abandoned, heels exchanged for flats—greeting old friends; making new ones. Sam Eaton, Kylie, and some other children were playing tag. The farmhouse and barn sat high on a hill and the view across Penobscot Bay was spectacular.

After the truly cinematic climax at Sanpere Shores, Alexandra had accepted Hans's invitation to stay at his summerhouse in Cape Elizabeth. He spent winters at his Manhattan town house and traveled extensively. He'd come to the wedding as her "plus one," and Faith had overheard her tell him that she had planned the whole thing. Some people never changed.

Looking around, Faith thought she was glad those here didn't, cherishing the Millers and extended family, all the island friends, and Aleford out-of-towners just as they were. And her own Tom, Ben, and Amy. Although she couldn't say that Ben and Amy hadn't changed. Ben was an adult now or near to it, and the events of the summer had affected Amy. She would always be Faith's little girl, but she wasn't one anymore.

A few minutes later, Sophie asked, "Are you thinking what I'm thinking?"

"Probably," Faith said. "Something along the lines of hasn't this been an incredibly hard-to-believe summer? A terrible one?"

Sophie shuddered slightly and sipped her champagne. "Exactly. But they didn't get away with it. Any of it. The Childses hadn't even gotten as far as Ellsworth, thanks to the APB that had gone out."

"Which was before the feds arrived, right?"

Sophie nodded and took another sip. "Strange that. After I had been questioned, I was alone with Earl, waiting for Mom to get me—not exactly in shape to drive—and he told me he'd received an anonymous phone call, muffled voice—didn't know whether male or female—describing the operation. I think it may have been Jenny, or perhaps Cindy. She's talking now. Hoping to make a deal—a different kind from the ones she was involved in. He also said the feds were already watching the Childses and Cal, too. The raid on all three places had been in the works for a while and was moved up when Cal was killed. They figured the doctor and his wife might make a break for it. They had been stashing money in offshore accounts for years it seems."

"But didn't Earl also say they insist they had nothing to do with Cal's death?" Faith said.

"Is that so?" The man himself pulled up a chair and freshened their glasses with the bottle he'd brought. "I talk too much and you never heard any of this from me, remember. But I do wish I could tell you one thing and that's who the DEA had planted at the Shores. In one of the writing courses, not the actuaries. I do know that much. Any ideas? Sophie, you were in the best position to spot the NARC."

She shook her head. "Not a clue. The people in my class were highly individualistic. Not exactly undercover material. If it were two agents I'd go for the women who were supposedly college friends. Or the couple writing what the instructor was sure was going to be a romantic suspense block-buster. But they clearly wanted fame, not anonym-ity. Same with George Finley and Jay Thomas. Sorry, it will just have to remain a mystery."

"Okay, ladies," he shrugged, adding, "happens a lot in my job. Keep the bottle. I'm going to go dance with my beautiful wife."

The sun was slowly sinking below the horizon and the scene in front of her was filled with the kind of brilliant long light that always reminded Faith of a stage set. Earlier the photographer had gathered everyone together, bride and groom in the middle, and recorded the gathering forever from the top of a stepladder. Click.

Faith looked at Sophie, content now, and out at the dancers. Click. At the beginning of the reception, everyone had joined in the horah as the bride and groom were hoisted up on two chairs, linked to one another by a silk handkerchief. Click.

At the moment Tom had engaged Millicent for what looked like some kind of waltz to an arrangement of "All You Need Is Love." Click.

And there they all were in the amber of the moment.

Author's Note

There are places I remember—the first line of the
Beatles' song "In My Life," on the 1965 *Rubber
Soul* album, has been running through my mind
lately. I find myself humming the evocative tune.
This year Faith and I have celebrated significant
birthdays—and no, we're not telling—so perhaps
that is why I have been thinking about all the
places I remember. And yes, some have changed;
some not.

Patrick, the memoir-writing instructor, asks the
group to go back to a first memory as a starting
point exercise. I gave Alexandra what was my own
mother's earliest memory, significant for the bril-

liant colors of the beaded curtain that Mom, an artist, recalled. My first full memory is of sitting on a sofa in the New Jersey farmhouse my parents rented just after the war—our first home—holding my brand-new baby sister. I had just turned three. Hopscotching through the years I've come to realize what John Lennon expressed so poignantly. That the places are all tied with the people, and I've loved them all.

A trip to the Jersey shore with my cousins, Uncle Charlie lifting me onto a carousel horse, pointing out the brass ring. To everyone's surprise my tiny hand grabbed it the first time around. Flash forward many years later to a week on Martha's Vineyard with my four close college friends. We'd rented a house and gathered from both coasts, leaving all responsibilities behind to celebrate a milestone birthday (what was it again?). After Oak Bluffs Illumination Night, we went to the Flying Horses carousel, and as we rode, laughing together, I stuck out my hand only to find I had grabbed the ring once more.

Seven months after our December wedding, I stood holding hands with my husband on a hiking trail high in the French Alps in the sunshine and knew I had grabbed the ring again.

Learning to swim from my Norwegian cousin Hege in the Hardangerfjord. We children, the smalls like me on up, were a tribe that summer.

We slept in an old sod-roofed granary and went to the main house for riotous meals when we could be coaxed indoors.

Sgt. Pepper summer, 1967, the Summer of Love, outside London with my sister working as au pairs, spending our days off at Hyde Park watching all the beautiful people. "When I'm sixty-four" was very far away. Thirty was a stretch. All those *Sgt. Pepper* songs and the others, too. For many of us, the Beatles were, and are, the soundtrack of our lives.

A cross-country trip with our newly graduated high school son. I snapped a photo of him with his dad arm in arm, overlooking Oregon's Gold Beach, a photo I look at on my desk every day.

Back to places . . . Hearth and home rooted here in Massachusetts virtually my entire adult life. Especially this house, our forever house. The walls echo. Many joyful gatherings, but the one we give each year for close to a hundred neighbors and friends, old and new, is special.

And this house holds another memory I go back to often. A private one of intense happiness when my mother was staying with us some years after we lost my father too soon. I fell asleep wrapped in the knowledge that the three people I loved most in the world were all under one roof.

And then there's Maine, always Maine. It is no accident that this twenty-fifth book in the series, a kind of silver anniversary, is set on the island I chronicle and created. The island where I have been going since I was eleven. I had intended the "Sanpere Island" location for this book quite a while ago. No place is more significant for me, nor the people. To list them—some are gone and some still living—would take another chapter. It is home in a way no other has ever been—and not just because we'll be there awhile: our plot is at the end of King's Row in Mount Adams Cemetery, next to a stand of pure white river birch, the spot selected by my parents long ago.

Think back to your own places and the people. Often stop and think about them as Lennon says he will. Listen to versions of "In My Life" that other musicians have recorded. It is an anthem of the soul.

In our lives we've loved them all. *I've* loved them all.

Thank you.

Coda: *Like the characters in this book, I—and my family—have been watching the drug crisis deepen with alarm for years. In Maine alone there was a 40 percent increase in drug overdose fatalities in 2017 over 2016, most due to fentanyl and heroin. The first six months of 2018 saw drug overdoses claim nearly one life each day. But also like the characters, we have hope* for the future. *This hope is due to the efforts of some extraordinary people at, to name a few, the Island Health & Wellness Foundation—https:// islandhealthwellnessfoundation.wordpress .com/, Healthy Acadia—https://healthyacadia.org/, Opiate-Free Island Partnership—https://www.face book.com/opiatefreeisland/, and one individual in particular, Dr. Charles Zelnick. Addicts are our friends, family members, neighbors—not criminals. Watch the documentary* The Hungry Heart. *Filmed in Vermont, it is every state, USA. https:// www.pbs.org/video/the-hungry-heart-b1sfbh/*

Excerpts from

HAVE FAITH
IN YOUR KITCHEN
by Faith Sibley Fairchild
with Katherine Hall Page

Summertime recipes!!

CHILLED GARDEN PEA SOUP

1 tablespoon olive oil
2 scallions (spring onions),
  sliced thin
4 cups frozen peas (Faith
  likes Birds Eye Sweet
  Garden Peas)

1 cup water
2 cups chicken or
  vegetable stock
Pinch of salt
$^1/_2$ cup crème fraîche
Fresh mint (optional)

Place the olive oil and scallions in a saucepan over medium heat and stir briefly. Do not brown the scallions.

Add the frozen peas and stir.

Add the water, stock, and salt.

Cover and bring to a boil. Check to see if the peas are tender.

Uncover, turn the heat down, and simmer for approximately 7 minutes.

The peas should be quite tender now.

Remove from the stove and let cool for about 10 minutes.

Puree in two batches in a blender and pour into a bowl. Cover with plastic wrap and refrigerate.

This soup is best made a day ahead.

Before serving add a dollop of crème fraîche or, using a pastry bag, pipe thin concentric circles of the crème and using the sharp point of a knife, draw a line through them to the side of each soup plate to create a web. Garnish with the mint.

Of course, if you are lucky enough to have enough fresh peas in season to make this, use them. You will cook them a few minutes less. Faith also uses her precious fresh peas for traditional salmon and peas on the Fourth of July.

For a variation on this dish, try garlic-infused or another flavor-infused olive oil. You may also add $1/4$ cup fresh mint leaves when pureeing.

A lovely first course or luncheon entrée.

Serves six.

FAITH'S FAMOUS LOBSTER ROLLS

2 lobsters, a pound and a half each
$1/3$ cup mayonnaise (Hellmann's or Duke's)
A squeeze of fresh lemon
Pinch of salt
Pinch of freshly ground pepper
2 tablespoons butter
4 split-top hot dog rolls

Cook the lobsters. (Faith steams them in a large pot of two to three inches of rapidly boiling water for 12 minutes.) When cool enough to handle, remove the meat and cut it into bite-size pieces, reserving the large claw meat for garnish if desired. Set aside.

Combine the mayonnaise (brand depends on where you live), lemon juice, salt, and pepper in a separate bowl. Season to taste, adding more salt, lemon juice, or pepper. When it's just right, add the lobster and mix well to coat.

Melt the butter in a frying pan—iron skillets are the best—and toast both sides of the rolls. Fill immediately and serve.

Other recipes call for celery, chives, parsley, scallions, and condiments like Tabasco. The Fairchilds are purists when it comes to lobster rolls, and this is the real deal. You may also use this recipe for crab rolls.

Serves four.

OLD-FASHIONED COLESLAW

1 ¹/₂ cups grated green
   cabbage
1 ¹/₂ cups grated red
   cabbage
1 large carrot, grated

1 ¹/₄ cups mayonnaise
   (Hellmann's or Duke's)
1 ¹/₂ tablespoons sugar
1 tablespoon half and half
1 teaspoon lemon juice
1 teaspoon salt

After grating the cabbages and carrot (a food processor works well and saves your knuckles), transfer to a large mixing bowl and stir to distribute the ingredients evenly.

In a separate bowl, mix the rest of the ingredients and stir well before pouring into the bowl with the cabbage/carrot mixture. Using a rubber spatula or similar utensil fold the liquids into the slaw. Cover with plastic wrap and refrigerate immediately until served.

While this is tasty right away, it is even better made the day before.

Serves a crowd.

BLUEBERRY BUCKLE

Topping

$^1/_3$ cup granulated sugar
$^1/_2$ cup all-purpose flour
1 teaspoon ground
   cinnamon

$^1/_8$ teaspoon salt
4 tablespoons unsalted
   butter, softened and cut
   into pieces

Batter

1 $^1/_2$ cups all-purpose flour
2 teaspoons baking powder
$^1/_2$ teaspoon salt
4 tablespoons softened
   butter, cut into pieces
$^3/_4$ cup granulated sugar

1 large egg
1 teaspoon vanilla
$^1/_2$ cup milk
2 $^1/_2$ cups blueberries,
   preferably wild Maine
   ones

Preheat the oven to 375 degrees F.

Grease a 9-inch-square pan at least 2 inches deep, preferably with butter.

Make the topping in a small bowl by mixing the sugar, flour, cinnamon, salt, and butter with two knives or a pastry blender. Set aside.

To make the batter, blend the flour, baking powder, and salt in a medium bowl. Set aside.

In a larger bowl, cream the butter and sugar until light and fluffy using an electric mixer or by hand. Add the egg, vanilla, and milk. Mix.

Gradually add the flour mixture from the medium bowl into the mixture in the larger one until blended. Fold in the blueberries. It will be a thick batter. Spread it in the pan and sprinkle the topping evenly on the batter.

Bake in the center of the oven for 40 to 45 minutes. Check with a toothpick or broom straw.

Serves eight.

A "buckle" has been described as a muffin that has mated with a coffee cake. The name comes from the fact that the cake "buckles" into a slight round when taken from the oven.

Buckles are an old-fashioned New England recipe. My friend and cookbook author Brooke Dojny—*Dishing Up Maine*, *Chowderland*, *The New England Cookbook*, and more—sent me the following about buckles: "In the same category as crumble (also called crisp), which is fruit with crumb topping; buckle is like coffee cake, then there's cobbler and grunt or slump (love those names) with biscuit topping that is steamed rather than baked so it sometimes heaves a sigh (grunt) and sort of slumps down into the fruit."

Whether you buckle, grunt, or slump, these are all delicious. A dollop of vanilla ice cream or whipped cream on the warm dish takes the cake.

SANDY OLIVER'S FRUIT SHRUB

Stymied by attempts that were too bitter, Faith and I turned to Sandra Oliver, food historian, essayist, cookbook author, and founding editor of *Food History News,* for what would have been a simple recipe used in colonial Down East and elsewhere for shrub. One of our country's first drinks, shrub is a mixture of fruit and sugar steeped in a vinegar. The name goes further back to the Arabic *sharab,* meaning "drink." Shrub has once again become a happening drink, added to vodka, gin, or other alcohols!

Fill a quart jar with fresh strawberries. Cover the berries with cider vinegar, put a lid on the jar, and set away to soak in a cool, dark place for two to three weeks. Do not refrigerate. The berries will get very pale.

At the end of the two- or three-week period, drain the berries, reserving the liquid and discarding the berries. Measure the liquid and put it in a saucepan. Add an equal amount of sugar as there is of the liquid (if you have one and a half cups of liquid, add one and a half cups of sugar). Heat until the sugar completely dissolves.

Cool and store in a bottle or jar, tightly covered, until you are ready to use it.

To serve, pour a few tablespoons of the syrup into a glass, add club soda or plain water to taste, and a few ice cubes. You can also add the syrup to iced tea, ginger ale, lemonade, or a similar beverage.

You can also use other kinds of juicy berries like raspberries or blackberries.

Note: Many of the recipes from previous books are found in Katherine's actual cookbook, *Have Faith in Your Kitchen* (Orchises Press).

ENTER THE WORLD OF
KATHERINE HALL PAGE

Katherine Hall Page, one of today's favorite authors, writes the well-loved, critically acclaimed and Agatha Award–winning mystery series featuring Faith Fairchild: transplanted New Yorker, minister's wife, mother of two, renowned caterer, and amateur sleuth. Faith has an uncomfortable habit of innocently entangling herself in murder, and a knack not just for puff pastry, but for unraveling a mystery. From Aleford, Massachusetts, to Boston, to Maine, to New York, to France, Faith grapples with killers, kidnappers, blackmailers, and arsonists, always managing to land on her feet. The pages that follow provide a quick glimpse into Faith's world.

Faith Fairchild, late of New York City, currently of peaceful Aleford, Massachusetts, is ecstatically happy with her much-loved minister husband, Tom, and infant son, Benjamin. Ecstatically happy, but bored, bored, bored. In Katherine Hall Page's Agatha Award–winning debut, **The Body in the Belfry***, Faith hasn't the faintest suspicion that the dark undercurrents of village life are about to rise to the surface and disturb her dull but pleasant existence . . .*

"It sparkles like a Yankee pond
on a bright autumn day!"
—*Washington Post Book World*

"A humorous and entertaining addition to the murder-in-the-village genre . . . Faith is a promising sleuth."
—*Booklist*

In **The Body in the Kelp** *. . . Faith buys a lovely hand-made quilt at an estate sale with her best friend, Pix Miller. But the quilt is not only patchwork; it's a map which leads Faith on a treasure hunt—toward her second taste of murder.*

"Great characters, a wonderful plot, and a puzzle laid out in the unfinished threads of a quilt."
—*Ocala Star-Banner*

*The crème de la crème of Massachusetts elderly go to Hubbard House. In **The Body in the Bouillon**, when a friend of Faith's favorite aunt dies there after hinting to her of scandal, Faith is duty-bound by family affection to investigate. If it means volunteering as a Pink Lady and trying her hand at standard New England cuisine (not her favorite), so be it . . .*

"Jaunty, breezy . . . *Bouillon* tastes great."
—Boston Herald

"The combination of crime, Faith's cordon bleu dishes, and New England in the snow is, as usual, irresistible."
—*The Drood Review of Mystery*

*In **The Body in the Vestibule**, the Fairchild family (soon to be increased by one) is spending a month in France, where Faith can indulge her passion for French culture, language, and most of all, cuisine. They're having a glorious time . . . until Faith finds a body in the entryway of the apartment. What's even more upsetting is that when she calls in the gendarmes, the body's gone. And no one, not even Tom, believes her . . .*

"Succulent . . . The mix of murder, wit, food, and drink remains irresistible."
—*Booklist*

*Faith's back in business in **The Body in the Cast**, with a brand-new daughter and a brand-new start in Aleford for her famous New York catering company, Have Faith. She's well on the road to success when she's hired by a movie company to cater their production of* The Scarlet Letter, *to be filmed in quiet little Aleford. But someone's playing nasty tricks, and when it affects Faith's cooking, she just has to get involved . . .*

"A lively read . . . The story really sparkles."
—*Romantic Times Magazine*

"Readers will find treasures aplenty
in these fast-flying pages."
—*Publishers Weekly*

*In **The Body in the Basement**, Faith's best friend, Pix, is irritated when she checks on the Fairchilds' new summer home and realizes the contractors haven't even begun—and there's nothing there but a foundation! And there's something wrong with the foundation . . . something very dead . . .*

"Unremittingly nice suspects and down-east recipes
establish a family-values backdrop for a killer
who faces the need to kill Pix by fretting:
'Our parents used to play bridge together.'"
—*Kirkus Reviews*

*Something's rotten in the town of Aleford. In **The Body in the Bog**, the village's peace is disturbed by the ubiquitous nemesis of rural tranquility—land development. Tempers run hot, culminating in a highly unpleasant death. Faith wanted to campaign against the development, but she's even more eager to work against murder . . .*

"Page's young sleuth is a charmer."
—*New York Times Book Review*

*In **The Body in the Fjord**, Faith's best friend, Pix, and her mother, Ursula, are off to see the natural wonders of Norway—or at least that's their story. In fact, Pix is going undercover, joining the tour group from which an old family friend has disappeared without a trace. Determined to discover the truth, Pix is drawn into a suspenseful world of intrigue, stolen antiques, secret histories, and deadly echoes from Norway's past and the Nazi occupation.*

"An expert at the puzzle mystery . . .
Page smoothly keeps her plot on course . . .
The Body in the Fjord is a solid example of her skill."
—*Ft. Lauderdale Sun-Sentinel*

In ***The Body in the Bookcase***, *Faith pays a parish call on the town's librarian and finds the gentle old lady's house ransacked. A burglary ring has targeted peaceful Aleford, and no one is safe, especially when the crime spree turns deadly . . .*

"A smartly executed excursion into the shady side of the antiques trade turns up all kinds of inside dope sure to fascinate—and infuriate— paranoid property owners."
—*New York Times Book Review*

"Peopled with entertaining and resourceful characters and sprinkled with mouth-watering recipes."
—*Dallas Morning News*

*For her tenth Faith Fairchild mystery, Katherine Hall Page goes back to Faith's beginnings. In **The Body in the Big Apple**, it's the 1980s, and young Faith Sibley is the up-and-coming caterer at a party where she runs into an old school friend, socialite Emma Stanstead. Hidden secrets have come back to haunt Emma, and she begs her friend Faith for help . . .*

"Enchanting . . . well-written . . . Page's style is entertaining and unpretentiously cultured."
—*Portland Press Herald*

"Fun . . . a little mystery with a big-hearted love of NYC."
—*Denver Rocky Mountain News*

The Body in the Moonlight *finds minister's wife Faith Fairchild catering her church's restoration campaign kickoff at historic Ballou House. But when a beautiful young woman dies moments after finishing dessert, Faith is suddenly in serious trouble. Never before have Faith's amateur sleuthing skills been more crucial, for her reputation—and her life—is at stake!*

"The final solution is clever and unexpected."
—*Old Post Gazette*

"A pleasant, light read, cast with just enough eccentric characters and red herrings to make the mystery interesting."
—*The Austin Chronicle*

Faith plays teacher in ***The Body in the Bonfire****, when she accepts a job running Cooking for Idiots at Mansfield Academy. But Faith soon finds that Mansfield is a seething cauldron of secrets, academic in-fighting, and unspoken rules. When somebody tampers with her classroom cooking ingredients, Faith realizes she must single out the culprit, or learn a deadly lesson . . .*

"This whodunit provides fully satisfying fare for a cold winter's night around the fire."
—*Publishers Weekly*

In ***The Body in the Lighthouse***, *the Fairchild family heads to their cottage on a Maine island for the summer. While Faith keeps busy with a local production of* Romeo and Juliet, *life imitates art as tensions run high between the island's two factions—the year-round residents and the summer people. It's small-town warfare, and Faith would like to keep the casualties to a minimum . . .*

"Page's literary concoction is satisfying
and surprisingly delicious."
—*Los Angeles Times*

"Spine-tingling."
—*Library Journal*

"Page's eye for detail adds to the appeal of a
book best read to the sound of the surf."
—*Boston Herald*

Faith's relocated to Cambridge in ***The Body in the Attic*** *while the Reverend Thomas Fairchild teaches at the Harvard Divinity School. Soon Faith is plunged into the past. A long-forgotten face reappears, plus she discovers a shocking diary in the old house's attic. Is it too late to uncover the truth—and too dangerous?*

"Faith becomes an ever more interesting character."
—*Booklist*

"Intriguing."
—*Bangor Daily News*

Catastrophe strikes at the Vermont slopes in **The Body in the Snowdrift**. *The Fairchilds take to the ski lodge to celebrate Thomas's father's 70th birthday. But even the hardiest of skiers don't stick around when they awake to find the slopes covered with red-hued snow. Somebody fell—or was pushed—into the snow-making machine, and Faith will have to work fast to solve this murderous puzzle, before the evidence all melts!*

"[W]ell told . . . close, careful observations of the complicated dynamics within large families . . . [Page] at her solid best."
—*New York Times Book Review*

Katherine Hall Page pays homage to And Then There Were None *in* **The Body in the Ivy**. *Faith Fairchild is asked to cater a very small, very private college reunion on an isolated New England island, but soon realizes she's trapped in a deadly game, with no phone lines, no cell reception, and no means of escape.*

"It's rare to get a writer who out-plots Christie, but Page does a fine job."
—*The Globe and Mail*

In **The Body in the Gallery**, *Faith takes over the café at the local Ganely Museum. Faith's friend Patsy confides her concern that the Romare Bearden painting she lent to the museum has been switched with a fake, and she wants Faith to snoop around to see if that's the case. When a corpse is discovered near a controversial exhibit, Faith can't help but think the murder and the theft might be related. With her knack for detail, Faith finds herself caught up in artistic facades to find an imposter and a killer . . .*

"Katherine Hall Page's intellect and wit shine through in every line . . . Hungry readers, enjoy!"
—Diane Mott Davidson

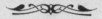

In **The Body in the Sleigh**, *the Fairchild's Christmas vacation is filled with many a Not-So-Silent Night. First, a dead body is found tucked among the mannequins in a local holiday display. Then, a spinster goat farmer finds a newborn baby boy in her manger. Faith must do triple-time as wife, mother, and sleuth to solve a beguiling holiday caper.*

"Page is adept at mixing charming narrative with page-turning mystery."
—BookPage

"This charming story, told with humor, warmth and wonderful characters, is a perfect holiday present for cozy mystery fans."
—Romantic Times Magazine

A moving, suspenseful tale, **The Body in the Gazebo** *is an evocative journey into the past, where the truth hangs by the thread of one woman's memory. Pix Rowe Miller, friend and neighbor to caterer Faith Fairchild, is preparing for her son's wedding out of town. However, she's nervous about leaving behind her elderly mother, Ursula, who is troubled by a dark family secret. While helping Ursula in Pix's absence, Faith gets drawn into solving this decades-old crime.*

"A pleasant, well-rounded story . . . A lovely dish."
—*Iron Mountain Daily News*

"Expertly crafted."
—*The Patriot Ledger*

The Body in the Boudoir *gives fans a flashback to 1990. Faith Sibley is a single young woman with her own catering business in New York City. But a chance meeting with the Reverend Thomas Fairchild is love at first sight, and suddenly Faith is engaged and heading north to New England to visit her future in-laws, not all of whom are friendly. Faith's path to the altar is made even rockier when she finds some-one is trying to call off the wedding—by eliminating the bride!*

"Enjoy the retro fun of perusing a vintage wedding menu, shopping at Bergdorf's bridal salon and having tea at the Palm Court in the Plaza Hotel."
—*New York Times Book Review*

The Body in the Piazza *finds Faith celebrating her wedding anniversary in Italy, where murder and mayhem mix with pecorino, panna cotta, and prosecco. Solving a murder in the Eternal City has Faith following a trail more twisting than fusilli.*

"Delightful . . . Hungry readers will rush to
the kitchen if not to their travel agent
to book tickets to Italy."
—*New York Times Book Review*

The Body in the Casket *finds Faith catering a birthday party for legendary Broadway producer Max Dane. While discussing the menu, Max reveals that one of his guests is going to try to kill him. As a storm brews overhead and the party begins, Faith must keep one eye on the dishes and another on her host to keep the birthday bash from becoming Max's final curtain.*

"Katherine Hall Page, who has written almost
two dozen culinary mysteries, has come up with
another smart twist on her cozy formula
featuring Faith Fairchild."
—*New York Times Book Review*

"A cracking good traditional manor house mystery."
—*Publishers Weekly*